FORGED UNDER FIRE

A.J. DOWNEY

BOOK EIGHT

COPYRIGHT

~

ISBN: 978-1-950222-22-3

Editing & book design by Maggie Kern

Cover art and Indigo Knights logo by Dar Albert at Wicked Smart Designs

Model - Ricco Bland

Photographer - JW Photography

DEDICATION

Happy Birthday, to the real Oz

PROLOGUE

z...

Pow!

Pow-pow-pow-pow-pow!

I looked up, a couple 'bangers' were trading fire in broad fuckin' daylight in the middle of the street. One was down, the other running this way; I didn't think – I reacted. I pulled my piece and screamed, "Indigo City P.D.! Drop your weapon!"

Fool drew down on me, popped off a few rounds, *Pop! Pop! Pop!*

I returned fire, *Pow! Pow! Pow!* The kick familiar, the vibration murder through my arms which I'd just finished working out.

He went down – I didn't. I stood there, shaking for half a heartbeat, but then my training overrode my shock; my feet carrying me up the sidewalk, gun still drawn pointed at the ground as I moved carefully around parked cars, aiming for the threat. I stepped off the curb between a Mercedes and a Lexus and kicked the dude's piece away from his hand.

He was staring up at me, eyes wide, teeth coated with blood, breathing way too fast. His chest rising and falling in short labored gasps before his eyes rolled back in his head and he let out a final one. There wasn't shit I could do for him. I relaxed marginally.

"Oz!"

I felt sick but held it in.

"Yeah, here, man! Over here!"

That's when a woman started screaming up the block and I had to turn and keep moving, keep doing the job that needed doing.

Some of the hose boys swooped in to render aid to the dead guy, a couple more catching me up as we surged up the cracked pavement to the screaming woman, my heart sinking as she pressed her hands against another woman who was down.

I was from the streets, but damn, I didn't *work* the streets... I was so out of my element with this.

1

*O*z...

Community outreach wasn't exactly my thing unless it was by way of the Knights. I kept to myself and there was a reason for that. One, while I *could* get along with just about anybody, a lot of the motherfuckers out here were fake as hell. Not the rest of my squad, though. The rest of my squad was here for it; here with me at Angel's church. Not for the funeral of the banger I'd shot, but for the civilian woman he'd nailed before I could take him out.

The other woman, her sister who'd been with her, was crying softly in one of the front pews leaning heavily into her dad's side. I felt like shit. It'd felt like months since the shooting, but it'd been less than a damn week.

The funeral was bought and paid for by the squad. We'd drained our charity account to do it, but the woman who'd died? She'd been young. Early thirties. Her whole life ahead of her and hadn't had anything to cover such a big expense. Her family was at a loss, her sister couldn't afford it, and I'd asked at the club meeting right after it'd happened, and the motion had passed with a unanimous vote.

We could always pull in more cash. A charity ride, a fundraiser, it's what we did… and if I couldn't save her like I was fuckin' supposed to, this was the next best thing… right?

We stood up again.

I didn't get this whole Catholic shit. I was raised in the south. Church every Sunday, but it was a far cry from this melancholy bullshit. Of course, I got that this was a funeral – but as far as I understood it, there wasn't much different between any of the Catholic services. Life, death, or just another Sunday – you couldn't tell 'em apart. Just a lot of up and down like a Yo-Yo on a string, the priest droning on and on, the message different, the delivery deadpan, and all of it the fucking *same.*

All this shit made me want to do was get on the back of my bike and just ride. Let the feelings get ground beneath my tires and into the pavement rushing beneath them. To let any of the rest of my worries or cares get carried off by the wind in my face.

I mean, this was fucking *bullshit.*

We sat down. A few more minutes of the priest talking and we were up again, only this time this was it. Showtime, as much as I hated to be in the limelight. I went up along with the dead woman's fiancé, her dad, and her uncle. Narcos and Driller taking up the rear.

She hadn't had enough people to be pallbearers so we'd stepped up for that, too. The weight of my failure, of her casket, of her missing brightness and soul was probably the heaviest burden I'd ever borne walking up that center aisle, all eyes trained on me – some misty, some angry, some… well at least to me, some accusing – and I deserved that.

I should have been quicker.

We set the gleaming casket carefully on the runners of the hearse waiting out on the street and slid Mia Köhler into the back. Her father shook my hand, then her uncle, and last her fiancé and I tried to hold my shit together, but it was hard when I felt so fuckin' gutted, so guilty. Then it was her sister, Elka, in front of me.

"Thank you," she murmured and leaned in to kiss my cheek and I couldn't help my own eyes getting wet.

It was pure chance that she and her family belonged to the same church as Angel and had made things a lot easier for us to help. I didn't think she was particularly religious, though. He said he'd known Mia's pops, not Mia or Elka. That they were Catholic CEO's as in Christmas and Easter Only. Probably to make their dad happy. I guess their mom had died a while ago. Heart attack or something.

"I'm just sorry I wasn't quicker," I told her, and she took my hand and gave it a squeeze.

She was pretty. A brunette with light brown eyes, the irises kissed with bronze in the right light. Like the direct sunlight, out here on the sidewalk.

Her dad came and collected her, and she cast her gaze back over her shoulder at me, something in her eyes. I vowed to follow up in a few days. Check and see how she was doing.

"You okay?" Skids asked me softly and I pressed my lips together and shook my head.

"Naw, man. I'm as far away from 'okay' as any dude can get, brother."

He nodded. "Wake is at the *10-13*," he said.

"Yeah." I nodded, eyes still fixed on the sister, Elka, as she spoke softly with Mia's fiancé up the block, next to one of the town cars.

Their family didn't do burial, so Mia was on her way to the funeral home to be cremated. Her dad had said something about putting her with her mother and it felt like someone was cracking my chest open with a railroad spike and a sledgehammer.

"Oz," Skids said and I snapped out of it.

"Yeah?"

"You coming?"

I nodded and glanced back up the sidewalk. Elka was looking at me.

"Yeah, I'm comin.'"

2

$\mathcal{E}$lka…

Everyone was being so nice, and all I could feel was this terrible nothing. Just numb. This hole scorched in the center of my being, silence flooding my veins, the edges still smoking. It was like my sister had been shot, but the hole was in the center of *my* chest and I couldn't stop the bleeding no matter how hard I tried… but nobody noticed.

I stared, sightless and vacant out the window at the restaurant and couldn't even drum up enough feelings to feel bad for my father. For leaving him to shake hands and deal with the murmured condolences for his dead daughter… all while his living one sat alone in the four-person booth by the front window staring out at the city street and the people and the cars going by.

"Ms. Köhler?" I looked up at the policeman who'd been there that day. Who'd shot the man who'd shot my sister.

"Officer Jones," I said and hated how faded and tired my voice sounded.

"Call me Hector," he said and set a cup of coffee on a saucer in front of me. "Or just Oz."

"Oz?" I asked, pulling the cup on its saucer closer to me, reaching for the sugar. "Like the Great and Powerful?" He set down a little stainless-steel carafe of creamer and slid into the booth across from me, batting at his tie to keep it off the table, smoothing it against his broad chest.

"Oh, ah, nah… like the T.V. show, about the prison. It's, um, what I do."

"I thought you were a police officer," I said adding creamer to the cup mechanically, stirring it in with the little spoon on the saucer for it.

"I am, with Indigo City but I don't work the street. I'm a jailer."

"Oh," I said softly. "But you…" I bit my lips together and reached for the sweetener.

"Yeah, I carry, but um, that's not my usual deal."

"I see," I said softly.

A silence lapsed between us and I swallowed hard, wrapping my fingers around the coffee cup, letting the warm ceramic heat my palms even though it was summer outside, and my hands weren't cold. I was cold. It just wasn't the kind of cold that a blanket or a warm drink could fix.

"I came over to check on you," he said evenly and I liked his voice. I dragged my eyes up from the coffee lazily spinning in the mug and fixed them on his face.

He was handsome. I didn't usually go for bald men, but on him it worked. He had a strong jaw that was shadowed by a light dusting of stubble, a pencil-thin mustache over his top lip. A bit of ink from a tattoo peeked out of the cuff of his shirt sleeve, a nice watch gracing his wrist. A definite conversation piece but I just didn't have it in me to comment.

"So, uh, how are you doing?"

"My sister was murdered right in front of me," I murmured carefully and gave a nervous sort of laugh. "I'm, um, not really sure how I'm supposed to feel," I confessed.

"I get that," he said.

I took a sip of the coffee and winced at the strong and bitter brew. It needed more sweetener. *A* lot more if I wanted it to be palatable.

"I'm not sure what to say," I said, reaching for another yellow packet.

"Just whatever's on your mind works," he said, leaning back in the booth, pulling at his suit jacket self-consciously.

"Nothing, really," I said. "It's like nothing will stick."

"I get that," he said with a nod and I stared at his blunt fingers pressed against the tabletop. He was light skinned for a black man, but I couldn't tell what he was mixed with offhand. His skin holding warm, golden undertones, genuinely like coffee lightened to medium with good cream. He moved again, adjusting his seat uncomfortably and I flinched, my gaze flickering back to his face which I rather decided was handsome, his brow slightly creased with a line of worry between his eyes. His darker freckles standing out in a scatter across his nose and cheeks.

"Nothing's gonna hurt you here," he said gently, and I gave a wan smile.

"There's really nothing left to hurt," I said gently, and I don't know where that had come from, but I didn't take it back. It was the truth. I let my eyes drift back out the window and kept them there, suddenly very disinterested in talking anymore.

Eventually, he slid a card across the table and said, "Do me a favor and call me if you need anything. Anytime. Day or night. Cell number is on the back."

I didn't say anything. I didn't know what to say. I just stared out the window, fresh tears leaking out of the corners of my eyes and wished this was over and that I could go home. Back to my paints and my little studio.

3

*O*z...

"Hey, oh, thank you..." Her dad took the card from my hand and I looked back towards the window booth and Elka. She stared sightlessly out onto the sunlit street, there but not really there and it bothered me.

"Do me a favor, anything seems off or you worry about her at all, call me first. Anytime, day or night. I'll drop what I'm doing and come out and check on her."

Her father followed my gaze and he nodded and put a hand on my shoulder, giving it a squeeze.

"Thank you."

"Yeah." I nodded and got out the way, more people hovering on the periphery waiting their turn to talk to him.

I went over to the bar, Skids behind it, and he wordlessly brought down the bottle of Hennessy and poured me a double, neat.

"How you doin', Oz?"

I let my gaze drift back to Elka, sitting alone with her barely touched coffee, gaze troubled and a million miles away and jerked my head that way. Skids followed the motion and gave a nod and a sigh.

"I didn't ask about her. I asked about you."

"I'm fine," I lied easily.

He gave me a frank look and an unconvincing "Uh huh," as he reached over and clapped me on the shoulder before moving down the bar to where the coffee service was set up. I watched him check it over and contemplated talking about it but then he put another pot of decaf on and I suddenly felt like I was in enemy territory or some shit. *Decaf? Really?*

I shook my head and took a healthy mouthful of the booze in my glass in silent misery, my contemplation switching back to Elka's somber silence from across the room.

I just had a feeling that something was on the horizon. A meltdown, a downward spiral, and I somehow wished I could spare her from it when really, I knew the only thing I could do was be there to mop up.

It was a commitment I was surprised to find I was willing to make. I couldn't tell you why. Maybe it had something to do with the first look I got of her, blood spattered and screaming, kneeling on the side-walk next to her dead sister.

I was beginning to wonder if it was what I was going to see every time I looked at her.

I sure hope not.

～

"You know, I hear you talk about this chick by like a metric fuckton since the shit went down – what I *don't* hear a lot is how are *you* doing, *Hombre*." I scowled at Golden.

"I didn't lose a sister," I said and he rolled his eyes at me.

"You just shot a kid," Narcos said and my gaze swung in his direction. "Watched him die in front of you."

"I realize that, genius." I *almost* felt bad for snarling but not quite. He put up his hands in surrender and leaned way back in his seat.

"Then how come you don't talk about it?" Driller asked smoothly and arched an eyebrow at me. I scowled and spun my dart between my fingers, stepping up to the line of tape on the carpet and taking aim at the board.

"What's there to talk about?" I demanded.

"How you're feeling, for one," Golden stated simply, and I brought my hand back, lined shit up and let fly. One, two, and three. I eyed my spread critically and turned, Narcos at the tall table our beers sat on, etching my score into the notebook Skids kept behind the bar for scoring. He nodded and tossed the midget pencil between the pages as a bookmark and gathered his set of darts off the table in one fist. I got the hell out of his way.

I slid back up onto the tall barstool and picked up my beer glass, swilling down a healthy mouthful.

"So?" Golden pressed, raising his eyebrows.

"Man, used to be I could count on you the most to avoid this touchy-feely shit. Lys has made you soft."

"Nah, man. Lys has made me realize that *not* talking about your trauma is the weakness."

"Look at you all profound and shit," Driller declared and sounded like some kind of a proud papa.

"Motherfucker," I said. "Not you too."

He gave me a half-assed shrug and plucked at the front of his tee beneath his cut. It wasn't his imagination, it was hot as fuck in here. I called out to Skids, "Man, your AC busted or what?"

"Looks like it," he grunted back.

"Shit," I muttered.

"Beer's still cold, though," he called back.

"At least we got that going for us," Golden declared, taking a swig of his own.

"Nice!" Driller clapped and turned back to the scorebook and I glanced over where Narcos was pulling darts mostly from the center of the board.

"Man." I shook my head. I hated not being the best at everything, but sometimes you just weren't. I'd like to say that's where my irritation was stemming from, but really it was the fact I didn't want to talk about what went down but these fools wouldn't let it go.

I mostly tuned them out, let myself get lost inside my own head, gaze fixed on the booth by the window where I'd last seen Elka staring sightlessly outside. There was a blonde woman sitting in her place right now, faking interest in some two percent tall glass of weak milk. Probably a first date, a failed Tinder match, who the fuck knew.

I wasn't into all that. Proudly divorced, I had no use for the opposite sex. Not even to keep my dick warm... *fuck*.

Except I really couldn't stop thinking about Elka. Couldn't stop wondering, couldn't stop worrying...

"You go check on her?" Narcos asked me and I shook my head.

"Why not?" Driller asked from over by the throw line.

"Not sure she'd wanna see me, man. I gave her my number. She'll call if she needs somethin'."

"Or, you know, she's just like you and don't know how to ask for help," Golden said bluntly. I scowled at him.

"I don't need help," I said flatly.

"Whatever, dude. We're here when you figure it out otherwise," Driller called, pulling his projectiles from the battered cork.

My phone started buzzing in the inside pocket of my cut, I pulled it out and scowled. I didn't recognize the number, but it was local and way too late to be a bill collector or a robocall. Usually, I made 'em leave a voicemail, or text me, but something made me wanna answer this call. Maybe it was just an excuse to get away from the guys and the topic for a minute.

"This is Hector," I answered.

"Officer Jones?" a man asked.

"Uh, yeah, who's this?" I slid off the stool and left the boys chatting to step outside where I could hear better.

"This is Albert Köhler, you told me to call you if..." his voice faltered but I could pick up the worry through the line, now that I was out of the restaurant.

"Yeah, yeah, Mr. Köhler, what's the matter?" I asked.

"It's my daughter, Elka. She's not answering her phone, no matter how many times I call. It's getting dark, and I can't drive so good at night –"

"Hang on, let me get something to write with, you can gimme the address."

"Yes, thank you," he said and the amount of relief in his voice told me I was definitely doing the right thing.

4

*E*lka...

I sighed, not that I could hear it through the music thundering in my skull. I gripped the back of my neck and tried to pull some of the tension out as I considered the canvas in front of my, loaded with paint. The oils slick and glistening, the high window of my basement apartment's master bedroom open to the city's night air. I'd claimed the master bedroom as my studio space. The adjoining bathroom more convenient for cleanup than trying to cart things through the hallway to the kitchen.

It was a weird little apartment, converted out of a street-level basement in an old, old building. Quaint, with its little wrought iron gates and climbing vines out of the little square flowerbed each ground-floor apartment boasted. The layout on the inside left a lot to be desired, though.

I stared at where my sister's face was taking shape and wrinkled my brow. I'd been painting this portrait of her for her wedding gift... but now it was for myself. A memorial... and that stung in ways I couldn't describe.

I felt a deep, bone weariness that had nothing to really do with being physically tired. I wasn't hungry. I had no appetite. I didn't want to deal with people – *at all* – but that wasn't especially new. I'd always been the introverted one. Mia had always been the better of the two of us, and that wasn't necessarily me being self-deprecating. It was simply the God-given truth of it.

Prettier, more outgoing by far – everyone had just gravitated toward my little sister and her vivacious personality and I was far from jealous. Oh, no... I was *blessed* because my little sister had always loved me best. Out of everyone in the world. Even her fiancé.

If I called her, Mia had been there and after what'd happened to me in college, I'd needed her, relied on her in ways that no older sister should rely on their younger one. It wasn't fair, but Mia had never, not once, complained.

I felt so incredibly and devastatingly alone and the only thing that even remotely soothed my hurt was my art, the love for it sustaining me, allowing me a place to disappear in swirls of color and the glide of the oils from the brush to the canvas.

Mia had always loved to watch me paint, and I only hoped that wherever she was, she was entertained watching me now.

"Shit," I swore softly and threw my brush into the little cup of solvent I had nearby to receive them.

I closed my eyes and tried to escape into the sound of the crashing drums and thrum of guitar in my ears, my favorite singer's melancholy voice soothing even as she seemingly understood my pain without ever having known me. Although, to be fair, she lamented the loss of some fictional lover – not a brother or sister.

A hand fell on my shoulder and I screamed, nearly hitting the roof, ripping the wires at my front, the noise canceling earbuds popping from my ears. Cool air rushed with harsh reality where warmth had been a moment before as I practically flew from my stool and spun.

"Mr. Jones?" I cried in confusion, chest heaving, hand pressed over my racing heart trying to get it to calm down.

"I told you to call me, Oz," he said like he wasn't standing in my apartment with his hands upraised in surrender. I glimpsed two uniformed officers out in the hall beyond him, one speaking into the microphone of his radio at his shoulder.

Cymbals crashed faintly from my headphones dangling useless near the floor and I reached down to reel the earbuds back up, wadding the thin, rubber coated wire into my hands as I demanded, "What are you doing here?"

"Don't you ever answer your phone?" he asked. "Your dad called me, he's worried sick about you. Says he's been trying to call you for hours."

I pulled my iPod from my back pocket and turned off the music, setting the little player on a spare corner of my easel, the headphones spiraling back to the floor, the wad of wire springing free. I rolled my lips together and felt myself color with guilt and embarrassment.

"How did you get in?" I demanded.

"Landlord doesn't believe in answering his phone, either," he said gently, and I blanched when he finished with, "We kicked the door in."

"You did *what?*"

"Your dad was worried, thought you might have hurt yourself. The lights were on but you weren't answering the door, exigent circumstances," he said, following me out and down the hall. I gaped at the wreckage and ruin of my doorframe, the door warped and twisted, the metal dented in the center, smudged black boot prints on the pale blue paint. It'd taken more than one hit.

"Oh, my God," I muttered aghast. "How am I going to afford to fix this?"

Officer Jones shook his head. "Don't worry about that. Just call your father right now, please?"

I nodded and he stayed put in the living room, turning to the two uniformed officers who had moved out of my space and were now lingering just outside.

I went to my bedroom and picked up my phone off the charger by my bed... *twenty-nine missed calls... holy shit.*

I called my father, thrusting everything else to the side for the time being.

One problem, one step, one breath at a time...

5

*O*z...

I cleaned up the remnants of her door while she talked to her pops on the phone in the other room. I couldn't make out her words through the short distance or the walls, but I could make out her tone. At points in the conversation, kind, at other points, exasperated, which I could feel her. I didn't have no helicopter parents, but I saw plenty of 'em picking up their little darlings from the jail.

This didn't exactly have that vibe, though. More like just your average concerned father and one hell of a mix-up.

"Damn," I muttered, shaking my head at the shards of doorjamb and the flimsy rumpled door. There was no getting it back in its frame. Not even for looks. Not tonight, anyhow.

"So, what now?" she asked, leaning against the wall of her hallway, arms crossed over her chest. She was in a pair of cutoff, paint-stained denim shorts that showed off her long smooth legs and I tried not to think too hard about that. That, or the skin-tight rainbow striped tank top that she wore up top, huddled in her plain white kimono-type wrap thing she must have grabbed out of her bedroom to cover up with.

"Uh, well, now I guess I'm staying on your couch until my guys can get here in the morning and fix your shit."

"Thanks for that, fixing my door, I mean… management is barely above 'slum lord' on the 'can you come and fix this' scale. Most of us do it ourselves."

"That's some bullshit," I said, and she smirked faintly.

"That's life in a cheap apartment in Indigo City," she said. "Although, when I moved in right after college, the neighborhood here wasn't nearly as bad."

I nodded. "Yeah, they been fixing up one of the poorer neighborhoods nearby, redevelopment, gentrifying the hell out of it – the poorer folks had to go somewhere."

"And here was it, yeah." She nodded and clutched her phone a little tighter near the opposite upper arm as she hugged herself.

"You got work in the morning?" I asked.

She nodded. "Yeah, my first day of a new job actually. We were…" her voice cracked and she cleared her throat. "Mia and I were coming back from her taking me to have my nails done to celebrate the new job. She was so happy for me…" she trailed off and bit her lips together staring hard at the ceiling as her eyes glassed over.

"They put off my start date so I could go to her funeral and help my dad. Get everything all arranged, you know?"

I nodded. "That was nice of them."

"It was, so," she dashed under her eyes and took a fortifying breath, "I really can't afford to be late my first day."

"It's cool, I'll uh – just go to bed. I'll crash here on the couch, a bunch of the guys, all of us are law-enforcement types, we'll get your door fixed and I'll lock up and bring you your new keys around lunch time. Sound good?"

"I guess that will do," she said but sounded wary all the same. I mean, I got it, who wanted a bunch of strangers up in your place when you were gone?

"Sorry I kicked it in, in the first place." She smirked at that again and eventually that smirk turned into a little laugh and a smile.

"A bit over the top," she agreed and I grinned back and shook my head a little.

"Naw, not really. Your pops seemed real freaked out."

The brief smile that'd lit up her face flickered out of existence, like a candle flame doused by a sudden and swift breeze.

"Yeah, well, I haven't always been the most stable of his two daughters," she said with an edge of caution in her voice.

"How's that?" I asked, Spidey-sense a tingling.

"It's nothing," she said finally, and she wouldn't look at me, just shook her head and found a spot on the floor to fixate on.

"Okay, well, you should probably get some sleep."

She nodded and said, "The bathroom is in the room with my paintings, I'll shut my bedroom door so you can use the light. *Please* use the light. I think I would die if any of my projects were damaged."

"I got you," I said and nodded. I didn't take any offense. I was a big dude, wide through the shoulders, I was forever smacking them into things – doorways, gym equipment – you name it. I'd be careful.

"I really don't know how to feel about any of this," she said frankly and looked torn.

"Then don't," I told her. "It's cool." Her brow furrowed and she took a deep breath and let it out in a gusty sigh. I didn't let her say anything else. I just kind of ordered her gently, "Go to bed. I got this."

She worried her bottom lip between her teeth and reluctantly nodded, turning and drifting back down the hall and into her bedroom. I heard a few quiet thumps and bumps and gave a nod, figuring she'd locked her door. That was a good idea even though she ain't got no worries from me.

I figured I'd be staring at her ceiling for a few hours, but surprisingly, I was out like a traffic light inside two minutes. Dead to the world and a shitty guard dog, because when I woke up next, it was to Backdraft smacking my boot with his hand, both hands going up as I drew down on him.

"I come in peace!" he declared and I pointed my gun at the ceiling letting out a long slow breath.

"Put that away, neighborhood's bad but ain't none of it *that* bad," Skids declared.

"Man, don't ever sneak up on a homie like that." I scowled at Backdraft.

He rolled his eyes.

"I called your name like six times. I'm surprised I didn't wake up the whole fuckin' neighborhood."

"What'd I miss?" Golden demanded turning sideways to squeeze past Skids in the open doorway.

"Oz being Oz," Skids declared.

"Still working for that Asshole Merit Badge, huh?"

"Fuck you, I invented that badge and I already got it on." I pulled my cut up and pointed at the round badge on the front.

"My bad, where's mine?"

"Pull any dick moves lately?" Backdraft asked, moving over near Skids and eyeing the ruined door frame.

"Is it a day that ends in 'Y'?" I asked, sitting up with a grimace. My body straight up hated her couch.

"Exactly my point." Golden threw up his hands. "So, where's my goddamned patch?"

"You ain't earned it yet," I declared.

"Pfft! If you weren't older, I would have been first," Golden shot back.

"Age before beauty." Backdraft grinned and stretched.

"You shut up!" I pointed a finger at the hose boy and scowled at him, even if he was right.

"What kind of dick move you pull lately?" Skids inquired and I laughed.

"Okay, okay, so get this. We got a loudmouth in the jail, decides he's gonna barricade himself into his cell, right? So they call us up, the good ol' Tactical Response Team and we go through all the hassle of gearing up to go extract him. So we get there, and he's all barking like this fuckin' little Chihuahua. He's all 'motherfucker' this and 'pig fucker' that and finally, I bust out my can of OC and hold it up and yell at him, 'Bitch, shut *up!*' and he just keeps on going so look…" I started cracking up before I could finish the story. I couldn't help it. "I unloaded that can of OC straight in his mouth like it was Binaca."

The guys fell out laughing. I think the visual spoke for itself. Nothing like a can of riot control mace right in the mouth kickin' you right in the back of the throat to shut your ass down. It had, too. He'd hit the floor choking and sputtering and we'd shown mercy and busted out the gallons of milk to put out the fire.

"I don't get it." her voice disrupted the laughter and we all turned. "What's OC?"

"Oil of capsaicin, it's the shit in jalapeños that makes them hot," Golden supplied.

"Oh, so pepper spray?"

"Yeah," Backdraft wheezed it out wiping a tear from his eye.

"Industrial strength," added Golden.

She pondered a moment and then asked, "So what's Binaca? I've never heard of that, either."

"Girl, how old are you?" Skids asked with a grin.

"Old enough," she said with a frown.

"No offense meant." He held up his hands.

"It's a breath spray, press the button on the top of the canister type," I explained.

"Oh! Like a brand name type?"

"Yeah."

She gave a nod, uncrossed her arms and drifted over toward the kitchen, but still, the troubled look didn't leave her face. "Coffee?" she asked politely enough, despite her sour expression.

"You'd be a savior and a saint," Skids declared.

She eyed her ruined door and said, "If you can get that fixed today, I could say the same thing about you."

"We'll get it fixed," Backdraft said affably, going back over to the door to inspect the shattered jamb.

"Thanks," she muttered and disappeared into her kitchen.

"So, what the hell happened here, anyway?" Golden asked.

"Later," I said curtly, and he held up his hands in surrender, jerking his head in the direction of the kitchen and raising an eyebrow in question. He was wondering – *what was her deal?* I would like to know too. So, by way of answer, I shrugged, dropping it for the moment, and watched as Backdraft knelt down next to his thick canvas tool bag and opened it up, extracting a handheld short foot-and-a-half-long crowbar to start prying the doorjamb away from the wall.

"This is going to take some doing," he declared.

"Yeah, I don't do anything half-assed," I shot back.

"No! No, you do not," Skids agreed.

Golden chuckled and we stood around for the most part while Back-draft, the expert in these types of situations, did his thing. Assessing the damage, prying the boards making up the door jamb loose, that kind of thing. When he wanted or needed one of us, he would say so.

Elka came out of the kitchen doorway a short time later with a metal travel mug in her hands. She paused to look at each of us in turn and declared quietly, "Coffee is in the pot on the counter. If you need more, I left everything out next to it. Mugs are above the sink, milk and creamer are in the fridge. I left a bowl of sugar out if that's your thing. I'm really sorry, but I have to get to work. First day and all."

"Naw, it's fine, we get it. Thanks for the coffee." Skids smiled at her kindly.

"I'll walk you out," I said.

"No, please. It's fine. Just… just if you need to use the bathroom please be careful of the paintings. I'd die if anything happened to them. They're oils so the paint's still wet."

"We'll be careful, I promise," I told her.

"Thanks again," she muttered and taking up her purse and shoul-dering her briefcase she squared her shoulders and squeezed past Backdraft and Golden, her posture rigid.

"She's not okay," Golden mused out loud when she was well out of earshot.

"No shit, genius. What was your first clue?"

"Knock it off and come help me," Backdraft grunted.

"What do you need?" Golden asked.

"Pull!"

Golden hooked his fingers in the doorjamb and helped pull it away from the wall, the already splintered wood cracking loudly.

Fixing her door was a pain in the ass. Regardless of its status as 'finished' or not, I had promised to bring her the new keys around by lunchtime and so with the guys still working on it, that's what I did. I swung by one of the local hardware places where they still had a guy behind the counter to cut new keys and had some duplicates made for her. I figured three sets would do. One for her, one for her management company and a set maybe for her pops or whoever she wanted to give them to. There was another set, left with the guys to lock up if they finished up before I got back, but that didn't seem like it was going to happen.

It was always something, man. *Always* something. With any kind of home improvement project or repair there had to be a hiccup or a pain in the ass hardware issue just something. This project was no fucking exception and at times I found myself seething unfairly at Elka like it was somehow her fault for not answering the fucking door.

Which, it kind of was, even though it wasn't exactly fair to level blame. You know what I mean?

Anyway, I was shit at these kinds of things. Repairs and the like. Put a gun in my hand that was having issues and I could fix that, but cages, bikes, and houses? Never been my thing. I just was all thumbs. I could tell you how to fix bad sports plays or how to handle any sport-related injury, but fixing people was way different than fixing a splintered doorframe.

I especially had this thought hit home when I saw Elka, bent over some painting painstakingly doing what, I didn't know to it. It was the look of grim concentration on her face, something about her stooped posture, her bent shoulders; the way she clutched her necklace to her chest as if she were trying to keep her damn heart from falling out.

Naw, with as many fits and problems fixing her front door had been giving us all morning long, fixing *her* was gonna be way more painstaking a process.

Not your problem, asshole. Just stay in your lane, I thought savagely to myself but as I followed the reception lady to Elka's fancy white plexiglass table glowing softly under whatever piece she had on it, I knew I was fooling myself.

Females ain't nothing but trouble, I reminded myself, but my internal voice was echoed by the lighter side of my soul reminding me that not all females were. She honestly didn't look like no trouble at all. Just… tired. Lonesome maybe. Hurt definitely.

"Ms. Köhler, this man is here to see you – he says he's the police."

She looked up from her work, setting her cotton swab full of goop aside and said, "Thank you, Katie. I've been expecting him."

Katie smiled and I swear to God, dipped some fancy ass curtsey before turning and striding back the way she came. I cocked my head and stared after her, looking from Elka before back in the receptionist's direction before looking back to Elka shaking my head.

Elka, to her credit, actually cracked a smile and tittered a soft laugh.

"Some of us art nerds are from a bygone era," she stated, and I blinked in amazement and said, "For real."

"How's my front door?" she asked, slipping off her stool and hugging herself, her white-gloved hands capturing her elbows.

"A pain in our ass but it'll be done before you get home. I wanted to bring you by your new keys." I pulled the ring with two keys on it out of my pocket and held them out to her.

"Oh," she murmured and pulled off her white cotton gloves and the latex ones beneath them.

"You have lunch yet?" I asked.

"No, um, not yet," she murmured, taking the keys and slipping them into her navy-blue lab coat's pocket.

"Come on, my treat. There's this bomb ass taco truck right down the street in the food truck grotto."

"I don't know," she said, rocking back in her low kitten heels a bit. "I'm honestly not even hungry."

"Come on, you gotta eat and it's my treat," I said.

Again with that look on her face like she was torn in two.

Finally, she nodded and said, "Let me just clean up my station."

I wandered closer to it and gave a low whistle at what she had laid out.

"Looks old," I said dryly.

"Not terribly," she responded. "It was painted in 1874."

"Dayum!" I stretched my bottom lip and took a step back from where I'd leaned a hip against the table.

She smiled and tried to keep a lid on her laugh as she said, "By far it's not the oldest restoration project I've done. Get into the mid-sixteenth century and there's where I find my nerves."

I couldn't even fathom to do the math, so I asked, "How old is that?"

"Five hundred years or so," she answered as she pulled on a fresh pair of latex gloves. I felt my eyes go wide as I shook my head gently back and forth.

"Mm-mm, you got nerves of steel working on something like that," I said.

She smiled genuinely, pride shining softly from her face as she did everything she needed to in order to be able to go to lunch. It was a lot, and I kind of felt bad all the steps she had to go through in order to start back up once she was back.

"Ready?" I asked her as she tossed her stripped off latex gloves into a nearby trashcan and slipped out of her lab coat, extracting her freshly cut keys from the pocket.

"Yeah, let me just grab my purse." She went to a line of hooks on the wall, her name above one etched into a brass plate that was shinier than the rest. I smiled and said, "They sure know how to roll out the welcome wagon around here."

Elka smiled. "They have all the equipment to make them in another part of the building for exhibits. I asked about it. They thought it was a nice touch in here."

"Yeah, it is," I agreed. She pulled her purse down and hung her lab coat in its place. Slipping the strap over her head and settling the little bag on her opposite hip, she dropped her new keys in the top of her purse and zipped it closed.

"Need anything else?" I asked.

"Nope," she replied and fell into step beside me. We stopped at the front desk to hand in my visitor's badge and away we went.

6

*E*lka...

We walked slowly along the block toward the fenced-in vacant lot full of food trucks that were ringing in a makeshift cafeteria area of picnic tables. The food truck grotto was almost a modern art installation in and of itself, a mere block and a half from the historical art museum. One of Indigo City's crown jewels, if I do say so myself – er, the museum not the food truck grotto – although it had held a special place in my heart too.

"So," Oz, said with a gusty sigh trying to start a conversation after around half a block of silence. "Wanna tell me why your old man called me up in the middle of the night to come kick in your door?"

"Wow, you don't beat around the bush, do you?" I asked, hedging for time but also knowing that it was likely a lost cause. I mean, he'd already done so much already. The least I could do was be candid now.

"Not especially, no," he said dryly, and I nodded.

"When I was in college, I was engaged," I answered slowly. Finding the words was surprisingly difficult, even now.

"And?" he asked after I was quiet for too long.

"It… it didn't work out," I finished lamely. What I wasn't able to say was just how straight out of a Jane Austen novel Robert Critchley had been. How I hadn't been rich enough for his rich family. How I'd been pregnant when he'd dumped me at his mother's behest and how they'd graciously offered to pay for the abortion – which I'd gone through with – which had crushed me and sent me spiraling into a deep depression.

"Bad enough you tried to hurt yourself?" he asked.

I pressed my lips together and nodded a little too rapidly.

"It was stupid. Really stupid, and I regret it… mostly because of what it did to my dad and to Mia. I don't think he'll ever believe that I'm okay again, you know?"

"And are you?" he asked, stopping in line at the taco truck that was apparently his favorite. I gripped the strap on my bag with both fists, twisting the faux leather against the palms of my hands uneasily.

"No, I guess not. I mean, I thought I was but now with Mia… I mean, he probably wasn't *wrong* to worry but…" I swallowed hard and met Officer Jones' warm brown eyes. "I won't do it again. I learned my lesson," I said faintly, and his eyebrows went up.

"Interesting way of putting it," he said, slipping a pair of wraparound glasses off of one of the breast pockets of his leather vest. He slid them over his eyes, and I felt like it was a way to cut me off, a way to take a step back and put some distance between us.

I honestly couldn't say I blamed him. I was a hot mess. I owned that. I mean, I had to own that. Had to live with it. Alone now.

Tears welled up and I looked away, dashing at them with my finger-tips. While I wasn't all-out constantly crying over Mia anymore or how horribly distressed I was about moving through the rest of my life without her just being there somewhere in the background, just a phone call away... These sudden bouts were still overtaking me at the worst and oddest little moments.

I had been proud of myself that I hadn't broken down while working, that I had been able to lose myself in the monotonous task at hand of cleaning the surface grime off of the Inness painting in front of me, but it seems my grief would not be denied for more than a few hours, and it was roaring to life even now.

"Hey, don't do that," Oz said with a warm and tender smile. "Don't cry," he said gently and then added sort of off the cuff, "Pretty girls don't cry."

I laughed, the notion patently ridiculous, one, that pretty girls didn't cry – I happened to know from experience they did – and two, that I could even be considered one of their ranks. I was a fine-art nerd and 'pretty' had never really been a descriptor used in my direction. I'd always been passably 'cute' but nothing more.

Mia. Mia had been the pretty sister of the two of us. Still, his way with dry sarcastic humor had its desired effect for now. The small bit of incredulous laughter he'd drawn from me had allowed me to get just enough of a grip to get my shit together to keep people from looking or getting worried. The last thing I wanted to do was cause a scene.

"You know what you want?" he asked to distract my mind further and I contemplated the menu board above the truck's open food service window. A sandwich board was off to the side with the day's specials and I let my eyes rove the colorful chalk letters and drawings at the edges. Whoever had done the sign had an incredible eye for detail and a fantastic capability with blending the chalks. It was almost too bad that the sign would be wiped clean to start again for the next day.

"I'm really not that hungry," I reiterated, but Oz would have none of it. He was seemingly determined that I eat something.

"You a taco girl or more into burritos?" he asked.

"A couple of tacos," I finally relented, the smells from the truck catching on the summer breeze and carried to my nose sort of waking my stomach.

"Pollo, carnitas, or carne asada?" he asked, his accent flawless. I blinked, not sure why I was surprised a black man would know Spanish and feeling like a racist white-privileged little shit right on the heels of the thought.

"Um, I don't know," I said. I mean, I didn't eat a lot of Mexican food and I wasn't entirely sure what any of those meant. I spoke fluent German thanks to my upbringing and high school classes. Even some college classes. It wasn't very useful here, though.

"Right." It was our turn at the window, and he turned and reached up to the guy manning the window and clasped his hand in greeting. That strange sort of male hand-hug that dripped with machismo and made it look like they were about to arm wrestle. Offsetting the gesture were the genuine smiles on their faces, the younger man's expression lighting up with utter delight at Oz's presence.

They spoke back and forth in rapid-fire Spanish and I couldn't understand a word of it. It was more than slightly uncomfortable when the young man eyed me up from his heightened perch from within the food truck as Officer Jones spoke, clearly about me. The young man crossed himself and my tense posture eased.

"Man, I'm so sorry to hear that," he said. "My condolences for your sister."

"Thank you," I murmured, and he called back into the truck.

The cook yelled something back and the young man frowned and snapped at the older man who could have been his father or uncle.

"I'll have that right up," he told Oz and then waved his hands at him rejecting the money Oz tried to hand him.

"No, no, no, man! Your money's no good here!"

"Ahhhh, thanks, Enrique."

"No problem, go grab a seat, I'll bring it out."

"You're awesome, man."

I followed Oz over to a vacant pair of seats across from each other at one end of a brightly blue painted picnic table. We sat and he grabbed a spray bottle of cleaner from the middle of the table and sprayed our section of it down, swiping some paper towels off the roll and sweeping them over the space between us before tossing them into one of the open trashcans made from some equally vividly painted, repurposed metal fifty-five-gallon drums.

"There," he said, dropping into his seat and I smiled at him a little gratefully.

"Seems like you and Enrique go way back," I mentioned as just a way to get the conversation started.

"Ah, yeah, he's a good kid. Got swept up in a gang bust a few years back when he was fifteen, was facing some pretty hefty adult charges. Wound up in my jail for processing. I got him into an after-school program I was working at the time, volunteer shit. Got him back on track and out of trouble. That's his uncle's food truck he's working. Few more years and he's set to take over the family business when the old man retires."

"Wow," I said impressed. "You do a lot of community outreach then?"

He shook his head. "Not so much anymore. If I do, it's usually with the club."

"How come? Seems like you're good at it, or am I a special case?"

He laughed slightly, eyes unreadable behind his sunglasses as he bowed his head. He shook it. "You aren't a 'case' at all," he said.

Then what am I? I wondered silently, but I wasn't brave enough to ask. Instead, I studied what I could see of his face. He was strikingly handsome, unique in a way that I had almost never seen before. I mean, he was definitely mixed race and one of those races was black, but I couldn't for the life of me identify what the other half was.

Whatever it was, it gave a wonderful, warm golden cast to his skin that was offset by all the black he was wearing. The tee shirt he had on was wonderfully fitted and molded to his chest and shoulders like a second skin. It strained at the sleeves to contain his biceps and I let my practiced eye rove the tattoos that sleeved one arm from shoulder to wrist. I let my eyes follow each loop and curve of thorny vine, the roses big and crimson at their edges. The entire piece of art wrapping his forearm and clambering up over his elbow bespoke a vehement desire for the onlooker to *back off*, while simultaneously touched on a deeper sadness. One I couldn't yet identify. A loneliness, perhaps… or, perhaps, I was just projecting.

"A'riiiight, here you guys go." Enrique arrived just before the bubble of question that'd risen to my lips had a chance to burst. I swallowed it back down, deciding it had been too personal to ask. *What do they mean to you…?*

It was none of my business. I don't know why, but it just didn't seem like a good idea to get too close.

You know exactly why it's a bad idea. You don't want another relationship. Not if it's going to end like your last… and you especially don't want a relationship based on… what? Pity?

It wasn't time to try again. Not by a long shot. Especially not now.

I stared down at the too-bright cardboard-like eco-friendlier clamshell Enrique had set in front of me. Eying the glass Coke bottle he'd set beside it.

"I'm just going to grab some napkins," I murmured, half rising from my seat while he and Oz chatted amicably.

"Hold up," Officer Jones said with a smile. "Stay in the truck, I got you."

Enrique pulled a spate of napkins and some plastic cutlery from the front of his stained apron pockets and handed them to me with a smile. I blushed faintly and accepted them with a quiet thanks.

"Hey, no problem. I gotta get back to the truck, but it was good seeing you, man." He nodded to Officer Jones.

"Yeah, glad to see you're doin' alright," Oz said with a nod.

"Better than alright, man. Life is great! It was nice to meet you Elka!" He waved at me and I had completely missed it when Oz had given Enrique my name.

"It was nice to meet you too," I said faintly, and he turned and jogged back to his food truck.

Oz was eying me over his open clamshell, pushing the sauce on whatever he'd ordered within it around with his fork.

"You ain't even here," he said and it held a slightly amused tone, though I didn't detect anything accusatory in it. "You're like a million miles away, aren't you?" he asked.

"I'm sorry…" I started and he sniffed.

"Don't be," he said, shoving a bite of food in his mouth.

He chewed and watched me steadily, his eyebrows going up behind his dark glasses. I opened up my clamshell and the smell that wafted up was divine. Meaty and green from the cilantro sprinkled on top. Rich and spicy, buttery and – and I was suddenly *starving.*

I tucked into my food and he smiled as he chewed his, as if he were pleased. He finished his bite, swallowing and said, "I got you one of each. Chicken, pork, and steak. Let me know which one you like best."

I laughed slightly and said, "I doubt I will get through all three, but I think this one is the pork and it's good."

"Good deal," he said with a smirk.

I made it through the pork and half of the chicken before I was too stuffed to continue. At least I had dinner if I wanted it later. We gathered up our things, tossed our recycling in the green drums off to the side marked with its stenciled triangle of arrows, and he walked me back to the museum.

"So, uh, we might still be at it when you get home. There's no tellin'. Just wanted to give you a heads-up."

"Oh, thank you. I'm sorry it's being such a pain in the ass."

"Not your fault. I'm the one that kicked it in," he said, dragging open the lobby door for me.

"Well, thank you."

"Have dinner with me!" he blurted out. "I mean, not tonight, but maybe sometime later this week."

"I don't know…" I said chewing my bottom lip.

"I do. No pressure but seems to me you need to get out a little bit. Bein' some kind of a shut-in is the last thing you need right now."

"How would you know?" I asked and immediately regretted how it came out, how it sounded. I was just becoming genuinely curious about him.

His eyes were unreadable behind the dark lenses and the glasses were starting to drive me crazy. His mouth quirked into this sort of half smile and he said, "Have dinner with me and I'll tell you."

I frowned. "Very well," I acquiesced.

"Good deal. Call me. Have a good rest of your day," he said and then he was gone, and I was left staring out of the tempered and UV protected glass of the lobby doors, watching the sun glimmer off the silver thread of the rays behind the indigo chess piece of the great big patch on the back of his vest.

It gave me a different flavor of food for thought as I returned to my work and before I knew it, it was time to wrap things up and to take the bus home.

My new door looked very new, the smell of freshly cut wood and new paint assailing me as I stepped through. There was a note on my dining room table and another one of Officer Jone's cards with his cell number on the back.

The note read:

Good as new. Text me or call me to set up that dinner.

My cell is on the back of the card.

Oz

I went to the fridge and slid the rest of my tacos from lunch onto the shelf, my stomach suddenly churning for a completely different reason. I mean, I hope he wasn't thinking this was going to be like… a date.

"God, get *real*, Elka." I groaned covering my face with my hands and scrubbed, pressing my fingertips into my closed eyelids. I sighed and with a backward glance at the card sitting on the table, took myself in for a hot shower.

7

*O*z...

The days ticked by, and it was finally on Thursday when I got my cell out of my locker to find that I had a text waiting for me from an unknown number.

Unknown: It's Elka, about that dinner... what did you have in mind?

Good question, what *did* I have in mind?

I set my phone on the locker's high shelf and changed out of my uniform and into street clothes while I thought about it. The guys I worked with drifted through here and there, grabbing their shit and taking off and I made passable small talk, but I wasn't really feeling it. I had this urge to go for a long ride just to get out of the city when it hit me...

I picked up my phone and shot back,

Me: What are you doing on Saturday?

Tucking my cell into my back pocket, I shrugged into my jacket and cut before slinging my big ass waterproofed messenger bag across my chest. I had some laundry to do when I got back to my place if I wanted clean uniforms. I dropped my work boots into the bottom of my locker and kicked it closed with my Harley boot. My cell buzzed in my back pocket as I ducked out of the locker room and headed down the hall to the jail's employee exit to the garage.

I checked the message and would have to wait to answer whatever it is until I got street side. Cell service was shit in the garage. We barely got two bars in the locker room as it was. No good for calls but texts did alright depending on your network.

Unknown: Nothing actually. Paint, maybe. Put on a movie. I hadn't really thought about it.

First, I fixed it so instead of 'Unknown' my phone read 'Elka' then I got on the front of my bike and stuck the key in the ignition. I let her rumble to life beneath me and settle into that regular chugging purr I loved so much while I stowed my phone and pulled on my fingerless gloves. My lid on and some clear safety glasses on to cut the wind in my eyes, I pulled out and made my way up the ramps and out under a sky to match the city's name.

I worked swing shift most of the time, so it was late by normal people's standards. I pulled over a few blocks from the jail where there was room, so I didn't keep her up much later.

Me: Sorry, I wasn't ignoring you. I was at work. Just got off shift and had to get out of the garage. What are you still doing up anyway?

I sat for a minute, glad the response was pretty quick.

Elka: Was just cleaning up, about to go to bed. I have a hard time sleeping since... you know.

I sighed. Yeah. I knew.

Me: Yeah. About Saturday. Come take a ride with me.

I was half afraid she'd say 'no' the other half of me afraid she'd say 'yes' as I shoved my phone back into my pocket and hit my signal to pull back out into traffic. I made it over six blocks before the damn thing buzzed again and I almost missed it from the thrum of the bike. I didn't pull over again, opting instead to take my ass home.

I pulled into the spot for me down the alley and behind my old brick building and took the rickety old wooden staircase up the back to the rear door. It was further away, my place being at the front of the building, but I'd rather do that than have to hurt some useless fuck lookin' at me like I was some easy target.

The neighborhood I'd moved into after the divorce was shitty, but it was all I could fucking afford. My lawyer had been next to fuckin' useless and where he hadn't wiped me out, Regina, my ex-wife, had. She'd taken the house, half my fuckin' retirement, and had left me all of the fuckin' tax bill on that plus her fuckin' credit cards.

I'd declared bankruptcy, which pretty much locked me into this shit-hole for at least a few more years. I'd barely hung on to my fucking bike in the split. Vindictive bitch had gone after that, too. I wasn't a violent dude for all my posturing – had never hit a woman in my life – but that? That'd made me want to put a fist to her smug face so hard. I'd resisted. Walked away. Thank fuck Skids and the rest of the squad had been there for the worst of it.

Their presence had held my ass in check. Not proud to admit that's what it took – but it did.

I'm not a good man. I'm just alright, I thought as I unlocked the three locks holding my apartment door shut. Which was why I didn't know what the fuck I was doing where Elka was concerned. I certainly didn't know what the fuck I was thinking in inviting her out to ride.

I pulled my phone out of my pocket and checked.

Elka: I've never ridden before but sounds intriguing.

Intriguing? Huh. Not the word I would have picked, but alright.

Me: All you gotta do is dress for the slide not for the ride and hang on.

I waited. Staring at my screen, but after several drawn out moments gave it up. She was probably in bed and asleep.

I sighed and pulled my messenger bag off over my head and dropped it on my clean if slightly tattered secondhand couch.

I lived in a one-bedroom and that was a joke. The bedroom, to its credit, was bigger than the kitchen and living room combined. Probably because the bedroom closet also had the water heater, the washer, and the dryer in it. Weird, right? Better than hauling my shit to the laundromat each week though. It'd been my one deal breaker when finding a place. Must have laundry in unit.

I plugged my phone in at the kitchen wall outlet and took my ass in to shower and get ready for bed. I had to get up early if I was gonna make it to work out with the hose boys at Backdraft's station. A nice change of pace from the cop gym I went to. The place had softened up since Angel's ol' lady had moved into the back room making it her studio. The eye candy she had parading in and out the back for yoga and her circus shit was distracting. Pretty to look at but not much else. At least not for me.

If it was one thing Reggie had proven, females were trouble and it was trouble I needed to stay the hell away from. I know, I know... not *all* females, but after the constant shit with Reggie, I wasn't lookin' for any repeat performances and was happy to stay in my fuckin' lane.

Of course, my cyclical thinking took me right back around off my ex-wife and back to Elka.

She was worlds away in difference. Cool, somber, and mellow to be around but with a hidden edge. By comparison, which I couldn't help but make, Reggie was a walking disaster. Always bitching, always complaining; *always* yelling.

"Man, get your head off it. She ain't lookin' to hook up with your ass," I mumbled, ducking my head under the shower's spray.

When I got out of the shower, I dried off, stood at the sink and shaved my head. The entire time, I couldn't help but keep listening for my phone from the other room. Hoping that she'd be up, still. That she would answer that last message and put me out of my misery. I felt like I was on pins and needles and kept second-guessing the hell out of myself on whether I should have even made the offer. Wondering if I'd scared her off the idea of going out with me on the bike with that last message.

I got nothing. She'd probably racked out.

"Ahhh, boy!" I shook my head at my reflection in the mirror and rinsed a washcloth under the tap to wipe off the excess shaving cream on my head and neck, making sure to get behind my ears.

I went to bed, but sleep didn't come easy. Not in the least because I kept turning it over in my head wondering if I'd fucked up.

8

———————

*E*lka...

I stared at the screen of my phone and sighed out, a rush of unsteady breath as I pondered his last words on the screen. I lolled my head on its pillow and checked the time. It was twenty minutes before my alarm was set to go off and I'd woken from another nightmare.

Another iteration of Mia's death where my sister's blood had coated my hands and no matter how hard I tried, I just couldn't get them to come clean.

Even now, I switched from gazing at my phone to my hands that clutched it and almost had to will myself to believe they were clean. That nothing spotted them or stained them. That it was all in my head.

I went back to that last message... Dress for the slide and not for the ride... what did that even mean? I mean, objectively it meant to dress in protective clothing, but I didn't own any. At least, not really. Also, did I really want to even try it? I mean, I had never been on the back of a motorcycle. It seemed dangerous.

Ultimately, I decided I was too afraid and quickly texted out: **Maybe we should just stick to dinner first.**

I hit send and squeezed my eyes shut.

"Well, that could be left open to interpretation, now couldn't it?" I muttered.

Ugh. I should really make sure I had at least one cup of coffee before texting anyone back.

I sighed and tossed my phone down at my side staring fixedly at the ceiling for a full two minutes while my mind raced over possibilities on how I had just screwed that up. I needed to break myself out of this anxiety loop, so before I let it get much worse, I forced myself into a sitting position and swung my legs out over the edge of the bed, dropping my feet to the floor.

Shower. I needed a shower before I did anything. A proper start to my day was definitely in order.

I dragged myself under a shower spray that was almost too hot to handle and camped there until at least some of the tension left my shoulders and back.

It was partially through my setup to get to work finishing up the cleaning of the Inness canvas that my phone lit up and buzzed against my work table.

With trepidation, I looked and sure enough the message was from Oz. I still thought it was strange calling him that, but it was what he liked to be called and who was I to argue?

Ofc. Jones: I'm cool with that. Dinner first. I'll come by your place. Got anyplace you wanna eat in mind?

Wow. It was just that easy? No guilt trips? No passive aggressive sniping? *He's not your ex, Ellie,* I reminded myself and the voice in my head sounded a lot more like my sister Mia than it did my own. Even using her affectionate and definitely more Americanized nickname for me.

I sighed and felt a knot of dread I hadn't realized was between my shoulders loosen. I tapped out my reply…

Me: I know a place near my apartment. Do you like Thai?

I waited, holding my breath, and just as I was about to set my phone down the message came through.

Ofc. Jones: IDK, I don't think I've ever had it before.

I smiled.

Me: Open to trying new things?

Ofc. Jones: Every damn day. When is good for you?

Me: Um, Friday or Saturday?

Ofc. Jones: It is Friday.

Me: Is it?

I turned red with embarrassment and checked my phone's calendar. Sure enough, it was. *Oops.*

Ofc. Jones: It is, so is tonight good for you?

Me: Sure… I can do tonight.

Ofc: Jones: How late is that place open, I can try and get outta work early but I'm usually not off until around 10.

Me: Would tomorrow work better for you?

Ofc. Jones: Yeah, probably.

Me: Okay, because tomorrow works for me too. I don't have any plans.

Ofc. Jones: I can do tomorrow.

Me: Seven work for you?

Ofc. Jones: Seven works just fine. I'll see you then.

Me: Okay.

I let out a slow and controlled breath and tried to decide how I felt about things. I mean, I shouldn't be this... *excited*, should I? I set my phone aside and went to lunch, finding myself back at the food truck grotto and smiling up at Enrique, shyly ordering a couple of chicken tacos.

He grinned back and said, "It'll be right up."

"How much?" I asked and he shook his head.

"Your money's no good here. Any friend of Oz is a friend of mine."

"Oh, no! I can't let you do that," I argued.

"Too bad, I just did," he said with a wink. "You want a Coke with that?"

"Depends, are you going to let me pay for it?" I asked.

"Nope."

"Then no, thank you. Water is fine."

"One Coke it is. Go on and find a seat, I'll bring it out to you."

I rolled my eyes but complied and when he came out with a clamshell and a bottle of Coke, he set them down and dropped onto the open expanse of bench beside me, pushing his sleeves up past his elbows.

"So," he said with a grin, "you seein' Oz?"

"Um... no. He just... um." I was flustered and didn't know what to say.

"He just what? 'Cause I've never seen him bring a woman around."

"He just was bringing me the new keys to my apartment," I said.

"Why would he have the keys to your place if you aren't seeing each other?" Enrique asked, bold as brass. I gave a long, slow blink in response.

"You sure do ask a lot of personal questions," I said.

He shrugged one shoulder and gave a rakish grin. "I got my reasons."

I frowned and opened up my food, pushing the taco filling around and mixing it with the plastic fork he handed over.

"He broke down my door. My dad couldn't get a hold of me and panicked. I had my headphones on and didn't hear him knock."

Enrique laughed so hard he almost fell off of his seat. Slapping his knee, he said, "Yeah, that sounds like Oz, and it also kind of answers my question." He stood up.

"What question? You haven't asked me anything."

He winked at me. "Not going to either, I know Oz. If you want, ask him about it." And with that, he was gone, back to his food truck and serving the hungry masses. I stared after him mystified for the moment before returning to my food.

The curious exchange was momentarily forgotten by the end of the day but resurfaced on the bus ride home. I played it and replayed it in my mind and for the life of me couldn't figure Enrique's odd behavior out. It'd done well to distract me, momentarily, from thinking about anything else for which I was sort of grateful.

When I reached my shiny new door, I had to sigh. My thoughts returning to Oz. I was surprised to find myself slightly disappointed I hadn't taken him up on a late dinner tonight, yet at the same time found myself apprehensive about tomorrow.

I was a war of emotions lately, and I had to confess, I wasn't coping very well at all, lately. I locked my door behind me and sighed with relief at being *alone*, dropping my purse and my briefcase on the floor right there in the entryway, stepping out of my heels and leaving it all in a pile.

I would take care of it all later.

First, I showered. Then, I fixed myself a salad and a hot cup of tea with some honey in it. Finally, I took it all into my living room, set my small plate and my cup and saucer on the coffee table and dropped onto my couch with a sigh.

I went for *Persuasion.* My favorite Jane Austen adaptation to film and truthfully, one of her only ones without the prominent theme of sisters.

Reading her books, watching the film adaptations of her work practically on repeat –they were my most favorite guilty pleasure.

I fell asleep, sandwich half eaten, tea less than half drunk and when I woke, it was to the DVD's menu screen playing over and over on repeat. I groaned, and pushed myself into a sitting position, my neck and shoulders in knots.

I didn't know what had woken me, but then my notification chimed again. An incoming text.

I pushed myself up and went to my discarded briefcase and purse by the door, rooting through them to find my phone.

Ofc. Jones: Just got off work. Wanted to check on you.

Ofc. Jones: Looks like you may already be asleep. Hit me up tomorrow.

I frowned at the phone, noting the eight-minute time difference between the two texts and heaved a sigh.

Me: I fell asleep on the couch. Thanks for waking me up so I could go to bed.

I didn't want him to feel bad for waking me up, so I figured that might help negate that. I put things to rights. My dishes in the sink, sandwich in the trash, and cold tea down the drain. My purse and briefcase went where they belonged, and my phone came with me into the bedroom as I got ready for bed.

It chimed just as I slid between the sheets.

Ofc. Jones: Sorry, I was riding to the 10-13. How are you doing? Okay?

I rolled my eyes and texted back.

Me: I'm fine. Just tired.

A few minutes later my screen lit up.

Ofc. Jones: We both know you ain't 'fine' but it's alright. You get some better sleep and I'll meet up with you tomorrow. K?

Me: Okay.

He wished me good night, I returned the sentiment, and then I flopped back into my bed and stared at the ceiling.

I was suddenly wide awake. Sleep doing its level best to elude me in every possible way.

Finally, frustrated, I got back up and went across the hall, flipping on the overhead light in the spare bedroom that I used as a studio.

Mia's unfinished painting sat on the easel, staring back at me. Forlorn, lost, and accusing. Three emotions I identified with all too well.

I was all three. Forlorn, lost without my sister and accusing both myself and God for letting it be her instead of me.

"I should have grabbed you, pushed you, I should have done something, *anything*, to save you." I covered my mouth with my hand finding it suddenly too hard to breathe with the overwhelming emotion swamping me. Closing my eyes didn't help. Slow breathing didn't help. None of the tricks I was taught to control and moderate my anxiety did anything. Instead, I drowned on dry land. Crumpling to my floor in the little studio-bedroom's doorway… giving myself over completely to my grief.

It was almost a miracle how cathartic a cry like that could be. Before I knew it, the storm had passed almost as fast as it had come on. It felt like hours had passed instead of only minutes and even though sleep had dodged me just moments before, I was suddenly *exhausted* and ripe for sleep.

Rather than fight it, I went with it. Snapping out the light and returning across the hall to my bedroom.

I fell into bed and went right to sleep, feeling guilty about lying to everyone every time they asked.

How are you doing? Are you okay?

Every time I answered 'fine.' Every time, the lie got easier. Every time it couldn't be further from the truth… and then there was Oz.

We both know you ain't fine… but it's alright.

It was something to think about.

It was something I couldn't stop thinking about, even as I fell asleep.

9

*O*z...

I pulled up to the curb between a couple of cars a couple doors down from Elka's place. I sighed out and undid the chin strap on my brain bucket. I was replaying some of the talk I'd had with Reflash and Skids the night before.

I still wasn't sure what the hell I was doing here, but it felt right that I keep doin' whatever it was.

The chief and deputy chief had pretty much reassured me I was doin' the right thing and to just go with the flow. So here I was, on time, about to do just that.

When she answered the door, I caught a whiff of something sweet, like vanilla. She looked up at me with those big doe eyes of hers and they just slayed me but I played it cool.

"Hi," I said, and she gave me a brave little smile.

"Hi," she said back in her quiet way as she stepped out onto the front stoop with me. I stepped back to give her some room and thought to myself, *okay, she wants to play it like that. That's cool, that's cool.*

She locked up her place and I let my eyes drift down her back. She was dressed casually in a women's cut light pink tee and a pair of jean shorts that did great things for her already out-of-this-world ass. The cuffs on the short shorts rolled up into a neat ridge making her legs look like they went on for days.

Her feet were tucked into a nice pair of white ladies' Adidas, which I could appreciate. I always appreciated some brand-name classic style kicks. She had them paired with some low socks that barely peeked at the edge of the shoe. Her long, shining dark hair was pulled up off her neck in a high ponytail and as always, her makeup was understated as she turned those large, bronze eyes back up to mine.

"Everything alright?" she asked, tucking her keys into her little cross-body bag at her hip.

"Yeah! Yeah, everything's good with me," I said.

"Okay." She nodded and gave me a nervous smile.

"So, where's this place you wanna go at?" I asked, sliding my sunglasses back on my face.

"Um, it's just a couple blocks this way." She jerked her head up the block and turned.

I grinned and nodded, falling into step beside her saying, "Okay."

We moved up the block and lapsed into a deep silence, doing it. I finally had to be the one to break the ice by asking her, "You finish that painting you were working on the other day?"

"What? Oh, no. A restoration effort takes weeks most of the time. I finished *cleaning* the painting, but I've just started the retouching process."

"Wow, how could it take so long, though?" I asked. "Doesn't seem like it has much that needs doin'."

"I can only work on it a few minutes at a time before I need to do something else. Retouching is suuuuuper tedious and really is unforgiving. I don't want to use more pigment than is required and you really don't want to rush so you do a little here, maybe twenty minutes, maybe as much as an hour, then you work on something else for a while. The cleaning process you can do for hours on end, it's just the retouching and the painting process that you really want to get right and not get lackadaisical about."

I smiled and listened to her talk. She was passionate about it. I think this was the most I'd honestly gotten her to talk about anything since I'd started coming around.

"So, you like your work," I said with a smile.

"I do," she said and smiled, blushing faintly. "Sorry, you probably find it really boring. I'm sure what you do is far more exciting."

I tried not to frown and wondered briefly who had abraded off some of her shine. Nobody should ever have to feel like they had to apologize for what they were passionate about in my book, yet Elka had. I pushed it to the back of my mind in favor of answering her supposition.

"It's a job, I mean, you know," I buried my hands in my pockets and shrugged my shoulders, "I guess you can call it exciting but it's not fun. It just is what it is."

I actually hated talking about work with non-LEO's. They just didn't get it and to be honest, my job was a shitshow on any given day. I dealt with people who were high, who were crazier than a shithouse mouse, who were belligerent and bein' total assholes on the regular.

I did a lot of work with the worst humanity had to offer and I tried to do my best on puttin' what little good I had to give in 'em before they hit the street again, but I couldn't stem the tide. None of us could. It was rough out there and dealing with the worst on the regular, you had to have a thick skin. Whether you wanted it to or not, that changed you.

I told Elka as much and she listened intently, nodding gravely, stopping in front of a shop door. I looked through the glass at a wall of bamboo and realized we were here. She looked up and asked me solemnly, "So how do you do it? How do you get through the day?"

I put out a hand and dragged open the door for her and said the God's honest truth, "I keep the bad people locked up and I know that I'm protecting the good people out here. People like you."

A smile flashed briefly across her lips as she stepped through the door and into the soothing atmosphere of trickling water and piped-in Asian music with its tranquil notes. The smell of chlorine in the lobby from the little fountain was a bit strong but creeping out from around it were some exotic smells that I just didn't know about.

"Two please," she murmured at the tiny little Asian hostess who slipped two menus out of the pocket on the side of her cart. I slipped my sunglasses up on top of my head as the hostess smiled and led us into the dimly lit atmosphere of the restaurant to a table under this great, carved wooden pagoda thing in the middle of the place.

"That's impressive," I said with a low appreciative whistle and I pulled out Elka's chair for her. She slipped into it and I gave the hostess a nod of appreciation. She flashed a smile, dipped into this weird little curtsey thing and left us to it. I slid into the chair across from Elka and picked up the menu.

"How am I supposed to tell what any of this is?" I asked as I ran my eyes over the unfamiliar names for things.

She laughed silently, face gently amused, shoulders shaking, and she went from pretty to beautiful in that moment. I had to reach under the table and adjust myself, hoping she didn't realize what I was up to because *awkward* and *creepy*, neither of which I was trying to be.

"There are descriptions in English under the names of the dish." She looked me over and asked, "You trust me to order for you?"

I felt my mouth turn down as I considered it and finally bobbed my head slowly. "Seems like a safe bet," I said.

"You allergic to anything?" she asked.

"Nah."

"Okay. They use a lot of peanut sauces and the like. Coconut milk and shrimp, too. I guess I should have asked before suggesting it, but I didn't think about it." She sounded entirely too guilty about the slight oversight and I just barely managed to keep the frown off my face.

Again, I wondered what was up with that and again I dismissed it as none of my business… at least for now.

She studied the menu intently and I took the opportunity to study her while she was preoccupied.

The more I looked at her, the more I liked what I saw. It was like one of her paintings. The more you looked, the more details you could pull out. The more beautiful she became. At least to me.

As she studied the menu, I could pick out more details about her. The way she bore the weight of her sadness on her shoulders with grace. The way the longer she perused the menu, the more the pinched look left her face. She looked tired, but there was an elegance to it. For all the shit she'd been through since I met her on that fateful day, I could see she still bore the brunt of a much older hurt.

She'd been handed more than her fair share, but she was handling her own and it was impressive.

In watching her, I leaned back in my seat and had mad respect for the woman in front of me. She looked up and closed the menu, the faint smile on her face slipping as she looked me over.

"What?" she asked, uncertainty creeping into her voice.

"You've been through a lot of shit," I said plaintively.

"Um, I suppose so," she said quietly, blushing faintly.

"You're killin' it, though. You don't think anyone sees it, but *I* see you. It's hard, but you're makin' it happen for yourself. You're doin' good. A lot better than most people would. That's for sure."

"Um, thanks?" she said meekly.

"Just speakin' the truth," I said with a shrug.

"Are you always so…"

"Blunt?" I asked.

"Direct?" she said at the same time and it was certainly more tactful, but I didn't care about none of that shit. I was past sugarcoating anything and I told her so.

"You ain't gotta sugarcoat nothin' with me."

"I – I – I was just being polite," she stammered.

I nodded. "That's cool, but you ain't gotta be polite with me."

"I don't want to hurt your feelings," she said gently. "You've already been so nice and done so much for my family."

I barked a jagged laugh. "I don't feel like it. I don't feel like I've done enough, honestly. And as for my feelings, not like you're gonna hurt all one of 'em I got left."

She tittered a light laugh and asked me, "Is your sense of humor always like that?"

"Dry, sarcastic and as black as my ass?" I asked and her eyes flew wide.

"Yeah," she said, caught off guard once more.

"Pretty much," I agreed.

We were interrupted by the waitress, coming to take our order. Elka ordered quietly in gentle murmurs and asked me, "Is it alright if I don't get it too spicy?"

"Sure," I nodded.

She turned back to the waitress who gathered our menus off the table with a smile and went back toward the kitchen to put our order in.

Elka was considering me silently and I let her. I didn't know what she was thinking and at the same time I didn't know what to say.

Finally, I asked her, "What are some of your favorite things?" figuring it was a safe enough topic.

"What, like raindrops on roses and whiskers on kittens?" she asked, and I was like, "Sure if you like." Her smile grew and she said, "Like bright copper kettles and warm woolen mittens?"

I frowned slightly and laughed a little nervous myself because it sounded a lot like I was missing some kind of a joke.

"Sure, uh, what else?"

She barely suppressed a laugh and *sang*, "Brown paper packages tied up with strings. These are a few of my favorite things!"

I chuckled and nodded. "Oh, she has jokes! I got you."

"You've never seen *The Sound of Music?*" she asked, laughing lightly and I shook my head.

"Can't say that I have."

"Oh, then that is so unfair, you're missing over half of the joke and why that was funny."

"Guess you'll have to educate me some time," I said laughing.

"Pretty sure by the end of it you would hate me, but sure. We could watch it sometime if you'd like. Actually, that *is* one of my favorite things. I really like watching the film adaptations of Jane Austen's books."

"She write *The Sound of Music* or whatever?" I asked.

"What? No! Um, sorry, that was probably somewhat of a non sequitur. I just meant that I liked watching films, not that I *don't* like *The Sound of Music*, I *do*; I just like the Jane Austen films a lot more. They're not even the same time periods. Sorry. I'm not being very succinct." She shook her heat and pressed fingertips to her forehead in her flustered state and I just waited her out, glossing over the awkward for now.

"They good?" I asked. "The Jane Austen movies."

"Oh, my God, *yes*. So good. She was so far before her time."

"I don't know anything about her," I said. "Never heard of her."

She gave a long slow blink like that just did not compute.

"How many movies are there?" I asked.

"Um, well, she wrote six books but not all of them were made into films. Movie-wise there's *Persuasion, Sense & Sensibility, Pride & Prejudice, and Emma.*"

"They a series?" I asked.

She shook her head. "No, they're all stand-alone stories."

I smiled. "I'm always up for new things. I'd watch one with you."

"Yeah?" she asked surprised.

"Yeah, why's that surprise you so much?"

"Um, they're not exactly car chases and explosions," she said blushing.

"What are they?" I asked. "Romance movies?"

She blushed and stammered, "Yeah."

I nodded. "Consider me forewarned. I'd still do it."

"Okay," she said and looked unconvinced and I suppressed a laugh and asked, "What you don't believe me?"

"Make you a deal, if you hate it, at anytime, you can tell me to turn it off and I will."

"Sounds good," I agreed and wondered, again, what kind of fucksticks she'd been hangin' with that she felt like she had to both apologize and hide and make all these deals and shit with me over the things that she liked. I mean, I wanted to know – it's why I asked her. I just didn't think it was a good time to go over that particular subject yet. I just got the vibe that it was still a little too early for that.

She was starting to open up and I didn't want to ruin what was clearly a good mood for her. I had to imagine that she hadn't had a feel-good time or day in a minute.

Our drinks came out and I raised an eyebrow at the glass. It was a rich brown at the bottom layered on top with white and between the two liquids it was a cascade of orange into the deeper brown coloring.

"It's Thai iced tea," Elka explained, stirring hers with her straw. "It's a strong flavor and not to everyone's liking, but if you hate it, I'll be happy to drink it. I love the stuff."

"Another one of your favorite things?" I asked.

"Ah, yeah, I guess so. I mean, I really do like tea. I drink it every day. Sometimes over coffee."

"What? Now how you gonna say that?" I demanded. "Man, I ain't had nothing negative to judge you on until you said that."

She hid her smile and laugh with her hand and I stirred my drink like she did before I took a sip.

It wasn't at all what I expected. Strong and smoky with a hint of sweet, it definitely was a rich and powerful punch in the mouth flavor-wise and I couldn't immediately say it was unpleasant, but it was *different*. Sort of in that realm of where I couldn't decide if I liked it or not.

"How is it?" she asked.

"I don't know," I said. "I'm gonna keep drinking it, might be one of those acquired taste kind of a thing."

"I definitely know all about that. There's a few dishes here that I wasn't sure if I liked it at first but finally realized I must after I'd ordered it for the third or fourth time."

"Aw yeah? Nice."

"Some of it is *definitely* an acquired taste," she said with a bit of a giggle.

We talked about the food and she was surprisingly knowledgeable about it. I was getting the impression that she was smart about a lot of things but that it was all book smarts. It made me smile on the inside, thinkin' that she had a good friend in my street-smart savvy self. That I might not be able to keep up with her on some things, but I could definitely give her a run for her money on others.

The more she talked, the more she seemed to relax. Opening up like a flower on a time-lapse video.

It was pretty sweet, and I was here for it.

10

$\mathcal{E}$lka...

Our food came and we dished up. He made a few intrepid faces, daunted by some of the fare and I suppressed a smile.

"You don't have to like any of it," I said, "but I *do* insist you at least try a bit of everything."

"I don't know if I even want to try this," he said pushing around a forkful of wet noodles on the edge of his plate.

"The Phad Thai? That is some of the most amazing stuff! You *have* to try it."

"No offense," he said, "but it smells like a whore that's sat too long."

I laughed and covered my mouth at the audacity of the statement and finally, shaking my head, said, "That's probably the fish sauce in the sauce that you're smelling. Just try it. I promise it's amazing."

"Alright, if you say so," he said dubiously, but to his credit he tried a bite, his eyes widening in surprise.

"That's good shit, Maynard!" he declared around his mouthful of food and I laughed.

"I have no idea who Maynard is."

"Seriously old commercial," he said. "Probably before your time. It was honestly before mine too, my mom and my pops used to say it back and forth all the time when I was a kid."

"Oh, yeah? Where were you born?"

"Virginia."

"Okay. I was born here in Indigo City," I volunteered.

"Ever get anywhere outside it?" he asked.

"On family vacations and the like, yeah. I also traveled to Italy for school."

"Oh, yeah? How was that?"

"Amazing! To see the greats in person was… I mean, seeing Michelangelo's David in person?" I put my hands over my heart, the echo of that long-ago flutter in my heart dim but still there at first laying my eyes upon it. "Ah, there still isn't anything like it."

He chuckled and said, "You look like you're in love over there."

"I mean, yeah, I guess that's not too far off the mark. Art will always be my first love, my passion." I shrugged one shoulder and tried not to think too much about what I had given up to keep it in my life as fully as I had.

Except I really hadn't… he'd given me up, had cited everything I'd loved and held dear as a *problem* and his betrayal had cut deep. I had already changed so much about myself for him and it had all been for nothing.

"You light up whenever you talk about it, you know," Oz stated staring at me intently from across the table, sticking a bite of chicken and veg from the Ginger entrée I'd ordered into his mouth and chewing it with gusto. Except his eyes didn't hold a smile. They held a calm, cool, and collected calculation as he observed me, and it thoroughly unnerved me.

"Yes, well," I took a sip of my Thai iced tea, "I love it, so."

"Yeah, and then it looks like your mind catches up and you look the saddest I've ever seen you. What's up with that?"

"Oh, no… it's nothing," I lied. "I just think about my sister and…" I trailed off and gave a weak smile.

He nodded but the look in his eyes said clearly that he didn't believe me, but he also didn't press.

I tried to change the subject by asking, "What do you love to do?"

"Me?" he asked, surprised.

"No, the other guy sitting across the table from me," I said dryly, and he raised his eyebrows, a sparkle of amusement returning to his eyes.

"Oh, again with the jokes. Alright, now. I'm really into fitness and bodybuilding. I'm into my club and riding. Pretty straightforward stuff."

"How is any of that straightforward to someone like me?" I asked.

"What you talking about 'someone like you'?" he asked.

I suddenly felt like I was caught flatfooted and didn't know how to answer, knowing that any answer I had to give would sound really bad.

"Oh, well, you know, um… someone who's *boring*."

He jerked his head back and looked at me like I was crazy. "I don't know who you let fill your head up with that nonsense but you're not *boring*. Far from it."

"I'm not?" I asked, surprised.

"Nope," he declared and went back to polishing off his plate with gusto.

The rest of the meal passed with idle chit chat about our days – well, mostly my day. Oz didn't want to talk about his day too much, just kept it exceedingly vague with how many reports he had to write though not what they were about – that kind of thing.

I could only imagine that he was trying to somehow spare me from the worst of it, and I couldn't really say I blamed him. It was how a lot of people acted once they found out someone close to you had died recently, though I couldn't help but worry that part of it was due to the fact my father had shared the very privileged information about my fragile emotional state from years back regarding my break up.

I'd always felt strongly, passionately, and deeply about things and when it came to my ex... well... some doors were just better left closed.

I imagined it was much the same for Oz, who had mentioned a divorce in passing during our meal, but by the careful tone that'd crept into his voice, the way he'd squared his shoulders, and the way he'd sighed heavily after the mention – I quickly got the impression that it wasn't something he wanted to talk about, and so I avoided the subject despite my curiosity about how the event had shaped him. Curious about what the event had potentially taken away from him.

I know my ex had stolen things from me. My confidence chief among them.

We walked back toward my apartment, the sun just beginning to set, hanging lower in the sky, the shadows beginning to deepen between buildings and stretch into the street, but still everything was aglow enough to see clearly.

"How about we watch one of them movies you was talkin' about?" he suggested when we drew nearer my door.

"What, now?" I asked.

"Yeah, why not? You can't tell me it probably wasn't what you were gonna do anyway as soon as I left."

I laughed and unlocked my front door. "Oh! I see how it is!" I scoffed.

"You're just mad I'm right."

"I'm not mad," I said with a smile and then added, "So what if you're right?" as I pushed through my door.

"That's the spirit," he declared.

"Go ahead and make yourself comfortable. I'm going to make a cup of tea, you want one?"

"Uh, sure, what have you got?"

I listed off several of the variants of loose-leaf tea I had in airtight and light tight containers on my kitchen window sill and he gave a long, low whistle of appreciation.

"You got a lot of shit," he said stepping into the kitchen doorway and leaning a shoulder against the archway.

"I like tea," I said and filled my electric kettle from the purifying filter on my tap.

"How about that Ruby Orange Ginger stuff?" he said nodding in the canister's direction.

"An excellent choice." I pulled the canister down. "Do you like sugar or honey with your tea?"

"Ah, nah," he said at first but finally backtracked and said, "Honey might be nice."

"Sure thing."

One thing I hated about my kitchen was the cabinets were so freaking high. I wasn't terribly short, but anything on the second or third shelf was pretty much painfully out of reach. I pulled the honey jar down from the first shelf, but the teapot I wanted and rarely used was on the second. It was clear glass and I stood on tiptoe to reach and Oz was suddenly there, right behind me, reaching over me and saying, "Here, let me."

His close proximity sent unexpected shivers down my spine and I sucked in a silent but sharp breath. With the breath came the smell of him – clean man, a hint of clean laundry, and over it all the pleasant smell of his cologne. A slightly sweet, spicy affair that held hints of my childhood. Not that he smelled like my dad or anything, far from it. But there was something…

"Thanks," I murmured, taking the teapot and its diffuser from his hands. "I need that metal housing, too."

He smiled and reached up, obliging me and just needing a moment of space between us I asked, "Can you put it on the coffee table?"

"This thing?" he asked with a wolfish grin and I knew that he knew the effect his proximity was having on me. I didn't like to be played with and I frowned slightly and nodded.

"Yes," I said pointedly.

His smile gentled from wolfish and teasing back to easy and his posture eased. *Message received* radiated out from his being even as he asked, "What is it?"

"Patience is a virtue." I smiled and said, "You'll see."

"Okay." He went out into the living room and returned shortly to resume his place in the doorway.

I went about plucking the container of tea down from its perch and measuring two tablespoons into the diffuser. I dropped that into the top of my glass teapot and waited on the water to finish boiling and for the kettle to switch off. I waited as Oz looked on curiously.

"You want the water to cool just a bit from boiling before you pour for the best flavor."

"Where did you learn that?" he asked.

I paused… "You know, I can't remember. Seems like something you would, but I can't remember where I picked that one up."

I got out the serving tray I used for when I wanted to bring more than a couple items to the living room and set the pot with its waiting tea on it. I put my little honey pot on it and brought down two of my favorite tea cups and saucers.

"Mia bought me these," I mentioned, turning so he could see the cups. Both of them porcelain, one a peacock, the other a phoenix, the handles of the cups the bodies and heads of the bird, the saucers teardrop shaped, the tails continuing from the cups onto the saucers. The look wholly unique to the both of them.

"Christmas, a couple of years in a row. She got me the peacocks, first. A set of two, and the phoenixes last year."

"Sounds like she was up to something there," he said quietly.

"She was *always* up to something," I said with a bittersweet smile. "Christmas was her favorite holiday.

"Oh yeah? And what's yours?"

"Mine?" I asked.

"Yeah."

I thought about it and for some reason was drawing a blank…

"I… I guess I don't know. I never really thought about it too much."

"You ain't got to have one," he said and smiled at me.

"Good thing, then, because I don't think that I do. What's yours?"

He gave a slow grin and said, "My birthday," and I laughed. I couldn't help it. The deadpan delivery was everything.

"Okay, well, I'll have to remember that. When is it?" I asked.

"November twenty-third," he said making a face.

"Oh, a Thanksgiving baby, not as rough as a Christmas Eve or Christmas baby but close."

"Yeah, those guys get a raw deal," he agreed. "I've had my fair share of 'this is for your birthday *and* Christmas, though. It's kind of bullshit."

"I absolutely agree," I said, pouring the hot water into the top of my teapot through the diffuser. I set my electric kettle back on its base and dropped the lid on the teapot and gave a bit of a melodramatic sigh of accomplishment.

"We good to go?" he asked, and I smoothly picked up the tray.

"Yes, we are."

"Great."

I set the tray on the coffee table and he dropped onto the couch. While things steeped, I went over to the DVD player and opened it up. I plucked out *Persuasion* and put it back in its case and then turned holding up the four Hollywood film versions I owned.

"*Pride & Prejudice, Sense & Sensibility, Persuasion,* or *Emma*?" I asked.

"Uhhh, which one goes first?" he asked.

I rolled my eyes. "They're all standalone, remember?"

"Oh, shoot, right, um, which one is your favorite?"

"I love them all, I don't have a favorite!"

"Who's in each one?"

"Um, *Pride* has Keira Knightley, *Sense* has a huge all-star cast –"

"That one, then," he decided finally, putting me out of my misery.

I nodded and slipped its case out from between the others and opened it up. He settled on one end of the couch and waited patiently while I loaded the DVD in the tray and I finally looked up and said, "You don't have to do this, you know."

He laughed and said, "I don't do anything I don't want to do."

"I'm just afraid you're going to be bored stiff," I declared and he laughed again.

"That's my problem, and I doubt it."

"Okay," I sang out as I dropped onto the other end of the couch and took up the remote to my T.V. I turned it on and exchanged remotes for the DVD player remote and arrowed through the menu and hit 'play.'

While the opening credits played and the gentle piano music drifted from my television, I doctored both of the waiting teacups with a dollop of honey in the bottom of each one and set up the tea warmer he had brought out to the table, slipping a tea light candle from the drawer in my coffee table along with a lighter.

"For real? Is that what's that's for?" he asked as I lit the candle and slid it into the base of the fat space between the metal discs. A whole cut in the top one to allow the flame of the candle to flicker below the bottom of my glass teapot, keeping the liquid remaining inside warm.

I poured the ruby liquid into our cups and set the pot on the metal stand and sighed saying, "That's what that's for."

I handed him his cup, the phoenix, and took up mine stirring its contents with the little matching feather-capped spoon that came with the cups and their saucers.

"Okay, so I don't get it..." he said after a few minutes. "It's their house, why they gotta get out?"

I smiled and said, "Because the husband and father died, and women can't inherit at this point in time. So, the father has asked that the son ignore his will which only leaves his current wife and three girls five hundred pounds a year and is beseeching him to take better care of them than that."

"Yeah, he's not, what a tool."

I laughed and agreed.

"So current wife and three daughters have to move while the son and his shrew of a wife are already moving and settling in before they're even out and they've invited the shrew wife's brother to stay while they are still finding a place to go."

"Jesus."

"Yeah, pretty much."

The whole movie went like that. With Oz growing confused by the antiquated speech patterns and alien way of life, frequently needing to ask questions. Rather than be annoyed by it, I actually delighted in the fact that he wanted to know and wanted to understand. I'd seen these movies a thousand times and needed no help in understanding them, though I had read the books long before encountering the films and I loved history and had a soft spot for the regency era.

"Okay, do what now?"

"Remember, they have a rich uncle who has invited them to stay in a cottage on his land. His wife died and he remains a widower but still has a close relationship with his mother-in-law who lives with him."

"That's creepy. I don't know about that."

I laughed over the ruckus of the jovial mother-in-law and teeming throng of barking dogs on the screen.

"Wait, so *that's* a cottage?"

"That's what I said when I first saw it!"

"It's bigger than my apartment building."

I laughed. "You must have a tiny apartment building."

"Yeah, it's not exactly the *Ritz* but it's alright."

He was actually drinking the tea I'd made for him and he seemed to be enjoying it and the movie, so I poured him and myself another cup.

"So, who is this bitch?" he asked as I was about to take a sip and I snorted and almost had tea go up my nose. He reached out and thumped me on the back, shoving a wad of tissues at me from my Kleenex box and I shoved them at my mouth and nose to catch the few tea droplets threatening the front of my tee.

"Okay, so you got that Hugh Grant was all into Emma Thompson, right?"

"Right."

"Then you got that he was trying to tell her something back in the stables at her old house."

"Right."

"Right, that something was that he was already engaged to someone else, but his sister interrupted before he could get that out."

"Oh," he made a face and finished with, "damn."

"Right? Well, that's here. She's told Elinor that she's heard so much about her from Edward and so she simply *had* to come out this way to where they live now to meet her – basically, she's here to check out the competition."

"What kind of high school bullshit is that?" he demanded and again I fell back against my end of the couch with laughter.

"Edward is rich, Lucy doesn't want to lose her meal ticket to a poacher," I said simply.

"God damn." He shook his head. "Not sorry for sayin' it but *fucking white people.*"

I died laughing all over again and I had to say, "I don't disagree! It was really bad back then for women though. Keep watching."

And to his credit he did, and what's more, the questions became fewer and further between as he actually became engrossed in the movie and I smiled to myself.

It was a rare thing to find a modern man, hell, *any* man to watch a Jane Austen movie with you.

11

*O*z...

She wasn't like other girls. I mean, most women, if you didn't get it, would be assholes about it all snippy and shit as they explained what was going on. Not Elka. She would just pause the movie and would explain it and talk about it like sharing it gave her life. She illuminated from the inside out with a glow of pride and pleasure when I caught on to what was happening and made a breakthrough on my own on what shit was going down on the screen.

She didn't make me feel stupid for not getting the old-timey speak or how they were talking about one thing while meaning something completely different. I didn't understand that shit. If you meant something, you said it, it was a different world I came from, but it didn't stop me from trying to understand someone else's.

"Wait, wait, wait," I said, confused, and she stopped it for the umpteenth time and looked at me expectantly, eager to answer my questions and it was adorable. I smiled and said, "What exactly is it with this Willoughby guy?"

"Ah ha, catching onto what a douche he is?"

I laughed. "I mean, he wouldn't even acknowledge Maryanne at the party, so yeah, kind of a dick. Look at her." I gestured to the sobbing Maryanne on the screen. Her sister trying to comfort her.

"Yeah," Elka said softly, her face changing, a sadness settling over her features.

"You and Mia a lot like Elinor and Maryanne?" I asked softly.

Elka choked on a laugh and cleared her throat. "Yeah."

"Let me guess, Mia was the Elinor to your Maryanne."

She cocked her head and shook it. "Everybody said the opposite, actually. I was supposedly the one with sense while Mia would let her sensibilities take her away."

I shook my head. "Naw, I think it's the other way around. You got a fire inside, get so passionate about things. You're definitely a Maryanne."

She blushed faintly and mumbled, "Keep watching, if I explain Willoughby now, it would be giving something away. I don't want to do that."

"Okay."

She started the movie again and I tried to wrap my head around it, but it had so many things going on, and it was like all these different threads were being pulled in and it was hard to follow.

Still, I exercised a little patience in hopes of a payoff and just generally enjoyed getting to know Elka more.

"Wait, what'd he say? Did that Willoughby guy knock somebody up?"

"Yes! Oh, my God!" She paused the movie and there was her infectious excitement again. I sat up and took a drink of the bomb ass tea she made me as she got ready to spill the tea.

"So, you remember when Brandon took off from the picnic like a bat out of hell, right?"

"Yeah."

She went on like a freight train plowing through the complicated morass of drama unfolding on the screen and the way she went through it? It made it sound like the most *fascinating* thing. I was all up in these character's lives by the time she had me straight and was genuinely wanting to know what happened next.

Me. A cop. A badass motherfucker. A biker. An alpha male among alpha males was sitting here watching a chick flick with this girl and I was actually enjoying it. I was suddenly rethinking and reworking this plan on why I suggested this.

I mean, my thought had been that I would do this and suffer through it just so I could get some leverage to get her out of her comfort zone. I wanted to take her for a ride, bad, and I figured if I did something she loved, I would be able to make a case to get her to do one of my favorite things.

It was still my master plan, but damn. Now it almost didn't seem fair.

She turned the movie back on, grinning like a kid at Christmas and guilt aside, I really wanted to show her something new. Something about me when she'd shared so much about her even in her wounded state. I mean, it took some time to find a crack in her armor, but it was like once this chick decided to let you in, you were *all-in* and that was kind of intense.

I wasn't like that, but I found myself wanting to try all of a sudden.

The brakes got pumped really fast when the waterworks started.

"What now?" I asked. "I don't get it, why you crying?"

"Were you paying attention to the carriage ride?" she cried.

"Yeah," I said stunned.

"Okay, so you caught the part where Hugh Laurie's wife was prattling on about Willoughby's house being *five miles* from their house, right?"

"Oh, shit, no I missed that, but why is that important?"

"Because! She walked five miles pining for that dumpster fire of a human being and Colonel Brandon is so in love with her, he not only walked five miles to go after her, in the rain, that man just *carried* her five miles back to the house. He loves her so much!"

She stared back at the television with the freeze-frame on Alan Rickman, soaking wet and looking helpless, standing in the doorway and I got it. I *had* completely missed that shit, and it made me think about some of the guys in the club, finding the women they would do that for. Happy with them, partnered up with them for life, and I felt a spike of jealousy.

I wanted that bad when I'd married Regina. I thought I'd had it. What I'd had was a younger prettier woman in my ex-wife who never in a million years should have *ever* become my wife in the first place. Her ass should have stayed the brother loving badge bunny I'd found her as.

Her appetites for brand-name expensive shit was way above and beyond my fuckin' pay grade but that hadn't stopped her opening up credit cards and shit in my name and running them up to their max.

When she'd divorced me, she'd stuck me with a lot of shit and had demanded half my retirement to boot. She was fuckin' lucky she got what she did. I was fuckin' lucky she hadn't gotten alimony.

That's what I got for marrying a chick fifteen years younger than me. It's part of why I worried so much about Skids hookin' up with a twenty-something-year-old girl when dude was in his fifties.

For a while, I thought some lessons were learned the hard way and I'd been right. Not about Coco and Skids. The two of them were solid. I'd learned *my* lesson the hard way about not being such a judgmental bastard. I was learning a lot of new tricks in my middle age and I guess I should be grateful I wasn't an old dog. At least not yet.

"Aw c'mere," I said, setting my tea aside and opening my arms. "Bring it in."

Elka laughed but scooted closer and let me hug her. I held her tight and she shook slightly before she really started to sob, and I think she just needed the hug. Had needed it for a while now.

"I'm sorry," she warbled pitifully, and I shook my head, resting my chin on the top of her head.

"Naw, you just go ahead and cry," I told her. "You ain't gotta worry about me."

And she didn't. I was right where I wanted to be. If I wasn't, I wouldn't have been there.

"What are you doing?" she asked when I shifted and snatched the remote off the table. I didn't answer immediately, manhandling her a bit so we were both cuddled in a pile on her couch. I hit play and held her tight and said, "I'm finishing the movie, and you ain't gotta go anywhere so settle down."

She laughed, and it sounded a bit watery.

"Thank you," she said and let me hold her. I smiled and breathed in her clean vanilla scent and said, "You're welcome."

12

*E*lka...

It was with great reluctance that I dragged myself out of the comfortable cocoon of his arms. I couldn't believe myself. I wasn't typically so audacious and now that my feelings were back under control for the most part, I didn't know how to feel anything except awkward.

For Oz, it was like water off a duck's back. He just didn't pay it any mind as the credits rolled and I pushed myself up off of him to clear our tea plates and to blow out the candle that was still going beneath the much-depleted teapot.

"Be right back," he said gently. "All that tea has caught up to me."

I smiled and murmured, "You know where the bathroom is."

He smiled back and pushed himself smoothly up off the couch. I gathered the tray and took it to the kitchen, taking my time to wash everything up by hand.

"So, what are you gonna do with the rest of your night?" he asked.

"Paint, maybe… go to bed, probably. What about you?"

"Definitely headed home and hitting the hay," he said.

"Well, thank you for this. I guess I hadn't realized how much I needed just a low-key night spent with company… sorry if I –"

He cut me off with, "Hey, no, you ain't got nothin' to apologize for. It's cool, alright?"

"Okay." I nodded and swallowed hard.

"Come take a ride with me next Saturday," he said, and I looked up at him like he was crazy.

"Me? On the back of a motorcycle? Yeah, right."

"Come on," he said with a wicked grin. "I did something you liked tonight, fair is fair."

I frowned at him and opened my mouth to protest but he was right.

I closed my mouth and took a deep breath and said, "I'm afraid."

He simply shrugged and said, "So? Be afraid but do it anyway."

I blinked in surprise and looked at him. I didn't have a retort. I mean… he smiled at me and said, "See you next Saturday. Text me if you got any questions."

And with that he backed out of my kitchen archway and throwing the locks back deftly, slipped out my front door. I rushed out of the kitchen and stood staring at the new wood for a second before taking the last few steps and locking up behind him.

I felt my shoulders drop as I asked myself, *What just happened? Did I agree to go for a ride next week?*

I moved automatically through the rest of my clean up and back into my little artist's studio where I flipped on the light and dropped onto the stool in front of my unfinished canvas. I picked up a brush and considered it before dipping the bristles into the pigment to resume my work as my mind raced.

What would Daddy think?

He'd throw an absolute fit. I was, after all, the only daughter he had left.

I paused in my work and stared at my sister's face, the only finished part of the painting.

"What do you think I should do?" I asked her, and my immediate thought was *go*.

I knew I was right. That Mia indeed would want me to go and was surprised to find that *I* really wanted to go. I mean, it was something new and something I would never do, and Oz's words had stuck with me.

So? Be afraid but do it anyway.

It sounded so *easy* when he put it that way, but nothing about this was going to be easy for me. I mean, *what if I fell?* What if I got hurt, or lost the use of my hands, or developed something awful like a permanent tremor?

What if, what if, what if! What if you actually had fun for once in your life?

I smiled at the face of my sister, eyes misting with tears as I replayed the familiar counter argument in my head.

"As always, when you're right, you're right," I murmured and then I set my brush down and covered my face with my hands and sobbed.

God, I wished my sister were here to have this petty argument with me. I missed her so much.

Out of the two of us, she had certainly been the Marianne. Passionate, vivacious, so much more passionate and fuller of life than I was. Always pushing me, especially after he-who-shall-not-be-named had broken it off with me and married someone more fit to his station in life.

I'd done everything he asked me to. Had become everything he had wanted or needed me to be in the moment, only for it to have never been good enough, and now? Now, I didn't feel like I was... for anyone. For anything.

Certainly not for someone like Oz, I thought derisively.

Oh, knock it off! I was really starting to wonder if it was still me conjuring my sister's voice or if she were indeed here.

"Mia?" I called out softly, and listened ears straining... but of course, there was nothing.

"Okay, Ellie. Enough is enough," I told myself. "It's time for bed."

I cleaned my brush, used the bathroom and brushed my teeth, and with one final lingering look behind me at my unfinished painting, snapped out the light and crossed the hall to my bedroom.

13

*O*z...

"Got a live one for you," Golden declared, as he and his partner dragged a hobbled man between them.

"Whoa, busted out the extra chains and a spit mask, huh?"

"Yeah," Golden's partner for the night grunted and I pointed over at single cell one.

"Let's get him in the restraint chair and into one. What's he on, anyway?"

"Fuck you! You fucking pigs! I'll kill you! I'll kill you all, man! Fuck you!" the man was screaming.

"I dunno, combo of alcohol and something. Could just be a head case."

We three struggled with the dude who kept trying to spit but was having no luck with the fine nylon mesh face hood he was rockin'.

"Hey, knock it off!" I put down the law. "Ain't nobody disrespecting you, my man! You done this to your damn self. Act like a man, you get treated like a man. Act like an animal, you get *this*. It's all up to you in here, buddy."

He went from screaming at us to hyperventilating but I'd seen this shit before. He was doing it on purpose. We got him unhooked and hooked back up in the restraint chair, but it was a fight. Hobbs, another one of the jailers had to get in there and help us, one of the jail nurses standing by and documenting with a video camera, writing the occasional note on her blue latex glove.

"You good?" I asked the dude and he hacked a fat one and tried to spit it at me, but again for the mask.

"Mm-mm." Hollis, the nurse, shook her head. "Another fun one."

"What's his name?" I asked.

"John Doe. Didn't have any ID on him." Golden shook his head and I sighed.

We locked dude up in the observation cell with its thick, scratched, but still serviceable glass door and I headed on over to the computer to do the intake paperwork. Golden and his partner stood by at the corner of the desk flipping through pages on their clipboard and marking things off.

I finished up my shit and went back over to the previous screen.

"What's that?" Golden asked.

"Tryin' to convince Elka to come out for a ride with me on Saturday," I said. "I think she will, now I'm just lookin' at a few places to take her."

"Whoa, hold up, you actually getting into a relationship here?"

I shook my head. "Just friends," I told him, half distracted, reading through what was on my screen.

"Uh huh, is that why you're looking at 'Fine Art Galleries Near Me' then?"

I shrugged. "She likes art."

"Yeah, but you don't," he said laughing.

"How do you know what the fuck I like?" I demanded with a frown. Motherfucker just laughed at me.

"Man, get on out of here with that mess." I waved him off. "Go do your paperwork in your patrol car. Get some coffee and a doughnut or some shit."

Golden guffawed and grabbed up his clipboard he and his partner wandered to the sliding doors that led to the garage and he shot me a one-fingered salute over his shoulder.

"Love you, too, my brother!" I called after him.

"Man, that's some gay shit," one of the prisoner's waiting in the DMV style waiting area for the rest of his intake called out.

I spun on my stool and pointed at him. "You, shut up!"

He cracked a grin that was more gums than teeth and I fought not to roll my eyes. Meth was a fuckin epidemic, same as the opioid crisis, only less headline inducing.

I spun back around and pulled my notepad out of my breast pocket and a pen out of the slim pocket on my sleeve. I flipped open the pad and jotted some things down then went over to google maps and plugged a few things in.

"Eh, a little rough for a first ride," I muttered, looking at the time and distance. "Go big or go home, I guess."

I had a plan, and I had all week to change it, so it wasn't a big deal. This was just one of a few ideas I had, but it was the best one I think I'd come up with out of all of them. I guess we would just have to wait and see.

"Hey, Jones!"

I perked up dragging my eyes off the screen. "Hey, yeah?"

"That don't look work related!"

"Just lookin' something up real quick, Sergeant," I called back, x'ing out of the google search screen. I went back to the intake form and heaved a sigh.

"That's what I thought," he grumbled, and I fought not to roll my eyes. Dude could be a real asshole sometimes.

I had no intention of telling Elka where we were headed on Saturday, but I did need to text her and tell her when I would pick her up.

The shift dragged bad when you wanted to do something and couldn't, and I tried not to let it put me in a bad mood. Still, between my sergeant and some of the inmates, they were a testin' me. I didn't let it show. It was one of the worst things you could do, letting either one of them get to you like that.

"Hey, man, what's it like bein' locked up in here with us day after day?" one of the inmates asked me. "It's almost like your dumb ass is in jail too, am I right?"

I looked over. "Yep, you got me there, buddy. Every damn day right up until I clock out, go home, and fuck my girl," I told him deadpan. The rest of the inmates in line fell out laughing at dude's expense, and the look on his face was pretty priceless.

"Man, that's why you don't mess with Jones," one of them said, still cuttin' up. "He's quick!"

"Alright, alright, you jokers! That's enough." Miller, one of the good dudes on my team, escorted this freshly turned batch back into the next holding area right before they went to their cell blocks. I gave him and Dewey, who was bringing up the rear, a nod and threw the switch to close the gate behind them.

I shook my head and jotted things down for the paper trail, my mind wandering not to my ex-wife, but to Elka which was both odd and wasn't. I mean, Elka, by far, wasn't even close to being 'my girl' and probably never would be, but the attraction was there and was pretty real.

I sighed.

I still felt like a perve getting hard every time I thought about her body pressed to mine. Hell, the smell of vanilla was enough to drive me nuts, now. I couldn't remember where I had encountered it between Saturday night and today, but I remember I'd breathed it in and had started low-key looking for her.

I think I was starting to realize how the rest of the guys felt when they'd latched onto their 'one.' I just hoped to hell that Elka wasn't mine. The girl didn't deserve any more heartache than she'd already been handed, and I was afraid it might be all I was good for. Handing out heartache and disappointment. I didn't want to or mean to even be that guy. It just was what always seemed to happen.

"You alright my man?" I looked up.

"Yeah, Miller, why what's up?"

"You just seem extra distracted today."

"Shit, man. I'm sorry. How much longer we got on this shift, anyway?"

"Something like about an hour, what's going on?" he asked. He crossed his arms and bounced on his feet, rocking from heel to toe and back again. It was just a 'Miller' thing to do and I smiled.

"Thinking about a girl, if you can believe it," I said.

"Oh yeah? That's awesome!" he said, and I frowned and shook my head.

"I'm not so sure all the time."

"Oh yeah? How come?"

"You remember that shootout I got caught in the middle of a while back?"

He frowned. "Yeah, what's that got to do with anything?" he asked.

"Girl is the sister of the civilian that got killed."

He sucked in a sharp breath and said, "Ooo, I can see why that might be complicated. How'd you get involved?"

I told him the story and he laughed and shook his head. "You kicked down her door?"

"I had it fixed the same day, but yeah. Her pops seemed really worried about her."

"And an unlikely friendship was born?" he asked.

I nodded. "Yeah."

He nodded slowly, the gears turning in his head.

"You're a good man, Jones. I think she's lucky to have a friend like you in her corner."

"Yeah?" I asked surprised. "You really think that?"

He slapped me on the back of the shoulder. "I really do, but the rest of us are going to need you to leave that shit at the door."

I nodded. He was right. Distraction was the fastest way to get hurt or killed in this profession and not just yourself, either. The other guys around you had lives and families too.

"You're absolutely right," I agreed.

"See." Miller gave me a dazzling smile, his blue eyes sparkling. He ran his hand over his silver-frosted short haircut, his hairline receding, but still lookin' good over all on him. "Told you, you're one of the good ones around here."

"Why, because I can admit when you're right?" I asked with a half-grin.

"Which is pretty much the exact same as admitting that you're wrong. Not every guy can do that."

"Thanks, Miller."

Surprisingly, the short talk with Miller helped a ton. In that I was both able to put this thing with Elka away for the time being and that I felt better about it. A lot better.

I made it through the rest of my shift and hit the locker room to go change. I checked my phone, pleased to have a waiting text from her.

Elka: Okay, I'll be afraid, but I'll do it anyway. What do I need to wear?

That's my girl.

14

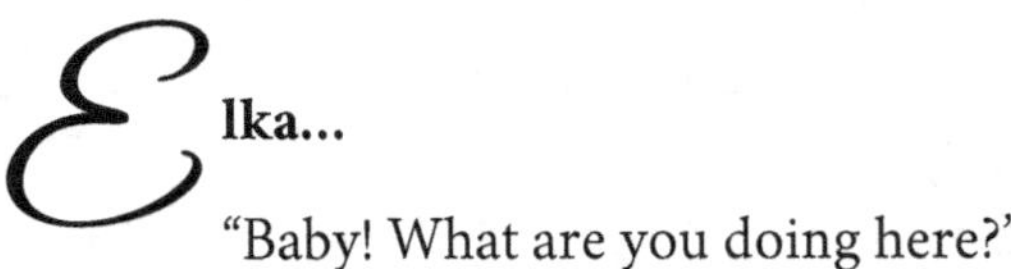

*E*lka...

"Baby! What are you doing here?"

Contrary to how it sounded, my dad was happy to see me, folding me into a tight embrace before I could even get through the front door.

"Hi, Daddy." I hugged him back tightly. "I told you, remember? I wanted to go through a couple of boxes of Mia's things. I think I'm ready now."

"Well, sure..." he said kindly. His worry for me lingering in his eyes. He stepped aside and I entered into the little townhome Mia and I had grown up in. Our pictures along with pictures of our mom scattered along walls and over every available surface.

"The boxes are in your old room, upstairs," he said, shutting the door tightly against the soothing summer night outside. He locked the door out of habit, and I drifted toward the bottom of the stairs.

"I picked up pretzels from *Hans' Delicatessen*," he said and I turned with a brave and brittle smile. *Hans'* was the German deli on the edge of the city and had been a family favorite since I was a little girl. When

Mamma had been pregnant with Mia, she had craved the big, soft baked pretzels from the little German deli and my dad's cheddar beer sauce to dip them in.

One of my very first memories was sitting on my daddy's lap at our kitchen table, happily munching on pretzel pieces, my little fists smeared with cheese sauce, my mother laughing.

The tradition had been born before my sister, but whenever things got rough, any kind of heartache or discord among the family, a trip to *Hans'* would be made, the pretzels brought home in the white box tied with cotton string, and Dad would stand in the kitchen making the cheddar beer sauce, pouring the beer, drinking the rest, while Mom set the table with napkins and prepped the pretzels for the oven.

Music would play, then there would be dancing in the kitchen, and before long we would be at the table indulging, laughing, and telling stories... we would be a family and the pain or whatever we'd been fighting about would be forgotten.

Pretzel nights had been a fairly common thing when we were teenagers. It broke my heart that Dad and I were the only ones left to carry on the little family tradition and it hurt even more that he'd been about to indulge in it all alone.

"Why didn't you call me, Dad?" I asked him.

"You showed up here and beat me to it," he said, waving me off.

I nodded. "Looks like it was meant to be, huh?"

"Looks like," he agreed, hugging me around the shoulders. "I'll get the sauce going."

"I'll get started upstairs, it shouldn't take me too long," I said.

"A little at a time," he agreed. "Steady as she goes. Nothing has to be done all at once. You take what you like, and we'll get it all sorted, eventually."

I nodded and he let me go with a pained look. Like he felt so guilty and I smiled bravely. I hadn't expected him to go through all of Mia's things. Just the weight of them in the rooms above him must have been an incredible thing. Bearing down on him, weighing him down. I went up the stairs and drew a fortifying breath, wiping at silent tears gathering on my bottom lashes as I stopped outside the familiar bedroom door.

I could barely get the door open, the boxes stacked and piled like they were. I squeezed through the gap and past the few boxes just inside and let out a shuddering sigh.

"Rome wasn't built in a day…" I reminded myself. Likewise, the rubble couldn't be easily disposed of or carted off any sooner, either.

I rooted through a few open boxed of curios and things stacked on top and sighed, flipping on the overhead light so that I could see better.

It was hard, sorting through the shattered pieces of a life taken too soon. Through the shards of my broken heart. I sat cross-legged on the woven oval mat between our twin beds and pulled a box marked 'purses' closer and opened the top, sliding the flaps of cardboard against each other where they'd been woven and tucked to stay closed.

"God, Mia. Why am I not surprised?" I sighed. It really was nothing but handbags and purses. From clutches to bags that could be more gym bag or tote than a purse. I picked a big, brown leather affair out of the mess and sorted the rest into two piles, a much smaller one to keep for myself and the rest back in the big cardboard box they'd come from.

I rooted around the night table between our childhood beds and came up with a marker from the drawer. Uncapping it with my teeth, I tried it against the flap of the box and was glad to discover it worked.

I x'ed out 'purses' and wrote 'donate' on the box and sighed.

"One down, half a million to go," I muttered and looked around. I hadn't made much of a dent at all in the big purse box, but then again,

I didn't have a whole lot of room at my apartment, and whatever I did take I had to carry on the bus tonight, so some would have to be set aside for later and I would have to find something to carry everything I did take tonight in to get it home. That, or I would just have to wear it and sweat. It was hot out and humid. An oppressive heat outside the townhome's walls.

I rubbed my temples and set back to the task at hand, going through a few boxes until I found the one I was looking for.

"Ah!" I made a triumphant noise and opened the top, pulling a couple of layers off the top until my fingers encountered the slick leather of my sister's coat. An expensive fashion piece for her, but I was hoping to get some functionality out of it.

"Knock, knock!"

"Yeah, Dad, what's up?"

My dad poked his head around the door and asked me, "You ready to take a break kiddo?"

"Yeah, Dad, I am." I looked up at my dad who frowned down at me a mix of sympathy, empathy, and worry on his face.

"Sauce is all finished. Come on down and let's get into these pretzels."

I smiled wanly and nodded, pushing to my feet.

"I still want to do a little more," I told him and he nodded.

"After pretzels," he said.

"After pretzels," I agreed, casting a look back at the mounting pile of things I wanted to carry home that night.

"So, uh, what are you doing this weekend? Going anywhere or doing anything?" my Dad asked once we were seated at the dining room table. I smiled a little ruefully at the careful hesitation in his tone, the halting lilt as he asked his question, as he both hoped for and dreaded the different answers that would come from me.

"Actually," I said, tearing off a bite of soft pretzel and dipping it in the ramekin of cheddar-beer sauce Dad set on the plate, "I have plans to go out."

"Oh, yeah?" he asked with a gusty sigh of relief. His voice tinged with surprise as he sagged with the former emotion in his seat. It broke my heart that I worried him so much and I didn't know how to tell him that it was okay… that I would, despite the excruciating pain of losing my only sister, be alright and that I wasn't going to do anything to myself.

I set my bite down in the sauce and leaned the pretzel against the side of the ramekin and looked over at my dad and sighed.

I didn't know how to tell him except to just… tell him. It was uncomfortable talking about such a painful moment of my past, especially dropping it in the caustic solution that was currently swirling in my heart over the murder of my sister, but I had to fix this – no matter how draining it was.

"Dad, I know it doesn't look like it, and I know things are really, really bad right now but when it comes to… *that*… I promise, I'm okay. I'm not going anywhere." My voice cracked on 'anywhere' I couldn't help it. "Okay?"

He sniffed. His eyes welling with tears and he reached out a hand over the top of the table and I grasped at it without a second thought.

"Okay," he agreed, squeezing it a couple times but not letting go.

"Okay," I reiterated, a little more strongly this time.

"I love you punk-in." He smiled tremulously and we both sat and drowned our pretzels in the extra salt of our tears.

"I love you, too," I said and thought if it hadn't been for Oz, for this damn ride coming up this Saturday, I wouldn't be here right now. My dad would be suffering alone, in this big empty townhome by himself. Eating pretzels and cheesy beer sauce – his wife gone, his youngest daughter gone, and feeling out of touch, out of reach of his oldest daughter… and that slayed me.

A deep well of gratitude opened up and swallowed me whole when I thought of Oz the rest of the week. I thought about it on the bus ride home, as I got ready for work, all while I cleaned a Dutch painting from the 1500s. Painstaking and downright terrifying work when it came to the shoddy conservation that'd been done to it sometime in the 1940s.

Still, I couldn't stop thinking about Oz. About the changes he'd brought to my outlook on life, about how he was still coming around despite my near-permanent status as a bona fide misery muffin lately. About every patient moment, about every hard-won smile, and I realized that even if he didn't realize he was doing it, just being around him was restoring me just as I was restoring the painting on my worktable.

It was a painstakingly slow process, to be sure, but he was here for it and even though the thought of getting on that bike tomorrow utterly *terrified* me… It was pretty much the *only* thing he'd asked of me in return for all of his kindness and it was so quintessentially him and what he loved above all else and in all reality, he was really asking me to be able to share that with him so as daunting as it was… as utterly terrified as I was… I would absolutely take his advice.

I would be afraid, but I would do it, anyway.

I felt a sort of satisfaction with that. Like I had made some sort of death-defying decision here and it honestly put something back that'd been taken out of my soul without my even noticing.

I felt myself sit up a little straighter, held my head a little higher, and felt somehow elevated… and I would *not* under any circumstances, listen to that foul little voice in the back of my head that tried to tell me that I was being foolish in my newfound strength and confidence because I knew that this time, it was utter bullshit whatever it had to say.

Instead, I rode the high of my newly mended relationship with my dad, and the feeling like some of the universe had somehow snapped back in place for me all the way back home after work where I fixed myself a healthy dinner, texted Oz that I was going to bed, and that I was sorry I would miss talking to him when he got off work, but that I would see him in the morning... and I slept well, for the first time in a long time.

15

Oz...

Her front door opened before I could even shut off the bike. I watched her turn and stick the key in the lock, twisting her wrist deftly to secure her apartment. I shamelessly took the opportunity to check out her ass in the tight jeans she wore. The medium wash denim fitting her like a second skin, tucked into knee-high, sturdy black leather boots that laced up in the front. They looked like some weird cross between riding boots and combat boots, but for getting on the back of an iron horse, they'd do just fine. She slung her neat little crossbody purse over her head, slipping her arm through and settling it against her hip, the strap laying neatly over the black leather jacket she'd gotten from somewhere.

I gave a low whistle as she came through the decorative little gate in front of her apartment and crossed the sidewalk coming toward me.

"Nice jacket," I declared as she tugged on the hem a little bit to settle it, the built-in belt rattling in the front.

"Thanks, it was my sisters," she said and shifted in her stance nervously.

"Fits you good," I said and nodded in approval. I smiled and slipped my sunglasses off my face and asked, "Not having second thoughts, are you?" at the look of apprehension on her face, her warm brown doe eyes traveling from me, over the bike before her gaze flicked back to mine.

"No," she said a little too hastily and I couldn't help but grin.

I said, "Hop on up here and put your feet here and here." I pointed to the foot pegs and she pressed her lips together and nodded. "I'm serious now, don't do what my ex-wife did the first time she came for a ride. She took her feet off the damn pegs and melted off the sole of one boot on the pipes. It was a damn mess."

She laughed and it was a good sound. Reggie had blown a gasket when the fellas and I had gotten a laugh at her expense. Not to mention, I'd had to replaces the boots and that bitch had liked designer *everything,* so it'd cost a pretty penny. It'd been a while before I'd lived the embarrassment down. As soon as the guys had figured out it bugged the hell out of me, they'd stopped, though. Not like Reggie. Reggie never knew when to quit.

"What'd you just think about?" Elka asked quietly.

"Nothing." I shook my head and asked, "You listening?"

"I'm listening," she said.

"Oh, yeah? What'd I just say?"

She parroted back what I'd told her with a serene smile and I nodded.

"Good." I nodded and went through the last of it and handed her my spare helmet. She took it between her hands and took a fortifying breath. I smiled and asked, "You got a bandana?"

"For what?" she asked.

"Keep the road grime and bugs outta your grill." Her eyes widened in the side-view mirror and I laughed, handing her back a spare of mine, an indigo blue one. She wrapped it around her nose and mouth, outlaw style and I handed her back a pair of clear-lensed safety glasses. She slipped them on over her eyes and got settled, her arms tentatively going around me. I picked up my sunglasses off my tank and put them over my eyes.

"Better hold on tight, now," I told her, thumbing the switch and starting up the bike. Her arms snaked around my chest and I pinched the material of the black bandana scattered in crosses and brought it up over my own face. It was just preferred when hitting freeway speeds to have the thin layer of protection on my face.

I kept it slow and easy for her down her street and felt her stiff posture ease slightly against my back. *See, yeah, it's not so bad,* I thought back at her and felt her look up at the tall buildings as we passed between them. At the last stoplight before the freeway on-ramp she called out to me, "Where are we going?"

I grinned and called back, "For the second-best ride of your life!" as the light turned green and I steered us through the intersection smoothly piloting the bike in a lane change to the on-ramp.

"Oz?" my name was a question, the alarm in her voice unmistakable and I just called back, "Hold on!" in response. Her grip on me tightened, the bike growled like a tiger in a cage, wanting to be let out and I twisted the throttle and we were all *free.*

I loved riding at freeway speeds. There wasn't a single damn one of my troubles that could keep up with me at sixty or seventy miles per hour, the wind washing over me, chasing off the black shadows of whatever mood whatever bullshit brought on.

It swept over and around us, the sun beating down on us, the music from my sound system loud and bass heavy, bright and enthusiastic, as we swept past cars and trucks at an easy glide. I checked on Elka, her eyes closed, her long brown hair whipping in the wind and smiled.

She was eating this up and I just knew it. I just knew there was something about her yearning to get free like this and even though she was afraid, I was just so damn proud of her in this moment. I reached back and gave her knee a squeeze and a bubble of laughter erupted from her as she nodded in the mirror, the material of the bandana I'd loaned her plastered to her hidden smile. Her eyes sparkling through the protective eyewear like I'd never seen them do.

I'd probably go through some kind of hell to see her eyes do that again and thought to myself it was a good thing I probably wouldn't have to.

The ride wasn't too bad, some traffic drawing it out the closer we got to DC, but overall it wasn't too bad at all.

I turned down the music and pulled up to the curb a block or two down from our final destination where the parking wasn't too bad and killed the engine.

The music ceased and the quiet left behind was almost deafening until the little city sounds managed to backfill things. The sound of a passing car's tires on the street, the shudder of a light breeze in the trees lining the sidewalk. Little things that slowly filled the absence of the rumble of the bike's engine.

"That was... *wow*," she said and laughed a bit unsteady.

I smiled and nodded, pulling my bandana off my face and going for the buckle on my chinstrap.

"Yeah? You like that?" I asked.

"It was amazing, but where are we?"

"DC," I said simply, and she gave me a light smack on the shoulder of my jacket.

"I *know* that, smartass... but *why* are we in DC?"

I grinned at that and said, "Ah now that you're just gonna have to wait and see. Come on, now, watch the pipes getting down." I held out an arm for her to grab onto to help her get off the bike and then followed suit, heeling down the stand and tucking both her helmet and mine into one of my hard-case saddlebags and locking them away.

"You good?" I asked her as she handed me my safety glasses back and tucked my borrowed bandana in the top of her purse.

"I'm good!" she said brightly, and I worried for half a second that she was just tellin' me what I wanted to hear rather than the truth.

"You sure?"

"I'm fine, Oz!" She rolled her eyes and declared, "I'm better than fine, actually. I'm feeling pretty good."

"Oh yeah? How's that?" I asked, locking the hard case and joining her on the sidewalk. I pointed in the direction we were headed, and we fell into step beside each other.

"I went over to my dad's the night before last and we had a good talk," she said.

"Yeah? That's great."

"It was," she nodded as she said it, her face thoughtful, but serene. "I think he was afraid that..." she paused, and I stayed quiet and just let her talk. I mean, she was talking, for real this time. Not some superficial bullshit. She was really opening up here and it surprised me... caught me off guard in a way I hadn't expected. I mean, wasn't the whole purpose of this exercise to somehow make her better? Make her feel better? Get her back on some even footing again so she could handle what came at her next? I mean... whatever that was.

"I think he was afraid still that I would be next. That I would do something to myself and that he would be all alone." She pursed her lips rubbing them together slowly and I stopped and looked at her. She stopped with me and looked at me quizzically.

"What?"

I shook my head. "You wouldn't have done that," I said.

"Done what?" she asked softly. "Killed myself?"

I nodded.

"I tried once," she reminded me.

I nodded again, slower this time.

"Yeah, and you're not that girl anymore," I reminded her.

"No, I'm not the same girl as I was before," she said, agreeing and I shook my head.

"No, you're not, you're someone different now, but that's part of life, isn't it? You go through some shit and it changes you. You go through some more, sometimes heavier, sometimes just the same kind of heavy but some different shit and it changes you some more."

"Yeah," she spoke quietly, her eyes softly unfocused as she stared past me.

"Point is, it's up to you on how you let it change you. Some of how things can change you is out of your control, but some of it? That's all you, baby. So, you gotta decide that for yourself. You know?"

"Not this, this isn't in my control." She said shaking her head. "Anyway, back to the conversation with my dad."

"What about it?" I asked her.

"I was trying to thank *you*," she said.

"Me?" I asked, putting us into motion, into a slow stroll again. We were coming up on it. The place I'd planned to bring her.

"Yeah, you… if you hadn't insisted on this ride, I probably wouldn't have gone over there," she said. "I didn't have any of the protective clothing you asked for but I thought Mia might and so I went over there to go through some of the boxes in our old room which led to my dad and I talking over pretzels."

The little smile that curved her lips at the mention of the pretzels led me to think there was a lot more there to unpack.

"What's a bar snack got to do with this talk?" I asked and she laughed.

"It's this thing my family does," she explained as I put my hand on the door handle to the National Gallery of Art. She explained, not really here but in her childhood home's kitchen, sorting shit out with her family and it sounded... nice. Definitely wasn't something that happened in home like where I grew up at. We didn't do none of that *Leave It to Beaver* June Cleaver, shit.

She finished her story and I said, "That sounds really good, actually," when she sort of woke up to where we were.

"Holy shit, Oz... is this where you wanted to bring me?" she asked and her eyes lit up again, just like when she'd let go and had fallen into the rhythm of the ride. Pride swelled in my chest at putting that look on her face *twice* in such a short span of time.

"Yeah. I figured you took the time to do something I loved, and turn-about is fair play or some shit... you like art, so I thought you might like it here."

She stared at me silently, mouth slightly open and the look she gave me was almost familiar. Like I'd seen it recently, I just couldn't place where. She turned back around and then this way and that way, and I smiled waiting on her to choose where we went first.

"They have Verrocchio on special exhibit," she said, a hint of awe in her voice. "Can we start there?"

I grinned and said, "It's all you, baby. We can start wherever you want."

She barely suppressed an excited squeal, reached out and took my hand, and dragged me into the museum. It's not like I resisted at all. It was my idea in the first place... and just like with her Jane Austen movies, she made this shit fun.

16

$\mathcal{E}$lka...

I let the art history nerd part of my major shine bright like a diamond, excitedly indulging in my passion, telling Oz everything I could remember about any given artist we encountered that I knew anything about. I held nothing back, not even the most trivial pieces of information. He indulged me in every bit of it, too. Listening with rapt attention, an amused smile gracing his full lips.

"You know a little bit about everything up in here, don't 'cha?" he asked and I smiled.

"Art is *life*," I said, throwing my hands wide.

He laughed a little and shaking his head said, "You know, all that tells me is you need to get laid!"

I scoffed in a I-can't-believe-you-just-said-that kind of way and hands on my hips, without even thinking, I blurted out, "You volunteering?"

His face lost that easy smile as he contemplated me, and I rushed out before he could answer, "That's what I thought."

I went to turn, but he stopped me with a hand on my elbow. "Hold on now," he said. "It ain't like that. I just... I guess I didn't think you were interested."

I swallowed hard, and dredged for something, *anything*, to say and finally said, "It's been a while. Sorry."

God, Ellie! Lame! Lame, lame, lame, lame, lame!

He gave a lopsided grin and let my elbow go. "Ain't nothing to be *sorry* about," he said. "I like that you're honest. It's like whatever comes to mind comes right out your mouth." He laughed at the look on my face, which probably looked a lot like I'd been sucking on a lemon.

"That's not typically an admirable trait," I said bitterly.

"Is for me," he declared.

"It doesn't matter," I said. "It was a stupid thing to say, I'm not looking for a relationship at the moment."

"Me either," he declared. "I don't need none of that."

"Good, case closed," I said with a false brightness.

He chuckled. "Not so fast," he said. "I'd be lying if I said the idea didn't appeal to me, Ellie."

I sort of froze. "What did you just call me?" I asked.

"Sorry," he said immediately. "I don't know where that came from."

"No, it's fine," I said. "It just surprised me is all... Mia used to call me 'Ellie' all the time. Since she was a toddler, actually. She just couldn't grasp 'Elka' and kept saying 'Ella' and it eventually evolved into 'Ellie.' I... I kind of miss it, actually."

"Then if you don't mind, I'd like to keep the tradition alive," he said and I smiled and nodded.

We meandered through the museum as we spoke quietly, reflecting and telling stories about our childhoods. It was nice, despite the low key sting of rejection from earlier and I was surprised to find that any advances that Oz would have made weren't unwelcome in the slightest… that it was just the opposite, in fact.

As we walked slowly, shoulder to shoulder, I wished for a deeper intimacy. Realized I missed it with a fierce ache in the center of my chest. It'd been some years since I let any man close and I hadn't realized how effectively Oz had slipped between the plates in the armor I'd donned my heart in after my last serious relationship.

"You okay?" he asked after a moment of my staring sightlessly at a Monet.

"I don't know how to say it," I said shaking my head.

"Say what?" he asked and I rolled my eyes.

"I don't know how to explain how I am feeling without looking like either a complete lunatic or pathetic as hell and neither one of them are a good look, you know?"

He stopped me again with a hand on my shoulder and turned me away from the painting to face him.

"Just say it like you do everything else," he said. "I judge you so far?"

"Not out loud," I said with a faint smile.

He smiled a little bigger and said, "Same for you when it comes to me."

I laughed slightly, and shook my head, cheeks heating with embarrassment.

"It's cool, you ain't gotta tell me," he said when I couldn't work up the courage to say it. "Just know I'm good to listen, anytime you need it."

"Thank you," I murmured.

"No problem," he said and we turned back to the painting on the wall.

"I would love to work on a Monet," I murmured absently, and I felt him looking at me. I turned and he stared at me and I stared back, and it was *definitely* a moment. The kind of moment that steals your breath and mutes your words like snuffing out a candle flame. The kind of moment with weight and promise. The hesitation, the pregnant pause, the universe holding its collective breath as if it doesn't even know what is going to happen next.

It was a moment that hung like the moon in the sky, both of us staring at each other, neither of us ready, both of us wanting, and finally he was the brave one. His hand came up gently and touched the bottom of my chin and he slowly brought his mouth to mine. I let my eyes close as his breath brushed warm against my lips and finally, soft as silk, his lips brushed mine.

I swallowed hard and kissed him back, trying like hell not to swoon. It was one of those earth-shattering kisses. One that left you feeling light-headed, one that curled your toes, one that left you practically levitating in your shoes.

"That alright with you?" he asked quietly, taking a half step back.

I flicked my tongue over my lips, tasting him, and nodded silently not trusting my voice.

When it finally came, it was confused as I murmured, "I thought you weren't looking for a relationship."

He chuckled and stared hard at the Monet in front of us.

"Just because a man ain't lookin' for a particular thing, doesn't mean that thing don't find him," he said.

I nodded, transfixed by his profile which was much better than the painting and said, "So… um… what now?"

He turned back to me and smiled and asked me, "You hungry?"

I smiled and grasped for the safe topic and nodded. "Famished."

"Got anything against hotdogs?"

I grinned. "Sounds fabulous."

"K, come on. There's a stand over at the Mall that's fuckin' awesome."

I nodded and took his hand automatically and he gave mine a gentle squeeze, curving his fingers around the back of it, holding it back as we slow walked through the museum headed for the exit.

That lighter than air feeling returned with every step we took and it felt nice. Really nice. New, sure, but *right*.

Finally, after so very long, that was it… something felt *right*.

We were still both nervous, though. Both careful of one another. We had lunch, we talked about everything… well, everything except the possibility of an 'us' for the moment. We rode back to Indigo City and he stopped in front of my apartment, close to the same spot against the curb that he had arrived at that morning.

The sun was beginning to go down, the shadows lengthening between the buildings and I hopped off the back of his bike, pulling the safety glasses off my face and handing them over as the engine of his motorcycle ticked and cooled in the muggy eighty-degree heat of the summer evening.

"You, um… you hungry?" I asked him. After all, lunch had been some time ago. We'd walked the Mall, had taken photos with our phones and had been in no rush to return home. My feet positively ached in my sister's boots and I was ready to get out of them, but if he maybe wanted to stay a little longer…

He reached out a hand and twined his fingers between mine, swinging our hands lightly between us, a charmed semi-smile on his lips. I waited for the smart-ass comment to fly from those lips and I wasn't disappointed.

"Yeah, but not for food… your pussy on the menu?"

I blushed to the very roots of my hair.

"You sure?" I asked softly. "I have it on good authority this bitch be crazy."

His smile got bigger. "Yeah, but your kind of crazy is easier to deal with," he said gently.

"Oh yeah? How's that?" I asked.

"Your kind of crazy just needs a little reassurance every now and again. It doesn't get pissed off for no reason and it doesn't hit, or make shit up, or any of that shit."

I think I felt myself pale as the implications became clear. I wasn't about to ask him, however. I didn't want to ruin the mood. Still it was on the tip of my tongue... *your ex-wife used to hit you?*

He pulled me closer and slid his hands against my ass and I threw a leg over the front of his bike, taking a seat in front of him even as he scooted back to make some room. Both of us sat there kissing quietly, falling carefully into each other, taking things slowly despite the barely contained passion in each touch. Hands sliding beneath coats, against ribs, over backs, hinting at diving beneath tees, the desire of being skin on skin mounting.

"Ugh, God! Get a room."

Oz and I broke apart giggling even as the stranger passed by on the street, a man walking a little toy poodle of all things.

"Think we ought to take the man's advice?" I asked, voice husky with desire.

"Fuck him," Oz declared, voice low, and pulled me back into his arms.

I giggled into his mouth and that giggle turned into laughter as he kissed the side of my neck, making noises like a mad dog, devouring its prey.

"K, yeah, come on. Let's go inside," he declared, adjusting himself between our bodies, through his jeans.

I laughed and got up. He followed suit and locked his helmets, glasses, and bandanas away in one of the hard cases on the side of his bike, swiftly. He rose and followed me to my door, pressing himself against my back, breathing me in, massaging my hips through my jeans as I fumbled with the lock.

"You better get that door open," he growled behind my ear and I very nearly fainted from the heat.

"Mm, having a hard time here," I laughed nervously.

"I can see that," he murmured, and his voice had gone all seductive.

"You're not helping," I sang out and the key *finally* turned in the lock. Twisting the knob, I shoved the door forward, relieved when we both practically stumbled into the apartment. Shutting the door behind us and shooting the deadbolt home, he spun me and pinned me up against the cool metal of the door, a knee between mine, hoisting me up. My legs twining around his hips unbidden, he fetched me back up against the door and pinned me there, trapping me like a butterfly in a killing jar, but I didn't care.

All I cared about was his mouth on mine, his hands on my body, and getting my hands on the rest of him.

"Oh, God," I whimpered. "Bedroom. Bedroom, now."

He carried me bodily down the hall and I loved it. It was everything every little girl dreams of, feeling like a princess, her prince carrying her away and I knew I was a hopeless romantic, but I couldn't bring myself to care. He threw me down on the bed and didn't even hesitate, covering my body with his, delving his hand beneath the hem of my white ladies-cut tee and cupping my breast through my bra.

I moaned against his mouth as he worked his jacket with its brightly patched leather vest off his broad shoulders. He broke the kiss and I whined about it when he knelt up and looked around, he stood and put the coat and vest on the top of my dresser and dug through its pockets coming up with a condom.

"Thank God you're prepared," I said, reaching for him and he came back to me.

"I'm gettin' too old to be a daddy," he said and I laughed. "Plus, I ain't gonna fit anything you got." I stopped laughing.

"What?" I asked, not sure I'd heard him right.

"Oh, you're gonna see," he said with a charming, smart-assed grin.

He pulled his shirt off over his head and my mouth went dry and I swear, my brain went out to dinner without me. Muscle moved under his deep honey skin, his tattoos coming alive as he wadded the tee up and tossed it on my floor.

I sat up slowly, transfixed by the play of the light from the setting sun through my high bedroom window as it shone over the hills and valleys of his physique. I wasn't worthy. I felt that insecurity deep, deep, and deeper still. *About as deep as he's gonna go*, I thought to myself. It was too late to back out now, and even if in all reality it wasn't… I didn't want to, as selfish as that might sound.

"What's wrong?" he asked, kicking off his boots.

"Nothing," I lied.

"You can't bullshit a bullshitter, Ellie. What're you thinking?"

"I'm thinking I'm not good enough," I whispered.

He snorted derisively. "Bullshit. You're perfect," he said and it was my turn to snort.

"Am not," I declared, shrugging out of my sister's coat.

He shrugged and cast my argument out of hand with a one-shouldered shrug and turning down the corners of his lips.

"And I say you are. Right now, you're perfect for me."

"Oh really?" My eyebrows went up.

"Yeah, really," he said, hooking his fingers into the waistband of my jeans and hauling me, giggling, toward him. "Now shut up, you think too much."

I laughed outright and he smothered my fit of giggles with another kiss, pressing his warm body over the top of mine, hands delving once more beneath my tee to caress my ribs. He didn't stop there this time, though. He didn't stop at my breasts, either. Instead he kept going, peeling the tee off, over my head.

I whimpered in protest at having to lose contact between my hands and the warm, smooth skin of his shoulders and back, but it was worth it, the way his warm brown eyes devoured what was beneath the simple white cotton. The way he hungrily ate up every inch of my exposed skin with his gaze, the way he trailed his calloused fingertips over my skin leaving gooseflesh in their wake.

"Oz..." the way I whispered his name was an impassioned plea, one he answered by unhooking my bra as he kissed along my jaw.

I didn't exactly have idle hands the entire time. I let my fingertips roam the smooth, sleek curves of his muscled arms. He was nothing like my ex. My ex had remained fit, but he had been all long and lean – a runner's build. Oz was something else. Oz was bigger, for sure, but also stronger somehow. Not in the physical sense, though there was that too. There was a serious confidence about him, a staunchness, a boldness that I found wholly appealing as he deftly stripped me out of the rest of my clothes.

I lay on my bed, vulnerable in the dying light, nude while he knelt between my legs still in his jeans and looked down at me, his gaze pouring over every exposed inch of skin rich and thick like honey, an almost physical touch, with nothing but appreciation in his eyes.

I was struck dumb, hanging on the moment for all it was worth, feeling it deep, as if a drop of his gaze had landed in the center of my soul, rippling out to the far edges of my existence, diffusing through my spirit as a drop of ink to a glass of water. It subtly yet profoundly forever changed me – that one look – and though I had no notion of what it was we were even doing right now, of whether this was a forever kind of thing or just in the moment, I knew that I would give anything for this moment to last forever.

"Kiss me," I breathed, and I wasn't asking. He smiled and leaned over me, kissing me solidly on the mouth, dragging his lips down my chin, worrying at the side of my neck until he found that one spot and had sufficiently exploited it to his own ends, leaving me shivering in his grasp, nipples pebbling into hard aroused points against his chest, the slightest friction against them sending delicious waves of sensation throughout my body but particularly aimed at my sex.

"Relax, baby," he whispered against my body. "Just relax and enjoy the ride." Of course, he didn't give me even half a second to process his meaning before he laid his tongue flat against my pussy and ran the tip between my folds from my entrance to my clit.

I arched off the bed, tangling my fists in my bedspread at both hips as he pressed his hands to my inner thighs to keep my legs open. He didn't pause for even a moment in his attack, mercilessly teasing my clit with his tongue, suckling on it gently, making me shiver, shudder, and shake as I unconsciously held my breath for so long, until I absolutely needed to breathe.

He chuckled against me, the vibration of it doing its own thing, adding its own sensation to the mix and I about died and went to heaven.

There was no comparison. Oz was absolutely *nothing* like my ex.

I made a strangled, frustrated noise at the errant thought. Low key angry with myself for even thinking of such a thing for thinking of my ex when I was with Oz now...

"That's it, baby," Oz encouraged, clearly thinking I was close, and he wasn't exactly wrong. I just wasn't as close as I'd been the mere moment before. I silently cursed myself and tried to relax, his voice encouraging me further. "That's it, baby. Breathe, just breathe."

He slipped a finger inside of me and I tightened around it reflexively. He hummed in appreciation around my clit and I thrashed slightly. He put a forearm across my hips and pressed me down into the bed and I cried out, sitting halfway up. He looked up at me from between my thighs, eyes dark and full of a nameless heat, a power behind them that I'd never encountered before but made me want to bend to his will like a reed in the wind.

"Yeah, like that, just like that," he praised, sliding his finger back and forth inside me. I moaned, biting my bottom lip at the sensation and he backed off of me and stood up, going for his belt.

I hadn't come. Not yet, but I'd been so very close. I lay, breathing deep yet uneven as he slid the leather tongue of his belt through the loops holding the excess. Watching him stand there, staring down at me with passion and intent as he undid his belt stirred a desire in me like no other and the anticipation was murdering me.

I whimpered, feet sliding against the covers as I pushed myself up and centered myself on the bed. He swept his jeans and boxer-briefs down his legs and his cock bobbed between his legs and I froze.

He was huge.

I'm not talking just length, either. He was *thick*. Like crazy thick, as in almost as big around as my wrist and I wasn't entirely sure how this was going to work. I mean, if it was anatomically possible for our bodies to *fit* one another... like... '*How am I supposed to do this?*' definitely crossed my mind.

"You alright?" he asked, tearing open the condom and I looked up at him.

"Fine," I said. "Why do you ask?"

"You keep eying my cock like it's going to jump off my body and bite you," he said and I couldn't help but laugh. He rolled the condom on deftly and *why* was it so *hot* watching a man get himself ready to fuck you like that?

"I've never been with someone quite so…" I trailed off.

"Big?" he asked with that rakish grin of his.

"Yeah."

"Well," he slid onto the bed with me and put a hand on one of my knees, "Now you know why they say, 'once you go black you never go back.'"

He winked at me and I burst out into a fit of ridiculous giggles at his utter audacity. I mean, he had every reason to be audacious and I still wasn't sure how…

"Hey." I swung my eyes back to his from where I'd fixed them to the tops of my knees, to his hand atop the one.

"Slow and easy," he said. "We got all night."

I nodded and he leaned up and kissed me, pressing his lips against my jaw, near my ear he murmured, "You ever want me to stop… you *need* me to stop, all you gotta do is say so." I nodded, not quite trusting my voice and he said to me, "Lie on your stomach."

"Why?" I asked, suddenly apprehensive.

"You trust me?" he asked. I nodded and began to comply, and he nodded too. "Good."

I lay on my stomach and he straddled the backs of my thighs. His hands fell lightly onto my shoulders and he rolled his thumbs against my back, gripping and kneading; combatting the tension that'd taken up residence in my muscles with my unease.

I groaned with a different sort of pleasure, then. I'd forgotten what it was like, the feel-good of simply being treated well. Of being taken care of… and I let him. I turned into proverbial putty in his hands, sinking into the mattress below me, the slight euphoric haze of pleasure, of relaxation, that my body had held before his pants had come off returning to me.

He teased me to a fever pitch, and I twined around him like a vine. I was so wet, so excited, I wanted him so badly and once again, he didn't disappoint. He pressed against my opening and I squirmed a bit, writhing against him, the dichotomy of excitement and fear intoxicating as he carefully eased himself inside me – stretching me, making me feel impossibly full.

I forgot to breathe, the connection impossibly deep and going far beyond physical. I bit my bottom lip and closed my eyes and simply concentrated on that feeling, that sense of unity, and nearly wept at the sense that I would never be alone again... even if it was merely an illusion, it was one I needed right now and I held onto it, onto Oz, for everything I was worth in that moment. I held onto this with everything I had and wished so deeply that it would translate into forever.

17

$\mathcal{O}$z…

God, the way she moved under me was so hot. Her hands on my ass, urging me to fuck her, her legs twining around my waist, her body arching into mine, it was all just so hot, and I couldn't deny her or myself anything.

I couldn't hold back, I thrust hard, losing myself in the rhythm of deep, hot, good and sloppy sex.

She was so wet, I glided in and out of her effortlessly, her walls tight around me, her pert breasts pressing against my chest, the way she plunged her tongue past my lips, it was like we were an endless circle – no telling where I left off and she began. Two sides of the same coin – and I *never* jived so completely with *anyone* in my life even with how different we were.

It was some kind of crazy, and I liked it. Couldn't get enough of it. Couldn't get enough of *her*.

"Mm, don't stop!" she begged when I slowed, but I couldn't keep up the punishing pace forever. As invincible as she made me feel, I was still just a man and fallible, my body giving up when I could have gone forever like she asked. I had an idea, though.

"Come on, baby." I moved her, posed her, laying her on her side, straightening out her bottom leg against the mattress, straddling it, bending her top leg, knee toward her chest. She twisted pressing her shoulders flat to the bed to watch me, as I pressed myself back into her, hands on her hip that faced the ceiling.

I knew she'd like that. I had a sort of side curve, a bend in my dick, and this position worked for me, shoving the head of my cock against the roof of her pussy, stroking over that spot that drove women wild but that most dudes, for whatever reason, couldn't seem to find.

Her head fell back, her hair fanning out over the bedspread like a halo and I gripped her titty in one hand, kneading it, concentrating on her face, every line etched deep with ecstasy.

She was beautiful. Organically sexy. Smart, funny, and even sassy when she had the nerve. She was everything I found attractive in a woman and right now, she was mine and the overwhelming sense of gratitude that I felt over that was something I couldn't fathom. I struggled with it but not enough to be distracted from my purpose at the moment which was to make the both of us feel so damn good it hurt.

I stroked deep, closing my eyes and turning my head as I listened to her soft moans that punctuated every thrust. Her voice was like music, her body wrapped around mine like iron. Her pussy was so damn good, I just wanted to get lost in the feel of her forever.

Damned if forever wasn't coming up on me faster than I wanted it to, though. I wasn't about to come early but she felt so good I might not have a choice. Didn't mean I was going to leave her unsatisfied – oh, hell no. That wasn't something I would ever do.

I struggled to hold myself back, but as any dude knows – you ain't really got no say in the matter. You gonna come, you gonna come.

Sometimes there just ain't no turnin' back. I was struggling now more than I ever did as a young buck and that was sayin' something. Except now, I didn't think Elka was the type to head outside and start talkin' shit about me if I busted this nut too early.

She tightened around me, and I fuckin' stopped for a second crying, "*Jesus* Christ!"

She just gave me this sexy little smile, biting her bottom lip and I was just done. I couldn't anymore, I just couldn't. The visual paired with her body gripping my cock, rubbing around me, slipping inside her, coated in her warm, sensual honey… I lost my shit, thrusting inside of her hard, losing control, the orgasm crashing into me, over me, electric current running from my skull down my spine.

I buried myself deep, spilling inside the condom, deep inside my woman, and it felt like coming home. Euphoria sweeping through me like somebody'd popped the cork on my champagne, my blood fizzing with it, whole body tingling from the inside.

This woman was a rush and the ride wasn't over, yet… even if it was technically curtains for me for the time being.

I held the condom on myself and pulled out, Elka shuddering beneath me, her pussy gripping my cock, twitching, and I knew she had to be close if she hadn't gone over already.

I didn't dispose of anything, I didn't care at the moment. The only thing I cared about was making this woman come, so I moved her, bodily onto her back, dragged her down the bed and set myself to feast.

She was so fucking wet, all purest velvet and core strength wrapped around my fingers as I fixed my mouth over her clit. She writhed, hands on her breasts, diving between them, caressing my head pressing my mouth tight against her and it was the hottest fucking thing watching her let go, watching her trust me, taking all of what I had to give her.

I watched her, eyes heavy lidded with passion as she watched me back, her pussy tightening around my fingers the closer she got. Her breathing, harsh, deep, but even until she got closer still and it lost its rhythm some until with a final cry of pure bliss, she came.

Watching her come apart was beautiful. The way she arched, the way she shook, the way her voice painted the room a deep erotic hue… I don't think I could ever get tired of seeing it.

She laid limp and spent in the middle of the bed, her chest rising and falling in an evening cadence, her face slack with peace like she'd somehow found God with that orgasm and I felt pretty damn pleased with myself. I kissed her hip, slipping my fingers from her gathering wetness and kissing her hip. She jumped at the slight touch of my lips, her skin warm and likely still oversensitive.

I climbed her body like a flowering vine, laying blossoms with my kisses, until finally I came to rest beside her, a hand on her stomach, just below and between her still heaving breasts. I propped my head on my hand and just watched her, smiling, because how could I not? It was hard not to congratulate myself on a job well done here. Especially when she turned those warm brown eyes on me, all aglow with good sex and a hint of something else in them that both scared me and didn't because I already knew deep down, I felt the same way.

"Welcome back," I whispered and she smiled, giggling, covering her mouth with her hands.

I took my hand off from over her calming heartbeat and used it to pull her hands away from her mouth.

"Don't hide that smile from me," I murmured, swallowing hard. "Not now, not ever, mmkay?"

She smiled and bit her bottom lip and went from shy to seductive nymph outta one of her paintings.

"Okay," she whispered back and reached for me.

We kissed, and I gotta say, my fate was sealed with it. Because damned if I wasn't destined to love this woman until the end of time.

"Stay the night with me," she murmured against my lips and I smiled.

"Baby, if that's what you want, I ain't going anywhere."

She laughed, the sound, one of pure, unadulterated joy, and pulled me into her arms, resting my head against her chest, ear over her heart and I was content to just lay in the circle of her arms and listen to it beat in her breast, sending life coursing through her veins. I honestly felt like her heartbeat sent it coursing through mine too, somehow.

18

*E*lka...

I stuck out my bottom lip in a pout and said, "I don't want you to go."

He laughed slightly and put a hand to my cheek, and I turned my face into it, planting a kiss on the heel of his hand. The smile he gave me was so full of emotion, so full of care.

"I'll be back," he murmured. "Don't you worry about that."

"Is it bad that I am?" I asked as he folded me into his arms.

"Yeah," he said simply. "Whoever put it in your head that you aren't good enough? I'd like to have some words with 'em."

"Some people just need a high five... in the face, with a chair." My voice was muffled where my face was pressed against his chest and his laughter vibrated through my whole body.

"You ain't lyin'," he said.

He kissed the back of my head where I had it tucked and bowed against his chest and he let me go. The step I took back from him was a reluctant one.

"You take it easy today, now. Y'hear?" He fixed me with a look, and I smiled a little sadly.

"Might go back to bed," I said honestly and he nodded.

I'd found him dressed and in my kitchen brewing coffee and now it was time to say goodbye for now. I hugged myself on my little front stoop in my satin robe and nodded.

"Think I'll paint, and I have dinner with my dad later."

"Well, you call me when you get home, okay?"

I nodded.

"What are you off to do?" I asked curiously and he reached out and brushed my cheek with his thumb.

"Club meeting later, work out with the hose boys for now – standing appointment."

"Ah," I nodded. "Sounds eventful."

He smirked at my sarcasm, gave me one final kiss goodbye and went over to his bike. I leaned against my doorjamb and watched him go with a deep, slow, rush of breath that was somewhere between a sigh and meant to decompress me.

I reached back and pulled on the back of my neck, rolling my head back and fixing my eyes on the eave over my apartment door.

I was slightly torn between sense and sensibility... On the one hand, a relationship with Oz could be a really bad idea given how we met, on the other hand there was a much bigger part of me that wanted to throw caution to the wind and just say *fuck it*.

Oz didn't just make me feel good, he made me feel *whole*. Like despite the Shakespearean tragedy that resembled my life as of late, he made me feel like I had my shit together and that I was *okay*.

I dipped back into my apartment and closed the door on the sun-soaked sidewalk outside, locking the door behind me out of habit and returning to my kitchen. I poured and doctored up a second cup of coffee and drifted from room to room contemplating what exactly to do with the rest of my Sunday before I was due at my dad's.

The answer was that I did go back to bed for a bit, napped for an hour, maybe two, before getting up, showering, and putting on some paint clothes to work on Mia's portrait.

Instead of the deep melancholy I'd felt every time I'd sat down since her death, I was surprised to find that a sort of hope and a deep affection had taken the negative emotion's place. I dipped my brush into some pigments I laid out on my pallet and said, "Well, Mia… it looks like something's changed. I don't know if it's for the better yet, or if it will be more of just the same, but for now, things are almost alright. What do you think about that, huh?"

Of course, there wasn't any answer but the feelings I was having didn't diminish in the slightest so there was that.

I painted until the hour before I had to leave, giving myself plenty of time to clean up, get dressed, and get to my dad's two bus routes away.

He opened the door with arms thrown wide and said, "Elka!"

I hugged him tight and said, "Hi, Daddy."

We sat at the dining room table and I was grateful not to be moving around too much. My body ached from so much good sex the night before, my hips a little angry at the unfamiliar treatment. I wasn't exactly used to spreading my legs so far.

It was slightly awkward trying to hide my discomfort, afraid that it was glaring across my face, in my eyes, as bright as a red neon sign. I definitely wasn't ready to explain things yet. I didn't even know how I was going to broach the subject with my dad.

"So, what did you do yesterday?" he asked after a lull in the conversation over our food.

"Mm, I actually took a trip to D.C."

"Oh, yeah? What'd you go there for?"

"Um, actually, Oz – I mean Officer Jones took me to the National Gallery of Art. They had an exhibit featuring Verrocchio."

"Oh? That's nice," he said, a wrinkle of concern in his voice and I thought to myself, *Here we go...*

"What's wrong with that, Dad?" I asked.

"What? Nothing! I said it was nice!"

I gave him a flat look and he had the grace to look embarrassed. "You… you spend a lot of time with Officer Jones?" he asked.

I shrugged. "We're friends… sort of." I felt so awful for downplaying it, but I was so afraid of things going south with my dad so soon after mending fences so to speak. It was frustrating because I knew he only meant well, but I wasn't a little girl anymore. By the same token, I didn't exactly have a good track record when it came to dating and relationships. Then again, my family had only ever seen what my ex had wanted them to see.

"Elka?"

I looked up.

"Yeah, Dad?"

He smiled at me and shook his head amused.

"You must really like Officer Jones."

"He likes to be called Oz," I mumbled.

"Ah, the Great and Powerful?" he asked, and I smiled and shook my head.

"No, after some television show, I guess. About a prison, because he's a jailer."

My dad nodded slowly and said, "Never heard of it."

I grinned. "Me either."

"You see him a lot?" he asked.

"Once or twice a week since he crashed through my front door," I said and gave him a fixed look. Again, my dad had the grace to look embarrassed.

"Ah, yes, that…" he said, trailing off.

"Would it bother you?" I asked carefully.

He considered me from across the table.

"What are you asking me?"

"I-I-if Oz and I were friends or maybe more than just friends?" I stared at my dad and felt two inches tall just for asking.

"Because he is black or one of the police?" he asked.

"Um… both?" I asked quietly.

My dad sighed and I knew he knew I was thinking about Oma. His mother, my grandmother. She was long dead but had strong opinions on both the police and people of color. My dad looked surprised for a moment, then angry, then… dismayed.

He set down his fork and folded his hands which shook with some unnamed emotion, folding them in his lap.

"Since when have you ever seen me, or your mother, treat any man or woman different from the next?" he asked gently.

"Never," I said quietly. "Although, to be fair, you and mom weren't exactly friends with many people of color, either."

His head jerked back slightly, and he blinked. "I had friends from work," he said defensively, and I cocked my head. He blushed and I know he knew we were both thinking of the same man. Frankie Johnstone was white, with a thick Boston accent, and unabashedly both sexist and racist and my dad and the rest of the guys from work always brushed his bad behavior off, stating 'that's just Frankie.'

"Daddy, your friends from work that would come to summer barbecues and our Oktoberfest celebration... none of them were any different in looks from you, or I, or Frankie Johnstone from work." And as Mamma had always been swift to point out, most of the men that had come from work to those things weren't my father's friends.

My dad sighed and sat back in his seat.

"Your mother is the reason you and Mia turned out so well. The reason you turned a blind eye to such matters as color," he admitted freely and the shard of truth in that statement pained me.

"Not blind," I said softly. "Just colorblind, I suppose. We always knew the matters were there, are still here, but Mamma always told us that in the grand scheme of things, God created all of us in His image and that God didn't make mistakes, He just had a fantastic love for every color and hue and thus painted us to match the land."

My dad smiled, ruefully, chagrinned. "That sounds like something your mother would say."

"So, it wouldn't be a problem?" I asked, feeling like I was on pins and needles, knowing that pressing for an answer might not be good, but not knowing the answer, for me, would be much worse.

"I just want you to be *happy*," he said and worried his napkin between his hands.

"I want to be happy, too," I told him. "I mean, I'm tired, was tired even before Mia, of being this constant misery muffin and with Oz?" I swallowed hard and fixed my eyes on my plate. "I know it doesn't seem right with how we met, and I know it probably doesn't even seem very fair given it's only been a few weeks but… I'm happy when he's around." I fell silent for a moment and said with more conviction, "I'm happy when I'm around him. Things are different."

My father nodded sagely, and an understanding passed between us.

"Do you think you love him?" he asked.

I did, but I wasn't quite ready to say it out loud. Not yet. It just didn't seem right.

"I don't know," I said quietly. "I think given more time it's more than a possibility."

My dad smiled at that and nodded, his look saying that he knew. He also knew that I had always been the more reserved of his two daughters. The more private of the two. I felt a flicker of sadness then. My voice of doubt making an unwanted appearance, speaking in low slithering tones from the back of my mind… *how awful it must be for him to be left with you.*

"I just want you to be happy, baby. I will take whatever makes you so and will welcome it with open arms." I smiled my eyes watering a bit. The voice in the back of my mind retreating back into the dark with its lies.

"I love you, Daddy. I just want to make you proud."

"Oh, Elka. You were and always have been my pride," he said and for the second time this week we added some extra salt to our meal through our tears.

19

*O*z...

"Hey, hey, where you been at the last couple of weeks?" Skids asked as I breezed through the door at the last possible minute for the monthly mandatory club meeting. We all tried to meet at least once a month, the whole club, and while it was a fuckin' struggle, we usually all made it to the monthly meet. If we couldn't do it, work was pretty much the only reason good enough and if it so happened that we all made it to a particular weekly meet that fell before the monthly one we had set, then we counted it as our monthly.

I slid into my chair at the table and said, "Oh, you know – doin' a little of this and a little of that."

"Tell me, this and that happened to be named *Elka?*" Golden gave me a savage grin and I felt more than a little protective of Ellie. She was too good, too shy, and still so broken. While some of her pieces were goin' back together, she was still so fragile, and I didn't know if she would be cool with sharin' her business with this pack of jokers. Not until she knew them like I did.

"C'mon, man. Don't do that. My business is my business," I said defensively.

"Ooo, good call Golden, looks like you're on to something." Backdraft winked at me from across the table, leaning way back in his chair, his hands folded behind his head.

"C'mon, guys. Leave it alone," Skids rumbled.

"Yeah," I nodded. "Girl's been through enough for the time being."

Yale fixed me with a scowl from down the table saying, "I agree, so do you think this is wise?"

"Slow your roll there, Turbo. You just go on and stay your ass in the truck, now," I said and he held up his hands in surrender. "Unless your ass knows something I don't," I said and my brother, the prosecutor, looked uneasy.

"Nothing I am at liberty to discuss."

"Shit, what's that about, Yale?" Narcos demanded.

"Nothin' he can talk about; didn't you just hear the man?" I demanded, taking up for him, even while I was saddled with this awful sinking feeling.

"Let's table this discussion for now," Skids said gruffly. "To order."

To order. The opening words to all our serious meets. Personal stuff got shoved aside and it was all club business. For now, that meant the Little Havana block party. We all attended, I mean that was my roots. Every summer the neighborhood in Indigo City declared as Little Havana had a barbecue and block party but part of having a block party meant that the residents in that hood were on the hook for their own security in addition to paying the city to close down streets and all.

Most of the residents of that hood were too poor for both, so as my act of charity for the month of August, which was the one I drew out of the hat, we off-duty cops of the Indigo Knights volunteered our time. In exchange, we got good food, an endless supply of cold non-alcoholic drinks, and we got to listen to some of the finest live entertainment and DJ's the Cuban community of this city has to offer.

It was more than a fair trade, and I was looking forward to bringing Ellie this year as it was in just a couple of weeks.

All the guys brought their women that had women last year, and all of them had a good time. We were all looking forward to it again this year and the guys were taking the security duties in shifts of three to have a chance to indulge. We just needed to iron out the logistics of everything.

"This thing keeps gettin' bigger every year," Reflash was sayin and he said it with a grin. He was a Cuban immigrant back when he was just a kid. Didn't become naturalized until he was eighteen, but he celebrated his heritage hard – like me, even though I didn't have much of a connection to it growing up.

My pops had never talked about it and he was where I got it from. After he died when I was a kid, I'd started digging for my roots, tryin' to keep that connection to his past, and by extension my past, alive.

We wrapped business and the guys fell off into pockets of talk, but my gaze fixed on Yale. He was starin' back at me and it was an uncomfortable weight to his gaze.

"How 'bout you got somethin' to say, you just say it, bro?" I said and the rest of the chapel fell silent.

"I would if I could, Oz. You know that." Yale looked fairly resigned and I didn't like this fuckin' game. I didn't like it one bit.

"You gotta give me a heads up, bro."

He nodded and looked at the rest of the club, asking, "Give us the room?"

"Whoa, there, Yale. You've never asked us for something like that before. Is Oz in some kind of trouble?" Driller demanded, leaning his elbows on the table, one fist inside the other, propping up his chin.

"I know," Yale said and again with that look like he was torn, the resignation visibly weighting his shoulders.

"Come on, now, boys. Ain't nothing against us. You know how the system works. Let's not put Yale between a rock and a hard place." Skids got up from the table and gave us both a nod.

"Thanks, guys," I said coolly, but my hackles were up. Something was going down and I was at the center of it and I didn't know what that something was. I didn't like it. I don't know anybody who would like it and I was hoping when it was down to just me and Yale, he could give me just a little bit of some insight.

As soon as the door swung shut, scraping against the lintel in its signature style, the noise of the restaurant outside cut off, Yale drew a deep breath. Without any real preamble he said, "Look, the only thing I can tell you is that there were some… inconsistencies discovered in the mandatory review process for any officer-involved shooting at the coroner's office."

"Fuck me," I said, leaning back heavily in my chair. "What inconsistencies?" I demanded.

"I can't tell you that. I shouldn't have even told you that much. The review should wrap up sometime this week, but Oz… we're going to come talk to you."

"We?"

"The prosecutor's office and IAB," he said.

"The rat squad is sniffing around this?" I asked and recoiled.

"Yale, I didn't do anything *wrong*," I said.

"I know that," he said, and I believed him that he believed me which was something, but it sure as shit wasn't everything.

"They looking to jam my ass up?" I demanded.

"No. Nobody wants that, Oz. I don't foresee any criminal charges or any disciplinary actions against you, at this point."

"I hear a 'but,'" I said.

"But stranger things have happened," he said carefully.

"Fuck me, what are they lookin' at?"

"I wish I could tell you, but even I am on a strictly need-to-know basis and IAB doesn't think I need to know – at least not yet."

"What the fuck?"

"About how I feel about it. Which is why I am just saying, for your own good, tread carefully with the sister right now."

"Ellie and I are just fine as we are," I said, and Yale's eyebrows went up.

"It's already too late, isn't it?" he asked.

"Just say it, dude. Ask it. Whatever!"

"You've, ah, already been intimate?"

"Fucked. You mean fucked. And yeah, just last night in fact."

"When were you planning on seeing her again?" he asked, standing, burying his hands in his pockets and hanging his head, mouth twisting in thoughtful contemplation.

"Tonight, as a matter of fact."

He nodded.

"Just keep things on the down low. Say *nothing* about what we've spoken of here. At least until we have anything definite to say about it."

"Dude, you swear you've told me everything about this that you know?" I bored holes in his lily white-bred ass with my gaze.

He nodded. "I swear it. I have my own thoughts on what could be up but it's all purely speculation at this point, so I would rather not share."

"Get to speculating," I said, crossing my arms.

"Now that I won't do," he said and I knew that look. I'd reached my limit on what the cagey prosecutor would say.

"Fuck, man…"

"It'll all be resolved, good, bad, or indifferent by the middle to the end of the week," he said, and it sounded like he was swearing on a stack of law books – which was Yale's version of a bible anyhow so I would take it as a gospel preaching.

I nodded. "Alright now."

He sighed and it didn't sound happy. I could feel for him.

"Thanks for tellin' me what you could," I said and he nodded.

"I shouldn't have even told you that," he said dryly.

"I know," I nodded.

"You know no matter what, we got your back, right?" He fixed me with a gaze made of twin hot coals.

"Yeah, I know. I got you, brother. Same as you got me."

"Good. You staying for a drink, maybe some lunch?"

I shook my head.

"Naw, man. I gotta get home and do some laundry, get ready for the work week."

"And go see the sister, right?"

I sighed and said, "She has a name. It's Elka."

"Fair enough," he stated. "Guess I am just doing the prosecutorial distance thing."

I frowned. "Sounds a lot like you think Ellie did something wrong in this, now."

Yale's eyebrows when up again. "Not at all and it's 'Ellie' now, is it?"

"I told you, we been spending some time together."

He nodded. "It's way past dire warnings, isn't it?" he asked frankly.

"By a long flat mile," I agreed.

He gave a long-suffering sigh and said, "That may or may not complicate things depending on the outcome of this review of the incident. Just do your best to be prepared."

I stood up and stretched, trying to keep it lookin' casual when really, I was tied up in knots on the inside.

"Hard to prepare for shit when you don't know what's coming," I pointed out.

Yale smiled a bit and said, "This is you we're talking about, Oz. You always find a way."

"Yeah, I'm a regular fuckin' boy scout," I drawled sarcastically.

Yale chuckled and I saw myself out, leaving him in the room on his own for the moment. The rest of the guys looked up expectantly from around the tables out front. Some of their ol' ladies who'd tagged along mirroring their men's faces. I felt like Johnny-on-the-spot, and I hated that shit.

"What's the word?" Youngblood asked, coolly assessing.

"I have no fuckin' idea," I told him honestly. "I'm out. I got shit to do today that doesn't include worrying about shit that ain't happened yet."

"You sure, brother?" Backdraft asked, concern wrinkling his brow.

"I'm sure," I muttered and waved back at them all over my shoulder as I reached the front door and stepped out onto the summer sidewalk.

So what if I took the long way home, favoring the ride as I puzzled shit out. I'd be lying if I said I wasn't worried, but I didn't know a single thing that I needed to be worried about. I'd done everything by the book. It was a textbook perfect takedown, if there was such a thing. I'd identified and stopped homeboy from shooting up the goddamn neighborhood any worse than he already had... so why did it feel like I was about to be punished for doing the right thing?

Damn.

20

*E*lka...

A knock fell at my door later that evening and I smiled to myself. I set my brush aside and wiped my slightly sweaty palms on the back of my paint spattered and streaked shorts and went to answer that knock, low key excited and knowing who it was likely to be on the other side.

I wasn't wrong. I opened my front door to Oz holding up a pyramid of Styrofoam clamshells in a knotted grocery sack.

"Thought maybe it was time for you to take a break and eat something," he said with a smile.

I grinned, biting my bottom lip to try and suppress just how stupid happy I was to see him.

"Your timing is impeccable," I said, stepping aside. "I'm famished."

"Well, alright then." He laughed slightly and stepped through the door and I had missed the small gym bag in his other hand.

"Oh, planning on staying the night, are we?" I asked.

"Damn straight," he said, setting his bag on the arm of my couch on the way by and pulling me up against his body the second his arm was free to do so.

I kissed him with enthusiasm and wrapped my arms around his waist.

"I do have to leave early for work in the morning," I reminded him.

"Yeah, I got a standing appointment with the hose boys to get a workout in before I go to work, so it's all good."

I felt my lips curl in a smile. "Hose boys?" I asked.

"The firefighters," he corrected and I laughed.

"I'm sure they just love that."

He shrugged. "Don't care if they do, don't care if they don't. I'ma asshole like that."

I laughed and shook my head. "You're the furthest thing from an asshole as a guy can get," I told him and he raised an eyebrow.

"You just say that because I'm nice to you."

"Okay," I agreed. "Touché." He had me there.

"So, what's for dinner?" I asked and he held up the bag.

"Chicken Teriyaki for you, with Gyoza and Chicken Katsu for me."

"Awww, I love Gyoza!"

"See, I knew that," he said and I giggled. It was something we had talked about, cuddling the night before. Different things we liked, which had mostly centered on food for some reason.

"What are you doing?" he asked when I headed for the kitchen.

"Getting plates?"

"To hell with that, why you gonna make dishes? Just grab some forks."

I smiled and said, "Yes, sir!" crossed my eyes and gave him a half-assed salute.

"Oh, okay! I see how it is now!"

Another fit of giggling and some silverware later, we were seated at my dining room table for four and a right angle to one another, happily munching our take away and discussing all manner of small things.

"How did your meeting or whatever go?" I asked not quite sure what to call it as he had called it something different from 'meeting' earlier that day.

"Church?" he asked.

"Sounds so sacrilegious, but yeah, that," I said, sticking a bite of teriyaki chicken breast in my mouth.

He grinned across the space between us and thumbed a bit of sauce off my bottom lip. I watched him suck it off the pad of his thumb and *why* was that so *hot?*

"It went okay," he said.

"Don't sound so enthusiastic about it." I rolled my eyes.

His smile was a good one and he said, "Wow, look at you go with your sarcastic self. No, really, it went alright the first half of it. Second half got boring real quick."

"So, Cliff's Notes it for me," I said.

"I can't tell you all of it," he said. "Club business is club business, but I can tell you what we're up to in a couple weeks. I was actually hoping you'd go with me."

"Oh yeah? You've got my curiosity piqued. What's going on in a couple of weeks?"

I told her about the Little Havana block party, and she blinked at me and asked, "And you want me to go with you?"

"Well, yeah."

"Like on a date? A for real date with your friends and everything?"

I was a bit taken aback. Just like that? That easy? *He's not your ex,* I thought once again and probably, most definitely, not for the last time, either.

"Yeah, Ellie. I mean, you have a problem with it?" he asked, and I shook my head rapidly, chewing furiously through the bite I had in my mouth and trying to swallow so I could speak.

"Slow down," he demanded. "You're gonna choke."

"Sorry, and no, not at all. I guess given my history with guys I'm just… surprised, that's all."

"What kind of fucknuggets you been with?" he asked, and I couldn't help it, the use of the word 'fucknuggets' was so unexpected, I cracked up laughing. I pictured my ex along with the label and laughed so hard I couldn't breathe! I mean, it wasn't all that funny, but it just struck my funny bone so hard I spent a solid few minutes gasping and wheezing between gales of laughter.

Oz waited me out a smirk on his sexy full lips and I shook his head as he took another bite of rice. "Wasn't that damn funny," he said around his mouthful of food and I rolled my eyes.

"Was to me."

"Didn't answer the question," he said.

"No. No, I did not." I didn't answer it then, either, and to his credit, Oz left it alone.

"So, what were you thinking on doing the rest of the evening?" I asked after a long, but comfortable, silence.

"Dunno. You wanna get some more painting in?" he asked.

I thought about it.

"No, I think I'm done for tonight on that front, but I do need to do a bit of clean up in there."

"Maybe watch some T.V.?" he asked.

"I don't actually have T.V.," I said. "I have a few favorite movies, and the DVD player, but that's about it. It's not even a Blu-Ray," I said and smiled at the look of horror that crossed his face.

"Damn. Okay. How about this, you clean up, I'll run down to the Movie Box at the corner store and pick up a couple of things for us to watch?"

I checked the time and bargained with him, "Mmmm, it's getting late. How about just *one* movie? Your choice."

He nodded. "Deal. Favorite flavor of ice cream?" he asked.

"Oh, now you're talking! Chocolate Chip Mint."

"Alright, now. You got it."

He got up and I did too, stowing my remaining food in the refrigerator. He watched me for a long minute and I paused. "Everything okay?" I asked.

"Everything's great," he said and smiled. It held a touch of longing, or sadness to it… something I just couldn't place. That just wasn't quite right.

"You sure?" I asked cautiously.

"I'm sure, babe. I just like lookin' at you is all."

I smiled and blushed, bowing my head.

"Takes some getting used to, I guess."

"Yeah? Well you better get used to it," he said and shrugged into his jacket and vest that was hanging on the back of his chair.

"Oh, I'm sure I will," I said with a pleasant smile.

"Be back before you know it," he said.

"Okay."

He went out and I cleaned up both the dining room, the few dishes I had in my kitchen sink, and put the kettle on for some tea while I went and dealt with putting my studio to rights.

Oz came back in calling out from the front, "Ellie!"

"Yeah?" I called out.

"C'mere for a minute."

I finished up quickly and went back out to the front where he'd set the bag with the pints of ice cream on the table. His jacket and vest he was returning to the back of this chair.

"What'd you forget to do?" he asked gently, and it immediately set my teeth on edge. The echo of my ex in the question. I had *hated* when he'd done that. Asking me something when I clearly didn't know the answer to just lord it over me – whatever mistake I'd done now – but this was Oz and Oz was different.

"I don't know, just rip the Band-Aid off and just tell me," I said, tense.

He flinched like my response was weird and to a normal person, of course it was but he answered me, anyway.

"Babe, you forgot to lock the door behind me. This ain't the best neighborhood. I don't want anything to happen to you."

I nodded slowly, and he came over to me and pulled me into a tight embrace.

"You alright?" he asked.

"Yeah," my voice was muffled in his tee.

"Liar," he said with a light chuckle. "Wanna tell me what's up?"

I swallowed hard and told him.

"Yeah, that's fucked up," he agreed. "I'll be careful how I phrase it next time."

"Thanks," I murmured.

"Hey, it's no problem," he said.

"What're we watching?" I asked, changing the subject.

"Oh, now I got one of *my* favorites," he said, handing over the flat DVD case.

"Spy thriller, niiiice."

We settled on the couch in a cuddle pile to watch and it felt good to have his arms around me. It felt even better when he would absently kiss my hair for no reason, or the way he had to adjust himself in his jeans simply from my proximity.

Midway through the movie, during a particularly spicy scene, I found myself both motivated and inspired. I twisted in his lap and climbed his prone form like a tree. He chuckled and smiled, reaching for me as I kissed him.

"Hi," he murmured and I smiled impishly.

"Hi," I whispered back, and my back went awash in a tingling euphoria when his hands slipped beneath the hem of my tee to caress my skin beneath.

Words failed, emotions took over, and our hands and mouths spoke for us for the time being. I let my hands push the bottom of his tee away, my fingers nimbly working his belt open, and the button through its loop on his jeans so I could finally lower his zipper.

"You want some of what I got?" he asked playfully, and I bit my bottom lip and grinned sliding down his body as he watched me, taking his pants down, his underwear with them, his cock bobbing thick and fully engorged in front of my eyes. It was a daunting task, giving a man his size a blowjob, but I was up for the challenge. Whether my jaw would hold out for long was a whole different bag of bricks, but I would go for as long as I could.

I took him into my mouth and the sound of his quickly sucked in, almost startled, breath that he took aroused me completely. I hummed in appreciation around his shaft and he gasped out, "Oh, God!" above my head in such a supremely satisfying way it just egged me on. I lay on my stomach on my couch, feet kicked up behind me, and fisted his base, working his lower shaft with my hand as I treated the head of his cock like an obscene ice cream cone or lollipop and I couldn't have been happier to hear just how much I was doing it for him.

I loved that about Oz. He wasn't afraid to be vocal. To encourage me to do it like that, yes *just like that,* or to direct me to where I would ultimately reach that particular praise. He was bold and beautiful in every way like that. He didn't care. He didn't sugarcoat things. There was no *guessing* with him and that was so precious to me, you don't even know.

It was easy to love him for that one quality alone, as much as it terrified me to ever love someone so completely again.

I wasn't sure I could handle another heartbreak, being passed over for something better when it came along had nearly crushed me… but Oz didn't make me feel like I was anything *less.*

The opposite, in fact.

He made me feel like I was *everything.* The careful attention he paid me was something I had never before encountered, and it was hard not to trust in him. Hard not to love him, and though I admit that I had been struggling with my feelings to a certain extent, right now, when we were like this, I didn't hold anything back.

The glow of positive vibes and emotion suffused me and brought me back to life as I worked him with my mouth. Sliding him back over my tongue, teasing him with my lips, carefully avoiding everything with my teeth. I slid into that Zen-like state where I could take him further and further in, touching the back of my throat just slightly, breathing carefully around him, holding my breath, stroking him in and out of my mouth in a timed rhythm. He fisted the cushions on my couch, one on the back, the other at his hip and held still.

I loved that he controlled himself; that he didn't grab at me, or force anything. That he just took what I had to give and that was enough. It was empowering. It was its own aphrodisiac and I found myself reaching for my own waistband, with him still in my mouth.

"Enough!" he cried. "Enough, enough, enough. Get up here."

He reached down and guided me up his body, my mouth to his and God, I'd never had a man hold me like this. Hold me against him as if I were his very last breath to breathe and he didn't want me to get away. It was possessive, but not in any way that made your skin crawl. Rather it made me melt into his arms, my mind delirious with happiness, scrambling in circles for the word, *what was that word?*

Safe.

I felt safe in his embrace, but not just in a physical sense. I felt safe in the sense that I knew he wouldn't hurt me. Not just physically, but emotionally. That as strong, as big and scary as he was, my heart was safe, beating in his gentle hands.

It was overwhelming. It was decidedly amazing, and my heart nearly wept with the relief of it.

"Hey, hey, what's that?" he asked and I blinked in confusion.

"What's what?" I asked softly, so softly I didn't think he had quite heard me over the film playing on the television.

He brushed a thumb along my cheek and took it away, his eyes locked with mine. I was vaguely aware of his hand moving off my face, the intensity of his warm brown eyes holding me fixed as he brought his thumb to his full lips and sucked the wetness of my tears from it. I swallowed hard and stuttered…

"I-i-t's not what y-y-you think."

"How you know what it is I'm thinkin'?" he asked with a soft, chiding smile.

"I don't, I'm sorry."

He shook his head, once back, once forth.

"Nothin' to be sorry about, Ellie. Just tell me what you got going on in there." He traced some of my hair behind my ear.

"I – um, that's to say…"

"Just be out with it," he said gently. "I ever judge you before?"

I swallowed hard and shook my head.

"No," I whispered.

He gave a lopsided grin. "Then tell me what's up, baby girl. Or you just gonna leave me with my dick hanging out all night?"

I snorted and gave a graceless laugh. He chuckled along with me as I slid down and rested my head on his chest. He put his arms around me and muttered, "Gimme just a second here," before reaching between us to adjust himself. "Okay, that's better."

I laid back down.

He waited me out for a few seconds and just as he drew breath to try and prompt me again, I spoke.

"I like this," I said bluntly. "Being with you like this. I like how it feels with you," I said, and I know my voice tremored a bit with my false starts but telling someone, *anyone*, other than Mia how I felt was diffi-cult. I mean, I guess, that was just another thing that my ex-who-shall-not-be-named did to me. He never raised a hand to me, oh no. He was always a perfect gentleman but… but for the cutting remarks and the what-do-you-call-it? That thing where even though something is true, is the situation at hand, the person you are with tells you different. Twists things so that you doubt yourself, start to feel bad and unreasonable and pretty soon *you* are the one apologizing.

"Ellie?"

I cleared my throat, and said, "I can be real with you." My voice was a little stronger and I let go of my last thread of fear of what he might say or how he might take it or *what if I'm wrong?* "I can trust you," I said.

"Well, yeah. Yeah, you can trust me. You know I got you."

"I know… and before you there wasn't anyone that did, you know? Except my sister. Except for Mia."

"Not sure who dulled your sparkle, beautiful, but I'm gonna find him and punch him in the mouth."

I couldn't help but smile at the images that evoked and I sighed.

"I'm sorry if I ruined the mood," I said softly.

He took my hand in his and shoved it between us, my fingers naturally just curling around the hot velvety softness of his straining erection.

"You ain't ruined anything. Shoot."

I smiled and he pulled me up to kiss me again. I melted into his touch once more, only this time I didn't let my head ruin anything with the thoughts of the past. No, instead, I let Oz tug me along and just let that shit go.

21

———————

*O*z…

    She was becoming more and more relaxed around me, but *goddamn*, I was fuckin' serious about punching a motherfucker out. It wasn't fair how she got bound up so tight. How her head took over where her heart should be leading the dance in her soul.

I didn't mind it for me, or delaying my gratification, but I wanted her soul to be on fire and *not* the fire of agony. I wanted to hold this woman in the palm of my hand, open it up and watch her fly free and that sure as shit wasn't going to happen on no narrow ass couch.

"Come on, let me take you to bed," I said, and she smiled up at me softly, her eyes warming to molten caramel as she nodded her assent softly.

"Okay."

Jesus, she made me hard without even trying.

I buried my hands in her hair and pulled her mouth to mine and she responded so beautifully, her lips parting underneath mine, welcoming, enticing; making me hard to the point of pain.

149

I groaned into her mouth and suddenly didn't want to move my black ass off the fucking couch. I mean, here was good. Here, right now, sounded really good.

I ran my hands down her frame, sliding over her thin tee and shoving down her paint crusted shorts taking her scrap of cotton panties with them. I relished in my hands smoothing over the swell of her perfect, ripe as a peach ass, helping myself to a handful of that pressing her body tight against my body. Our mouths feverishly worked at each other, her light whimpering moans driving me wild as I kept shoving at her shorts to get them down her legs and *off*.

She laughed, squirming awkwardly in my arms, trying to help, trying to get naked from the waist down and finally with a frustrated and impatient sound at the uncooperative denim we had some success.

"There we go!" I said triumphantly as she flung the offending clothes over the back of the couch.

"I thought we were going to bed," she said against my mouth and I smiled against her lips.

"You can sleep on a couch, can't you?"

She laughed and it was high and joyous, transforming her face from beautiful to just plain... I don't know... like she was some goddess or something and I was totally cool with that. It would be even cooler if I was up inside her. I fished in the front pocket of my jeans, which was harder than it sounded with them being half way down my thighs from her out-of-this-world blowjob of earlier.

"You had a condom in your pocket this whole time?" she asked incredulously.

"Always be prepared," I deadpanned and she rolled her eyes.

"Oh, yeah. I can totally picture you a real boy scout."

"Man, my family was too poor for that shit. We were more like the hood rat rangers."

She laughed again and I handed her the condom.

"Do me a favor, let me watch you put this on for me."

"Of course," she murmured, charmed.

Fuck that was hot.

She slid the condom down my length and her hands on me felt so good, her long hair a satin sheet behind her face, framing it up nice, the slight smile on her lips, her soft, milky white skin, the slight shadow of very light freckles across the bridge of her long straight nose, her lips lush and swollen with my kiss, branding her beautiful face as *mine.*

Mine to cherish, mine to protect. Mine to hold and to love and to spend the rest of my life making her happy... if she would let me.

I shoved the creeping fear of whatever Yale had half-assed warned me what was goin' on in the background *to* the background and let myself fall for her. Despite his warning that it might not be a good idea.

Fuck it.

I'd made a lot of piss-poor life decisions in my forty-plus years on the planet and falling in love with the beautiful creature that was Elka Köhler, currently lowering herself in a sensual glide over the top of my cock, her body hugging mine in a perfect chef's kiss of two bodies becoming one. Loving her was definitely not the worst thing I had ever done. She was definitely the exact opposite of the worst thing I had ever done in my life.

She was quickly becoming my fucking *everything,* and I honestly never thought that was something that could happen to me.

"Fuck yeah, baby," I praised her through gritted teeth, my hands drifting to her hips, caressing her soft skin, drifting up her body to whisk her tee outta my way. She wasn't wearing a bra underneath, and I weighed her perfect full tits in my hands, caressing her stiff nipples with my thumbs, lightly pinching them between my thumbs and the sides of my hands, rolling them, watching her lose herself in riding me. She threw her head back, that shining fall of long dark hair cascading down her back, sweeping along her skin, tickling the tops of my thighs just above my knees as she arched into my touch.

It was erotic art in motion watching her move above me and I just couldn't get enough of it. I watched her, totally enraptured, smoothing my hands against her skin, thrusting up inside her when she began to falter from fatigue.

I could lay like this forever with her above me like this, but there wasn't any holding out forever. My body just plain had other ideas.

Whatever ideas my body had, I would be damned if I was gonna come before her a second time, so I licked the pad of my thumb and slid it between the mash of our bodies. Her eyes fluttered closed in sweet ecstasy, her head tipping back, her back arching and I wished someone would carve her, just how she looked right now, into one of them big blocks of marble because she was so beautiful to look at right now. It was the type of beautiful everyone should see, and I was somehow honored it was just for me as I teased her clit with the pad of my thumb and felt her body tremble finely over mine, her pussy clenching around me.

I gritted my teeth and remembered to breathe even as she seemingly stopped, time stopping with her.

Finally, after a long hanging moment that shone with anticipation she cried out, her pussy spasming around my dick and it was just enough, it was too perfect, both of us launching into mutual orgasms – riding the waves of release.

She collapsed against my chest, her skin almost cool to the touch, her breath warm against my shoulder where she panted. I held her as she shuddered above and around me and this felt so much like *home* it was indescribable.

I held her close against my chest and tried to keep my mind here, on her, and off of whatever investigation was goin' on in the background. I couldn't change whatever it was that was going on. I couldn't do anything about it.

What I could do was right here in my arms and was the most positive thing I think I had ever done.

Restoring Elka wasn't like restoring one of her old paintings. It took a totally different skill set, but no less time and care. Plus, it wasn't like something you could do and it was done, you know? It was something that was going to take continued care; a lifetime of love, to maintain.

It was something I had never pictured myself wanting in my life. Was never something I had ever wanted before, but there was something about her spirit… maybe it was her resiliency, or maybe it was the fact that despite all the shit she'd been through she hadn't let it make her bitter – yeah, that was it – whatever it was, it made me want to stick around. Made me feel, I don't know, *secure* enough to want to stay.

I'd had my fill of bitter ass women in Reggie and I recognized how precious that Elka's willingness to stay soft through everything, soft but not weak – I wanted that in my life. Wanted *her* in my life, and I didn't expect anyone to understand it.

"Oz?" her voice was hesitant, worried.

"Yeah?" I asked, stroking a hand up and down her back.

"You okay?"

"Yeah! Yeah, why? Why wouldn't I be?" I asked.

"You're just uncharacteristically quiet," she murmured.

"Just enjoying you, baby."

"You sure it's nothing else?" she asked.

"I'm sure," I lied and I felt like shit doing it, but I didn't want to worry her. I kissed the top of her head and she melted against my chest.

"Okay."

She sighed out and we just laid limp and satisfied on her couch, the rest of the spy movie playing out on the screen.

It said more than I wanted to that sex, one of my favorite flicks on the screen, and a beautiful naked woman draped over my chest still didn't take my mind off of things.

THE HAMMER DROPPED the middle to the end of the week, just like Yale said it would.

"Hey, Jones. Acting Sergeant wants to see you in the Dog Pound. He's got the prosecutor with him."

I looked up from the computer screen on the intake and frowned.

"Almost done here," I said and Lagina shook his head.

"I'm supposed to relieve you immediately."

"For real?" I asked and dread weighted my heart into the pit of my stomach like a lead balloon. I spun in my chair and stepped down and Lagina took over.

"You good?" I asked, making sure he didn't have any questions. He scanned the screen in front of him that I'd just been on and nodded.

"All good here, man. Good luck."

"Heh." I gave him a dubious laugh and shook my head as I went back to the back office, or the Dog Pound as we called it. No officer ever got called to the Sergeant's office over anything good.

The only good thing was that our Acting Sergeant tonight was Miller. Our usual dude was on a disciplinary rip courtesy of a shit ton of union complaints about him being the asshole he was.

I stuck my head in the break room and saw Miller and Yale talking outside the little back office. The breakroom mercifully empty except for them.

"Yale, what's up brother, why you here?" I held out my hand and Yale shook his head.

"Not exactly a social call, Oz. Not good news, but not worse news either."

"You might want to sit down," Miller followed up, arms crossed over his chest, hands tucked under his armpits. He rocked back and forth on the balls of his feet but the set of his mouth and the troubled look in his eyes had me on the defensive.

"How about one of you fuckers just spit it out?" I growled.

"Oz..." Yale's tone held a bit of conciliation and I didn't give a fuck. I wanted this over – whatever it was.

"Just tell him, it's fine," Miller said, and I realized Yale might have been worried about my mouth in front of who was supposed to be my boss.

"Have to wait for IAB," Yale said unhappily, just as the door behind us opened and the rat squad appeared as if by magic. I rolled my tongue in my mouth, but the bitter tang remained at layin' eyes on 'em.

"Oh, good, you got him here already." Kratanski gave a polite nod in my direction.

"I need my union rep?" I demanded.

"No, uh-uh." Kratanski's partner, some woman that looked like Mrs. Trenchbull outta that Matilda movie closed the door behind them.

"Someone just spill it already? Jesus Christ," I said.

The rat squad moved into the room and I put my back against the wall by the door, crossing my arms.

"First, I'd like to say, you are absolutely not in any trouble," Kratanski said, adjusting his light gray suit jacket. He was a tall, fit white guy, his hair almost a perfect match for his suit, his blue eyes vivid and sharp.

"Okay, so what's going on?" I demanded.

"The coroner review found some... inconsistencies in the initial report," the Trenchbull looking bitch said.

"Inconsistencies with what?" I demanded.

"A coverup," Yale said dispassionately.

My eyebrows went up.

"Covering *what* up?"

Kratianski sighed and Miller threw up his hands. "Maybe stop beating around the bush and just tell him!"

"Upon reviewing all the evidence, they found that the trajectories were off. Again, you're not in any trouble. It was a righteous shoot, you were trying to save lives –"

"Just get to the damn point man!" I barked.

"Your weapon was the one that fired the bullet to kill Mia Köhler," Yale said calmly.

His words echoed in my ears more fiercely than the gunshots had that morning and my vision streaked, flashing at the edges as I felt a surge of... I don't know what. So many things.

I sagged against the wall behind me and slid to the floor on my ass, bringing up my knees.

"Whoa, easy there, big guy," Kratanski said and Miller knelt down next to me, fingers against my wrist, eyes against his watch as he timed my pulse.

"You're sure?" I choked out and fought not to vomit.

"It was double and triple checked," Yale said, full of concern as he looked on but giving me space.

"Anyone else know?" I asked.

"No, but this department leaks like a sieve, it's only a matter of time before it hits the street." Trenchbull made a face and it said she hated the thought. Not for what it would do to me, but more like what it would do for the department.

"I gotta tell Ellie," I said and struggled to my feet.

"Take the rest of the week," Miller ordered.

"You sure?"

"Yeah, man. I'm sure. You aren't here, and you can't be here until you process this shit."

"Again, there's no further action to take. We just thought you should know," Kratanski said and I struggled to my feet.

Yale didn't say anything. He didn't have to. His face said it all, as shuttered as his look was, he couldn't silence his eyes which fixed on mine and asked the silent question, *are you good to ride?*

I shook my head but didn't care. Ride I would. I had to tell Ellie, I had to be the one she found out from.

I had to be.

It couldn't come from anybody else.

22

*E*lka…

I savored one of the final bites of soup I had in my mouth, attention rapt on the television as I watched *Persuasion* for the millionth time when the knock fell at my door. I set my near-empty soup bowl on the coffee table next to my empty salad plate. I snatched up the remote, pausing the movie and rose as a second more insistent knock fell.

"Just a minute! I'm coming!" I called politely and went to my front door.

I was surprised to see Oz through the peephole, his head bowed, his face cast in shadow from the last rays of the sun behind him. I opened up the door quickly, a smile on my face which faltered and died the moment I saw his expression.

"Oz? What's the matter?" I demanded and he just looked at me, the expression on his face almost longing, his eyes haunted, his mouth set in a grim line and whatever it was, he seemed… haggard.

"Oz, what's wrong?" I demanded again, stepping aside and grabbing

158

his hand, pulling him inside, closing the door behind him. His eyes were red rimmed as he struggled to speak, and alarm bells swept through my mind, their peal deafening despite their physical silence.

"You're scaring me!" I cried, and tears welled in my eyes from my anxiety even as twin crystalline drops fell from his, cascading down his cheeks.

He gripped my shoulders and smoothed his thumbs over my upper arms and the soft material of my work-blouse. The look on his face desperate and frightened and I nearly shook him, wanted to scream at him to put me out of my misery and –

"It was me," he stammered. "Ellie, I'm so sorry – but you had to hear it from me. It was me."

"What?" I asked sharply. "I don't understand, Oz. What are you trying to tell me? What is going on?" My voice trembled as I stared up into his drawn and sallow face and the words that fell from his lips impacted my heart like a meteor strike.

"It was me, Ellie… It was my gun. I shot Mia. I killed your sister."

Devastation.

His words rippled out from the center of my being leaving such a silence in their wake. I stared at him.

"That's not funny," I uttered, and I don't know why I said that. I mean, Oz wouldn't joke about something like that.

His face crumbled and he began to cry in earnest, and I stared up at him.

"That's not funny, Oz! Why would you say that?" I shoved him and he let me go.

He fell to his knees in front of me, his shoulders wracking in great heaving sobs and I stood there, chest heaving as panic swirled through my breast.

I sank to my knees, shaking and tried to think but thinking was impossible.

It was me.

It was me.

It was me.

I put my arms around him, desperate for comfort, for something to cling to, and he wrapped his arms around me, burying his face in my shoulder, in my hair, sobbing like a child into the crook of my neck and the tears slipped down my face as I sat there, numb and in shock.

It was me.

It was me.

It was me.

The words echoed through my mind, sinister, insidious, and I stared into space.

I shot Mia.

I killed your sister.

I trembled and he clung to me, ravaged by grief and all I could do was sit there until the universe finally decided to breathe in once more and suddenly, *I* could breathe and all I wanted was to make it stop. All I wanted was to make the pain stop. To it make it all okay again, for me, and for this man who had painstakingly spent the last few weeks of his life making it okay for me again.

"It's okay," I whispered, and it was a lie. We both knew it was a lie, but I didn't know what else *to* say. I mean, it wasn't *okay*. It would never be okay – but strangely I wasn't mad. I was hurt, but not because of him. I was hurt *for him*. I hurt for *us*, and for what this could mean for us, but I wasn't mad, and I didn't know *why* I wasn't mad. The only explanation I had about my strange, almost calmness about the situation is that in my heart of hearts I knew...

Oz didn't mean to. There was no intention to ever hurt me. There was no intention to shoot my sister. He was trying to *stop* the madness of that morning. He was the hero of the story in so many ways. He was one of the good guys – a good man, and I loved him.

"It's okay," I whispered, and I held him close, kissed the top of his head, and finally, I wept too. I wept with him, because just what did you do with something like this?

"Oh, God, forgive me!" he cried, and I held him tighter still.

Forgive him?

I held Oz close, hushing him consolingly.

He didn't do anything wrong. There wasn't anything to forgive and I knew that was exactly what my sister would have told him were she here in my stead.

"It's not your fault," I said through my tears. "It's not your fault."

And it wasn't.

It wasn't my fault, or Mia's fault, or Oz's fault at all.

The men whose fault it was were both dead. Oz had stopped them. Oz had killed them. It was nobody's fault that we were in the way.

My heart broke for the circumstances of that morning all over again.

For my sister. For my dad. For myself. For the man I had grown to love, weeping inconsolably in my arms.

My heart broke all over again and we wept, but our tears watered the seeds of understanding, of forgiveness, and the roots went deep into my heart come what may.

"It'll all be okay," I whispered, rocking him on my living room floor as the storm of emotion passed.

～

"I DON'T KNOW why you would forgive me like this," he murmured an hour later.

We lay in my bed, atop the covers, close but not touching except for our hands, fingers twined between us.

"Did you mean to shoot my sister?" I asked bluntly.

"No."

"Then what is there to forgive?" I asked quietly.

"I *shot your sister...* She died..."

"It was an accident," I said and sniffed, fresh tears welling. Accident or not, it was one of the hardest pills to swallow knowing that the man you had fallen in love with had killed your little sister, intentional or not.

I was still processing, he was still processing, and things were difficult to say the least.

"I don't want to lose you," he said and closed his eyes, swallowing hard, as if the confession had cost him.

"I'm right here," I whispered. "I'm right here."

I shifted, leaning forward, and I kissed him. His hand found the side of my neck where it hovered just above the bed, his other hand found the curve of my body, along my ribs just before the swell of my hip and he pulled me closer, held me tight, as if he never wanted to let me go and my heart wept all over again for a different reason this time.

This time it wept with something almost akin to relief. Relief at finally being loved so well for who I was – arts of depression and heartache and all.

"I love you," I whispered fiercely, and he jolted slightly as if the words had shocked him with a very real electrical jolt.

"Don't say that, baby. Not now, not after this. It could get so bad..."

"Bad how?" I asked.

"People judging –"

"Fuck 'em," I murmured.

"What?" he laughed slightly.

"I can take a page out of your playbook, can't I?" I asked.

He smoothed a thumb beneath my jaw and searched my face in the close dark of the room. The lights were out and there was barely any light to see by coming through my bedroom window from the street outside, but we could see each other, barely, through the gloom and it was a comfortable dark.

"Yeah, yeah, you can," he said, his tone hushed as he stared at me in an almost wonderment.

"It's gonna be you and me against the world," he whispered.

I nodded slowly, carefully.

"I-I think I need that."

"What?"

"You. Me. A partnership of sorts. I… I don't want to go back to being alone." It was my turn to be vulnerable – for the tough confession.

"I don't care what happens, mkay? I'm always gonna be here for you." He captured my face between his hands and pulled my forehead to his lips. The tension just drained from me at the touch of his lips and I relaxed, sighing out into the dark, pulling myself close to cuddle against his chest. He held me tight, back in the driver's seat so to speak and it spoke to me of just how much he trusted me to be vulnerable like that in front of me.

I loved him and I was afraid of what the fallout could be surrounding this new information, but I meant it. I would weather the storm, come what may. I would be a silly ideological little girl if I thought there wouldn't be *any* fallout, but there would honestly be no telling just how bad it would be until it made landfall in our lives, if it ever did.

I shoved those thoughts to the side and kissed Oz, let him hold me, and I know it is so action movie cliché, that things like this weren't supposed to happen in real life, but we fell into each other's arms. The kissing becoming more heated, hands grappling with clothing as I worked at the buttons of his uniform shirt and he pulled my blouse from the waistband of my slacks.

"Oh!" I stopped at the unfamiliar vest below his shirt. "You wear a bullet-proof vest even in the jail?" I asked.

He gave me a sad crooked smile and kissed the corner of my mouth.

"Stab vest," he murmured, sitting up and peeling his uniform shirt off from over it, letting it fall to my floor with a metallic click from his badge. "Yale helped get the grant to fund buying 'em."

"Yale?" I asked.

"Damien Parnell, the ADA. He's a Knight."

"How did I not know that?"

"Don't know, but it tells me I got some things to fix, like bringing you around the guys and into my life."

"Oh?" I couldn't help the surprise, but I did manage to twist it with a questioning lilt at the end.

"Yeah." The sound of Velcro giving way was loud in the cozy space of my bedroom.

I pulled my blouse off and lifted the satin camisole I wore beneath it over my head. We quietly stripped to our underwear and got between the sheets, naturally coming together. Holding onto one another, battered spirits connecting just as much as our lips in our emotional exhaustion.

Hands sliding over each other's bodies, soothing hurts that went soul deep. He loved me slowly, cocooning me in a protective embrace whispering to me, "I thought I would lose you."

I smiled sadly and cupped his face in my hands murmuring, "I can't lose you, too. I just can't. I –" I choked up and he silenced me with a kiss and kept me close, cradling against his heart which needed to beat for the both of us for a scant moment as different emotions swirled in my breast, stole my breath, and tried to suck me down into a maelstrom.

I clung to Oz, anchoring me to the earth, body, heart, and mind, back in control, holding me close, and sheltering me from any more harm.

"I got you, babe," he whispered against my hair, and I believed him.

"I got you, too," I said and we held each other tight.

23

*O*z…

"How she doing?"

I sighed and bowed my head. "Better 'n me, bro."

"That was my next question."

I heard the shower shut off and said, "Can I come by?"

"Yeah, man. You know I got you."

"Okay, be there as soon as I can. She's got to get to work, I'ma give her a ride."

"Good deal, keep the shiny side up, brother."

"You got it."

I hung up the phone with Golden just as her bathroom door opened. She had gotten up in the middle of the night, had left me sleeping, and had finished the painting of her sister. I looked over at her, dragging my eyes off the painting with some trouble.

She smiled a little wanly and immediately came to me, wrapping her arms around my waist. I hugged her close. Didn't even care that my tee soaked water from her wet hair. It'd dry out. We both stared at the perfect rendition of her sister on the canvas, so real it looked like a photograph, and had a little impromptu moment of silence.

"I don't know whether to give it to my dad, or if I should keep it. I mean, should I give it to her fiancé?" She seemed troubled and I sighed.

"Why don't you keep it?"

She shrugged against me and said, "I could always paint another one."

"Well, yeah, you got me there," I said.

We were silent for a few, regarding the beautiful piece of art she'd created in front of us and she shook herself as if waking from a dream.

"I'm going to be late."

"Nah, I got you. I'll give you a ride over. It's not far and with traffic, we shouldn't go too fast. Just get ready and we'll get goin'."

"Okay," she said softly.

I finished getting dressed, putting on everything I'd had on last night getting here. It wasn't exactly comfortable, and I wasn't *technically* allowed to wear my uniform in public – safety reasons – but I would have my jacket and cut on and would head back to my place after dropping her off.

A knock fell at her front door as she was putting in her earrings and I swung my jacket on. She walked across the carpet in her kitten heels and had her hand on the door knob when my head caught up to the situation and it was too late to warn her.

She opened the door. I expected a gang of reporters on her doorstep, flashbulbs going off like in the movies, but it was just one woman with a notepad and a pen.

"Hi, Ms. Köhler. I'm Mindy O'Donnell and I'm with the Indigo City Register – can I have a moment of your time?"

"No, I'm afraid not. I'm going to be late for work."

"Are you aware of the –"

"Let me stop you right there, Princess."

Ellie opened the door wider to reveal me and I stepped up behind her and asked her "You ready to go?"

"Yeah, let me just grab my stuff," she said unhappily. I was unhappy too. Vultures were quick to a fresh kill this morning, golll-ee!

"Yeah, she knows. No, we don't wanna comment, you go on and have a nice day now, you hear?"

I stepped out onto the stoop with Elka while the girl just wouldn't quit. Peppering us with questions all the way to the bike. I fired it up, drowning the reporter out and without even putting helmets on, pulled away from the curb. We stopped briefly a couple blocks up and around the corner out of sight to get our lids on.

"You alright?" I asked her as she took her helmet from me, hands shaking. I stood from locking up my saddlebag and watched her carefully.

"Yeah."

"You watch yourself today," I said. "Call me right away if anything happens."

"I will," she vowed and I got back on the bike. I took her to work, and I waited until she was inside and past security before I sighed and rolled my head on my neck.

I didn't even fuckin' bother going home. I went straight over to G's brownstone and cut the bike out front. His front door opened and I looked up.

"Jesus Christ, you look rough, brother."

"Yeah, I feel it," I said unhappily.

"Come on inside. Lys is cookin' up some breakfast."

I hauled a leg over the bike and stood, my hip flexors and hamstrings bitching from the sex last night.

I took the steps a little stiff and Golden smirked as I crossed through the door past him and into his home.

"We figured when you dropped off the radar you went to your girl's place last night."

"Yeah, was gonna stop home and change but man, the vultures are already at it."

"Oh yeah? How's that?" I looked further back down the hall at Back-draft sittin' at the kitchen counter. Lys set a plate in front of him but was lookin' at me and Golden curiously. He shut the door and we moved down the hall and into the kitchen.

"Fuckin' reporter for one of the local news rags was camped out in front of her apartment this morning."

"Shit."

"Yeah. Makes me glad I went and told on myself before anyone else could do it."

I pulled off my jacket and cut and hung it on the back of one of the chairs around the kitchen table before sliding onto one of the breakfast barstools. Golden took up the one on the other side of Backdraft.

Lys set a plate of bacon and eggs in front of me and I gave her a crooked smile.

"Thanks, girl."

"You're welcome, and how are *you* doing? Really?"

I sighed.

"I feel like shit – obviously."

"Yeah but you have to know it's not your fault," Backdraft said.

"The fuck it ain't," I said, shaking my head, food forgotten for the moment, my stomach roiling with unease.

"My dude, there's no way you could watch all your shots in a scenario like that. It's not like you were aiming at a stationary paper target at the range. Remember, I've been there. Real-world scenarios are wild, unpredictable, and one of our worst fuckin' nightmares."

"Yeah, well, I wanna wake up," I said miserably.

Silence descended on us and Lys reached out, empathy radiating from her eyes as she covered my folded hands with one of her own and gave them a squeeze. She turned back to the pan of bacon on the stove and sighed.

"So, what did she say?" she asked and the guys looked at me expectantly.

"That it wasn't my fault, that I didn't mean to kill her sister – which, you know, I *didn't* but that doesn't change the fact that I *did* kill her."

"She forgive you?" Golden asked like he dreaded the answer.

"Pfft! What is there to forgive?" Lys demanded. "Oz did the right thing, we all know that. It was an accident."

"That's exactly what Ellie said," I said quietly.

Backdraft nodded and said, "She's a good woman. A smart lady. You should listen to her and believe her."

"She said she loves me, but I don't know how," I said.

"That there are your own issues talking," Golden said with a heavy sigh. "You're all twisted up inside with guilt, and I know how it is.

Nothing any of us say is going to change that, *Hombre.* You gotta come to that conclusion on your own and that shit takes time."

I rubbed my forehead and sighed.

"Yeah. Yeah, man. I think you're right. I'm just not ready to hear it right now."

"Eat your food before it gets cold," Backdraft said around a mouthful and I tried a forkful of eggs.

"Good stuff," I mumbled at Lys, who seemed pleased as she set a plate in front of Golden. "Where's Lil at?" I asked the big corn-fed country hose boy to change the subject.

"Writing," he said. "She opted to stay in her ivory tower to get some words down. Didn't want to overwhelm you or fuss. She gets it, somehow."

"Yeah," I nodded and crunched through a piece of bacon. "Yeah, she gets it."

"You didn't even change out of uniform last night, isn't there some kind of rule against that?" Backdraft asked.

"Yeah," I mumbled.

"You love her, too. Don't you?" Lys asked softly and I looked up and nodded.

"Yeah."

The three of them nodded as if something was confirmed and I scowled.

"What was that look for?" I demanded.

"Just realizing it's not just you we gotta take care of on this one," Golden declared.

"I don't need no one to take care of me," I said. "I'ma be a'ight."

Golden smiled and nodded. "First thing you've said since coming in here that's made me believe that, man."

"First thing you've said that's sounded like you," Backdraft agreed.

I sighed and nodded.

"I'm just tired, man."

"You want, head on upstairs. Little man is in school, you can crash and burn in the guest room."

"Nah," I shook my head. "I'm just gonna head back to my place. Get a hot shower and some sleep."

"You sure you ain't got reporters parked there?" Backdraft asked.

"Shit," I muttered. "I do, I'll tell 'em the same thing I told miss thing this morning."

"You can go to hell?" G. asked.

"Damn right."

He and Backdraft laughed a bit.

"Exercise that asshole merit badge," Backdraft agreed.

"You know that's right," I said, and Lys set down a cup of coffee with some creamer in front of me.

"Thanks," I told her and she smiled. "And thank you, fellas. I think I needed this."

"That's what we're here for, my brother," Golden said. "That's what we're here for."

24

*E*lka…

I threw myself into my work, carefully cleaning a layer of grime from the paint with a mild solvent and thick, handmade cotton swabs. Protective eyewear and breathing mask in place, I would have to pause periodically as my eyes welled and the safety glasses would fog up. It was frustrating but wasn't affecting my work terribly enough for me to warrant going home early.

Now if I were in the process of retouching a piece? That would require some rethinking on the matter.

I had to shut off my phone. The calls were coming in, incessantly. One after another after another. I sent a text to Oz telling him that I was turning it off and why, and that if he needed to reach me to call the museum front desk and what extension to dial.

Two hours into my day, my boss arrived at my desk to check on me.

"Mattias, hello," I murmured as soon as I got the protective gear off.

"Elka, how are you faring?" he asked kindly.

173

"I'm alright," I said breathing deep and evenly, the acrid tang of the solvent I was working with biting at the back of my throat.

"If you need anything, please don't hesitate to ask," he said and I smiled reassuringly.

"I'm fine, Mattias, I promise not to let it affect my work."

"I'm not concerned about your quality of work, though I probably should be – I'm more concerned about you."

"I'm fine, I promise you," I said, and he looked me over, the grave concern he was feeling etching lines into his forehead where it wrinkled his deep blue eyes searching mine out.

"Very well. Simply call if you need anything." I nodded.

"I will."

It was some time after that and just before lunch when Emily, one of our front desk girls, led a man I didn't know back to my work space. I frowned and removed my mask and glasses.

"Can I help you?" I asked frowning.

"Mr. Rivers said he knew you," Emily said and her voice faltered.

"Ha, yeah, I may have given that impression – I'm Anthony Rivers with the Indigo City Citizen Accountability Blog."

"I don't want to talk to you or any other reporter," I said curtly.

"Just a few questions," he said.

"I said no."

Emily put her hand on his arm but he shook her off, eyes on me.

"Just a few questions," he insisted and I stood my ground.

"I said no."

"What's it like to fuck the man that murdered your sister?" he asked loudly.

Everything stopped. People turned from their workstations and Emily's mouth dropped open, aghast.

I picked up my phone from my work table and calmly, despite the slight tremor in my voice said, "Emily call security," and turning to the next work table over and to Jonas who was scraping polyurethane from his work asked him, "Can you take care of this for me?"

My voice had to rise at the end as Anthony River's voice rose, his questions pointed, his language growing more vulgar, bringing Mattias from his office.

Mattias rushed over and put himself between me and Mr. Rivers as I turned to make my escape. I went for the ladies' restroom, choking up, turning on my phone, panic seizing my breath and making the bile rise to burn the back of my throat.

I called Oz.

"What's the matter?" he answered thickly, his voice dense with sleep.

"Can you come get me?" I warbled.

He was awake, instantly.

"Ellie, what's the matter? What's wrong?" I dissolved into tears and slid down the bathroom wall, weeping so bitterly, I couldn't form a coherent sentence.

"I'm coming. Someone will be right there. Just hold on."

The line went dead and I cried. I cried and cried at the unfairness of it all and I let myself have this moment of weakness because we all became stronger after the break.

"Elka?"

I shoved both of my hands against my mouth and nose in a bid to silence myself.

"Elka?" the bathroom door opened, and my humiliation was complete.

"Oh, Elka. I'm so sorry. I didn't know!" Emily knelt down beside me and though she was practically a stranger to me, she wrapped her arms around me, and I took the comfort because what else could I do?

I wept, bitterly, until I was all cried out and to her credit, the slightly younger woman said nothing. She simply rose and wetted some paper towels and handed them to me to wipe my face.

A knock fell at the door and Mattias called out, "Ladies, is everything alright?"

Emily went to the door and cracked it.

"Fine, we're all good here. Maybe just a moment."

"Yes, of course. There is a gentleman at the front desk, an off-duty Indigo City policeman, who is insisting he will not leave until he speaks to Ms. Köhler."

"I'm here, it's fine. I'll see him," I said hollowly. Emily opened the door a little wider and Mattias looked in.

"Yes, well, Jonas has taken care of your piece. Please, take the day – the rest of the week for this all to die down and blow over. Please. For the good of your health."

"I don't know that I have enough sick leave accrued for that yet," I said hesitantly.

"Give her mine," Emily said without hesitation.

"Oh, I can't let you do that," I said.

"It's my fault. I let him in. I insist."

"It's already done," Mattias said kindly, waving me forward. With a death grip on my phone I sighed and complied.

I wasn't ready to walk through the gauntlet of shame waiting for me in the work area. I wasn't ready for the hush and for the staring. Some of those eyes sympathetic, some smug – which I didn't understand, but noted nevertheless.

I took down my purse and swallowed hard, lifting down my briefcase and my jacket. Mattias and Emily walked me out. In the atrium, one of the Indigo Knights stood up from one of the chairs against the stairwell.

"Thank you," I murmured to Mattias and Emily.

"Of course," my boss said. "We'll see you next week."

I nodded and went up to the Knight who said, "I'm Poe, I'm supposed to take you home. I was the closest, so they called me."

"Hi, Poe. Thank you for coming," I said and sniffed, eyes welling again.

"It's not a problem. I'm parked right outside."

"Any reporters out there?" I asked with a feeble laugh.

"If there are, they're fixin' to have a real bad day," he said dryly.

I smiled and let him help me into my jacket, slipping my phone into the pocket, slinging my purse and my briefcase across my chest.

"Ready to go?" he asked. I nodded and with more than some mild trepidation went out onto the street.

It was like any other idyllic summer afternoon. I raised my face and closed my eyes, the sun shining fiercely through my closed lids. I opened them, buildings stabbing upwards to a perfect blue sky and I swallowed hard.

"It doesn't seem fair," I said, and Poe nodded at me from over by his bike, a helmet perched on his denim and leather clad hip. He stared at me, expression somber, his green eyes patient.

"What doesn't?" he asked.

"That the day should be this perfect when it feels like my life is a house of cards and is about to completely collapse."

He nodded slowly and said, "You and Oz both, you've been through a lot."

"Too much," I agreed.

"You wanna go home or you wanna go to his place?" he asked.

I didn't even hesitate.

"Take me to him, please?"

"You got it," he held out the helmet. "Let's get out of here."

It was scary riding behind Poe. I don't know, it wasn't anything he did. I just didn't know him that well at all and he just didn't feel as safe, as solid as Oz.

We rode the opposite direction of my apartment to the edge of the city. A rundown part of town that was just on the edge of gentrification.

Poe pulled down a fairly narrow alleyway between two buildings which surprisingly terminated in a small parking lot of subcompact cars and Oz's immediately recognizable bike.

"Hey!" We looked up as Oz came out of a door at the top of some thick but old wooden timber stairs. "What you bring her here for, dude?"

"Ladie's request," Poe called up and shut off his bike. "Your chariot has arrived, milady."

I got off the back of his bike and handed over his helmet.

"Thank you."

"At your service," he said with a smile.

"I'm gonna take off!" he called up to Oz who was on his way down. "You call me if you need anything else!"

"Will do, brother." Oz stepped off the bottom step and strode over to Poe, clasping hands and bumping shoulders in that hyper-masculine hug/not-quite-a-hug thing.

"Thank you again," I said and Poe gave me a sharp nod.

"Anytime. Don't let them get you down."

"I won't, thank you." I wasn't entirely sure I could give him enough thanks at this point.

Oz reached for me and pulled me tight against him.

"For real, brother. I owe you."

"You don't owe me shit," Poe said with a smile and started his bike. Oz and I stepped back and watched him go.

"Come on inside. There's no tellin' who is out here," he said and guided me to the bottom of the stairs.

He smelled clean and I took shelter in his arms and let him lead me up the stairs.

"Talk to me," he urged.

I groaned.

"It was so embarrassing!" I cried.

"What'd that dude say that got you so upset, baby?"

I told him everything and by the time I finished we were standing inside his apartment, the front door shut tight against the outside world.

"You're fuckin' kidding me!" He looked as affronted as I felt.

"Dead serious," I murmured, slipping off first one heel, then the other, burying my toes in his carpet as I looked around his sparsely furnished but super clean apartment.

The first thing that struck me was the utter lack of art on his walls. It was a bachelor's pad, through and through – just with a decidedly more grown-up touch. The couch was gray and a bit threadbare, but clean and serviceable. The coffee table scarred and something that likely came from the curb.

The end tables were much the same, and didn't match one bit, but the television mounted to the wall was, by comparison, very nice and was fairly large as compared to mine.

A gaming system was on the floor and seemed to serve as both gaming and movie or streaming service to the T.V.. As for the rest of the place, it seemed empty.

"What's wrong?" he asked, and I realized he was watching me look around his place.

"The walls are so… bare."

He laughed slightly and with a smile said, "So paint me something to put on 'em."

"I can do that," I said softly, and he sighed and said, "C'mere."

He pulled me into his arms and I went willingly, suddenly just exhausted, both mentally and emotionally. I felt numb and all cried out and I said, "Is it really awful that all I want to do is take a nap?"

"I did just as soon as I got here," he said and sighed. "It's not awful. I get it. You're just as tired of the bullshit as me."

I made a rude snort and said, "Not a good sign considering it's just beginning."

"You got that right."

"What do we do?" I asked. "I mean, where do we go from here?"

It was a valid question, I thought, yet Oz remained silent.

"First things first," he said finally. "How about you come in here, lie down, and take a nap?"

"What will you do?" I asked.

"Me? I'm fixin' to make a few phone calls."

"To who? About what?" I asked curiously as he led me into his bedroom.

"Don't you worry about that," he said. "Let's get you tucked in, here."

I sighed. As much as I wanted to argue, I was tired and it felt nice to have Oz take care of me and so, against my better judgement, I didn't press the issue. I simply nodded and let myself be led into his bedroom where he stripped me out of my clothes and slipped one of his tee shirts over my head.

He led me to his bed which was larger and way more comfortable than mine and tucked me in gently.

"Get some sleep," he whispered and kissed me one more time.

"Okay."

He stared at me from the doorway to his room for several moments before slipping out and shutting the door behind him. I sighed and closed my eyes and it wasn't but a breath or two before the sweet oblivion of sleep claimed me.

25

*O*z...

"How is she?" Skids asked over the line.

"Exhausted, and man, I'm tellin' you. I'm right behind her."

"What do you need, brother?"

"Honestly, to get the fuck out of dodge through the weekend would be nice," I said.

Skids sighed through the line and said, "Can you both come in tonight?"

"I could make it happen, though it's dicey, Chief. I feel like every time we step out, there could be a fuckin' ambush waiting."

"Fuckin' reporters," Skids growled in disgust.

"Ain't *no* love lost between a lot of us and them," I agreed, thinking about Youngblood's woman and that thing with Backdraft and his girl. "Why can't people just mind their own fuckin' business, man?"

"That is the sixty-four-thousand-dollar question, isn't it?" Skids asked.

"Man, who you tellin'?"

"Just bring your asses in here tonight. Might be we can come up with a temporary solution to your problem."

"Ten-four, Chief. Received," I said and Skids chuckled.

"Over and out," he said and we disconnected the call.

I sighed and sat on the couch, propping my feet on the table. I turned on the T.V. and lowered the volume immediately before I picked up my controller and flipped through some menus.

I didn't see the point in trying to play anything right now, so I put on a movie instead. I didn't watch much of it though. I was thinking about Elka, about us, and what would happen next.

I didn't know where to go or what to do, I mean, I had a few options – but I wasn't entirely sure bringing her home to my momma was a good idea right now. Shit, I was pretty sure the news would reach as far as my hometown. If not from the major outlets then some homie from back in high school told that homie who told *his* momma, and it would definitely be the talk of the barbershop or the beauty parlor by the end of next week.

I pressed fingertips into my eyes and rubbed them. The phrase *no good deed goes unpunished* coming to mind. That was exactly how I felt. That I was somehow being punished and at the same time, I felt like I deserved it. I mean, that little girl hadn't hurt nobody, and I didn't care what anybody said, it *was* my fault she was gone.

My phone buzzed. Unrecognized number. I rejected the call. They could leave a message. Buzzing filled my apartment and it wasn't my phone. I tracked the sound to Elka's jacket pocket where it hung off the high bar chair at my kitchen counter. Her phone was going off, *also* an unknown number. I rejected the call only for it to light up with a different number just as soon as I'd done it.

"Goll-ee, man!" I whispered harshly, keeping my voice down so I wouldn't disrupt her sleep.

I rejected the call off her phone and turned it off before it had the chance to ring again, just as my phone started going off on the arm of my couch. I shook my head, went over, and rejected the call.

Probably took them longer to find my number being as I was law enforcement. I didn't have any attachment to my number, so I would be getting that shit changed. I would see about having Ellie do the same.

I shook my head and stared at the back of my jacket and cut hanging off the chair next to Ellie's and sighed. I didn't know what I would do without the guys in my corner on this one. I didn't know how I would keep it together. Hell, I wasn't even really all that sure I *was* keepin' it together.

This was a hot mess and the only real comfort I had was layin' in the next room and I knew how *not fair* that was to her, but it was the fuckin' truth.

I went over and turned off the television, set both phones on the coffee table and slipped into my room. She was asleep, a little line of troubles, of worries, marring her forehead. I would give anything to smooth that line away, to ease the tension riding her fine as hell body beneath the sheet.

I stripped down to my underwear and got into the bed behind her, pulling her back gently into the curve of my body. She wiggled that ass against my cock, and I closed my eyes and savored the sensation as I curved my arms around her, sliding the one under her pillow and neck. Holding her close as if hanging onto her like this would make it enough, would *be* enough to hold on to her forever.

That's what killed me the most. She was under my skin like no other female I'd ever been with or encountered before and she was a balm to my wounded soul. If I lost that? It would be a special kind of hell, one I wasn't prepared to walk through but one I better get on board with it being a possibility.

I mean, I knew she was strong, but just how much could any one woman take in such a short span of time?

I kissed the back of her shoulder, nose buried in her long hair, and breathed in her soft vanilla scent.

She threaded her fingers in the spaces between mine on the arm that came over the top of her and hugged it close, pressing back into me and I whispered, "Sorry, baby. I didn't mean to wake you up."

There was no response.

"Ellie?" I whispered after a moment.

Again, no response and a bit of my anxiety loosened somehow. I relaxed and closed my eyes and even though I didn't think I was tired, I was out in probably the space of a minute.

I WAS BACK on Ellie's couch, her perfect body arched above me, her tits thrust toward the overhead light, my hands smoothing over her milk white skin, thumbs tweaking her rosy nipples as she moaned, my cock erect, as hard as it had ever been but something about it wasn't quite right, wasn't as fulfilling as it'd been that night, in real life, and when I woke I realized why.

I was lying on my side, still spooning my lady, her ass grinding against my cock, her little whimpering moans drawing me fully awake and like in my own dream, I was hard to the point of pain.

"Ellie, baby?" I said thickly, pulling my arm from beneath her slightly so I could prop myself up.

She whimpered again, dreaming like I had been, her guttural moan ending on a gasp as her liquid brown eyes with their hints of warm bronze flew wide. I chuckled and swept her long hair out of my way, kissing the side of her neck, sliding my hand under the borrowed tee she wore, sliding my palm along her warm skin, over her stomach and beneath the waistband of her thin scrap of panties.

"Oh, God!" she cried, voice throaty, her hips flexing, shoving her sweet pussy against my searching hand.

God, I loved the way she telegraphed her wants and desires with her body. The way she writhed against me, the way she pressed against my probing fingertips, the way she moaned breathy and light and couldn't get enough of my touch.

She was wild and the most alive I had ever seen her when she was like this. Her body twining around my darkness like a vine, breathing life into my withered soul, my bleak outlook on life. When she was in my arms like this, begging for my touch, begging me to fuck her, I was the most alive I could ever remember being and that was Ellie's magic.

She felt so deeply, and she had this power to drag all the feels outta me. A feat I hadn't realized, until I met her, was even possible.

She twisted onto her back in my arms, her mouth finding mine, her one hand the side of my face, her tee riding up to just below her breasts, her legs falling open to give my questing fingers better access. I teased her clit with a few more light strokes, her back arching her body taut with a need for more, for a final release I was having every intention of denying her for as long as possible. Not out of a need to be a cruel-assed motherfucker, but out of a desire to make it one of the best damn orgasms of her life.

I took two fingers and slid them up inside of her and she cried out, her hips bucking against my hand, trying to take them deeper. I smiled against her mouth and kissed her deep as I found that spot inside her and made a come-hither motion against it with the pad of my thumb firmly against her clit, slick with her desire, making everything go smooth and easy. I controlled the amount of friction, slicking my fingers in and out of her wetness, my dick having something to say about not being the appendage to please my woman.

I ignored the throbbing in my cock and just concentrated on her. This wild sprite in my bed, her body a playground I could get lost on for hours. She moaned in futility against my mouth as I fucked her with my fingers, teasing her to a fever pitch, whipping her into a frenzy of need.

She tore her mouth from mine and murmured, *"Hector!"* and it was the sweetest sound I think I'd ever heard. My true name from her lush mouth.

"That's it, baby. Just a little bit more," I whispered.

Her walls clenched around me, making it hard to thrust my fingers inside of her, but that was alright. I recognized this, was so in tune with her by now that I knew she was close. So goddamn close, it wouldn't be long now.

Her body rippled around my fingers and she sucked in a sharp breath, her cry of pleasure hitting the ceiling and running down my walls in a beautiful wash of pure emotion of all that was good, all that was still right in our world that had been turned upside down and inside out on us.

She lay panting, staring sightlessly, legs spread and twitching, shuddering as I withdrew my fingers. I smiled, chuckling decadently, as I got to my knees and shoved down my boxer briefs. I sucked my fingers clean of her essence while she watched, her eyes dilating with desire, stroking myself slowly with my other hand.

"God, I want you…" she breathed, and I grinned and took the time to strip her of her panties, following through and stripping off the tee shirt I'd lent her. She ran her hands over her skin, played with her breasts for my benefit and the woman knew just what would drive my ass fuckin' wild.

I got into my bedside table, pulled out a condom, and double-timed getting that shit rolled on.

Kneeling between her legs, looking deep into her eyes, seeing the light of desire in them; the want, the *need* to have me with her – it was more than enough to seal my fate. I would fight to stay by her side, always. Ours was a love forged under blue fire. Hot to the touch and stronger than steel.

I would do anything for her to make it right, and if that meant starting over somewhere else. If that was what she wanted? Then so be it.

26

*E*lka...

I held onto him. His body moving over mine, thrusting deep and deeper still, his hands in my hair, his cock deep inside me loving me languorously, slowly, and purposefully. The way he loved me cemented his place in my life wholly. I held tightly to him and met his drive with my own and somewhere in the midst of it all we ceased to be two and became one being and it was beautiful.

"God, Ellie..." His voice was subdued but intense. Just like the rest of him but not like the rest of him. There wasn't really anything subdued about Hector Jones and the way he did things, except when it came to me. When it came to me, he was reserved, as if he saved every bit of his tenderness for me and me alone and I felt so graced by this gift from him.

We lost time. Minutes could have been hours, hours could have only felt like mere minutes. I didn't know, and I didn't care. All I knew was this felt good. He felt too good to be true, and when it was like this, I never wanted it to end.

When I came again, it was a gentler thing than it had been before, and

189

it touched off Oz's orgasm as well. He collapsed over me, holding me tight and I kissed his shoulder reverently.

We lay, clinging to each other for several minutes, catching our breaths, trying to cope with the fact that reality lay beyond his apartment door and that eventually we would have to go back to it.

"You okay?" I asked gently and he nodded, not trusting himself to speak just yet. He pulled out and vaulted my one leg to stretch out beside me. I immediately cuddled against his side, my head on his shoulder; my arm across his stomach.

"I'm good," he said finally between breaths.

We cuddled close and he sighed out eventually, piquing my interest.

"What was that about?" I asked softly.

"Oh, nothing. I called Skids while you were out."

"Oh, yeah?"

"Yeah, we're headed to the *10-13* for dinner, see if me and the guys can't cook up someplace for us to go through the weekend. You know, just to get away for a bit. Let things die down."

"Oh, Oz, I don't know if I'm ready to go out in public so soon after today..."

"Don't do that," he said sharply, disapproval in his voice. "Don't let these motherfuckers win. They don't know what's up. The only people who matter in this are you and me. How you feel about me and how I feel about you. Don't let anyone else have their say in that, that's not how it works."

I was left speechless by the passion in his tone and swallowed hard.

"I'm not letting anyone tell me who to see or who to love here, Oz. I'm just *tired*. Tired of the judgement and the ridicule. Tired of everything I do and anything I say being met with pity. Like, I *understand* it. I was *there*. She was *my* sister! I don't need anybody and everybody prying into my life, tearing it apart any more than it already has been especially when you've spent so much time and care stitching it back together!"

He gripped me tight against his chest and kissed my head and said, "Alright, alright now. Easy. I didn't mean anything by it."

I huffed out an exasperated breath and said, "I know you didn't. I'm sorry… I'm just…"

"Sick of the bullshit," he finished for me when I couldn't find the words.

"Yes. That."

"I hear you, but you better get your hip waders on, now. It's only gonna get deeper while these reporters smell a story."

"There is no story here," I groaned.

"Not to us," he said. "But the rest of the world? They gonna be all up in our business until they're satisfied, they get bored, or something else more entertaining pops up."

"I hate that you're right," I said after a long silence.

"I hate it too," he said. "But I'll be damned if they stop me from livin' my life."

I rolled my lips together and nodded slowly.

"Okay."

"Okay, you'll come with me to the *10-13?*"

"Okay, I'll come with you, but I totally reserve the right to say, 'I told you so' if disaster strikes." I pointed a finger at him, and he nipped it playfully, holding the tip between his teeth gently, smiling around it.

He let it go and said, "Deal."

"And we have to go talk to my dad at some point," I said. Worried about him, wondering if buried in the myriad of messages from reporters in my voicemail box, if I had a few waiting from him. I was also glad he knew about Oz.

"You want to call him?" Oz asked.

"Let me check my voicemail and see if he already knows."

Oz nodded and went out to his living room, coming back with my phone which was turned off. I frowned.

"Was blowing up. Mine too. I shut 'em both off."

"God, now I'm almost afraid to turn it back on," I said as I hit the switch. It took a few seconds for the device to boot and when it did, I had a ridiculous amount of voicemails and text messages start to flood through.

"We're gettin' you a new number," he said and I nodded.

"Yeah, I do not want this to be the rest of my life. Holy shit."

"It ain't gonna be, babe. I've seen how this works."

I nodded and scrolled through the transcripts of the voicemails on my phone deleting all the reporters and requests for interviews as I went. I sighed when I landed on a voicemail from my dad.

"He call?"

"Yeah."

I rejected a call before I could put one through to him and blessedly, he picked up on the second ring.

"Elka?"

"Yeah, Dad. I'm sorry if I made you worry. It's been kind of a day..."

I filled my father in on all the gory details and he listened patiently.

"And where are you now?" he asked.

"With Oz. I mean, Officer Jones," I said, leaning back against the head-board of his bed, pulling the sheet to my chest.

"Elka…" My dad's voice was warm with concern but also held an edge of disapproval. Not, I think, because of Oz and what happened – although maybe that was it. More about what this might mean, what people would think. I don't know.

"Daddy, I love him very much, and nothing was done on purpose. He didn't mean to hurt Mia," I said.

"I know that!" My dad sounded affronted, like my words stung and I had to concede that this was an extremely complicated and delicate situation.

"Elka, come home," my dad begged, and my heart broke slightly.

"Not right now, Daddy," I said. "I'm safe, and I'm not talking to any reporters. I might get out of town for a few days. I don't know yet, I'll have to see."

"Elka…" again with that disapproving tone.

"It's okay, Dad. I'm okay. I just need some time to process and I think you do too."

"Well, yes… I will concede that point," he said unhappily.

"Just…" I raised my gaze to meet Oz's. "Just promise you don't hate him," I said, and the pain crept into my voice despite my best effort to contain it.

My dad sucked in a sharp breath on the other end of the line and breathed out slow.

"I don't think your mother, or your sister would want that," he said after a time. Which wasn't exactly a statement on how my dad actually felt about the situation, but it wasn't an outright condemnation of Oz, either.

"I love you, Dad."

"I love you too, my sweet girl."

"Talk to you soon."

"Okay," he said, defeat in his tone.

"I promise," I added.

"Alright. Just be safe."

"I will."

I ended the call and turned off my phone.

"Big mess," Oz remarked, and I nodded without looking at him.

"Big mess," I agreed.

"Right, then let's go sort it out," he said and held a hand down to me.

I let him haul me to my feet, up off his bed. We showered together, dressed in silence, and when it came time to leave, I stopped him with a hand on his back at his front door.

"Wait."

He turned to look at me and I took a deep and fortifying breath.

"You good?" he asked and I nodded.

"I'm good, just don't leave my side, okay?"

"Wouldn't dream of it," he said and opened the door to the outside world.

27

*O*z...

I took us down the alley on the side of the *10-13* and to the small little courtyard and delivery space behind it and parked the bike out of sight from the street. A lot of the brothers were already here, parked along the brick wall making the alley narrow as fuck, but I got around 'em. Didn't even have to make Ellie hop off to traverse the skinny aisle between front bike tires and the opposite brick wall – I was that good.

Ellie kept nervously eyeing the corner where the alley turned back here as she divested herself of her lid and handed it over to me.

"Hey," I said sternly but not unkindly. I wanted her attention for this. She turned to look at me and when I didn't immediately say anything, raised her eyebrows. Satisfied she was really listening I said, "I know it's hard, but relax. Mkay? Ain't nothing gonna come back here and bite you."

She smiled but it didn't hold her usual brightness and I got that. I really did, but she seriously needed to try and chill. She was starting to make me nervous.

I put a hand to her lower back and guided her to the kitchen door and rapped out the seldom used Indigo Knights' pattern. Typically, it was reserved for Narcos or Driller when they were undercover so as not to be seen waltzing through the front door.

Reflash himself opened it up. "C'mon, the both of yah," he said, and we were ushered into his kingdom, line cooks and dishwashers looking on curiously.

"C'mon!" Reflash cried. "What am I payin' you for! We got people that need to be fed!" The crew fell back in line and started working as quickly as they'd ceased their activity and Reflash led the way through calling back over his shoulder, "Don't touch anything."

I smirked, and steered Ellie in front of me, hands on her shoulders, dropping one to her hip as we stepped through the tidy kitchen over rubber no-slip mats and avoided the guys and gals back here who were feverishly creating Reflash's culinary masterpieces.

"How you doin' sweetheart?" he asked kindly, holding open the kitchen door out into the restaurant.

"Oh, um, alright I guess," she said, blushing faintly.

"Yeah," he said like he didn't believe her. "You're alright now, at least here you're among friends. Head on up to the fishbowl. We got it curtained off."

"Thanks man." I held out my elbow and he tapped it with his as I passed. It was a thing we'd adopted. Pounding fists just made him have to go wash his hands again, which even though I knew he was going to do it anyway after opening the grimy back door, I was just trying to be considerate.

"See you in a few," he said and I nodded.

"Thanks, my brother."

"Anytime."

"This way," I murmured behind Ellie's ear and I stepped around her and in front of her and went right up to the fishbowl which was, indeed dark, from the thick black curtains that had been pulled along the rails on the inside to cover the thick glass for privacy.

The door gave that familiar scrape along the lintel and it felt like coming home – for real. My apartment by comparison was just the place I went to crash. Right here, with this pack of loveable assholes, was my real home. Until Ellie. I was more excited about introducing her to this part of my world than I cared to admit. I just wished it was under better circumstances.

"Hey, hey!" Skids lumbered up from his seat at the head of the table, Coco slipping out of his lap and my eyebrows went up. I wasn't used to the women being up here, but this wasn't exactly club business in the full sense of the words. Plus, the rest of the guys must have had their reasons.

Skids gave Ellie a hug and a kiss on the cheek. "Welcome to our tiny little slice of utopia, darlin'. How you holding up?" Skids asked.

"I, um, could be better," Ellie said with a nervous laugh.

"Come on in and have a seat," Youngblood said. Chrissy was standing up right behind him and gave Ellie a hug before she could move past her.

"I know *exactly* what you are going through," Chrissy said. "Me and Lil both."

"Hi." Lil waved from across the table.

"If you need anything, to scream, to cry, to kill a bottle of wine and commiserate, we're here for you."

"Wow, um, thank you," Ellie said with another nervous laugh.

I smiled and nodded to Chrissy my thanks as I greeted Youngblood. Clasping hands and tapping shoulders.

It took a while for everyone to greet each other and to get settled. More chairs had been brought up here and it was definitely crowded. A few of the girls just resorted to their old man's lap, like Coco. We all made it work, though.

"Whew, gol-lee! What. A. Day," I said and Skids called down, "What 'cha drinkin'?"

"What do you want, babe?" I asked Ellie and she bit her lips together.

"Do you know what a Golden Gimlet is?" she asked.

"I rightly do, a German drink, right?"

She smiled and nodded.

"Alright! Now you're speakin' my language," Golden declared with a grin.

"You shut up!" I thrust my chin at him and everyone laughed.

"What're you having?" Skids asked.

"My usual."

He gave a nod and turned to Coco who bent down and gave him a quick kiss before heading out to the bar. I caught Elka blushing faintly and trying to hide it and smiled. It took me quite a bit of getting used to myself. They had something like a thirty-year age difference between 'em and I let my failed relationship with Reggie color my opinion. I really showed my ass when it came to Coco and Skids getting together and getting it on, and looking back – I honestly had to admit to myself that it was probably that I was some kind of jealous. They were solid in some kind of way I had never had before.

I looked over at Ellie who was trying to take it all in and thought to myself, *Until now.*

"So, what's the big plan?" Driller asked from across and down the table some.

"Honestly, we've got no fucking idea," I said with a big sigh. "I still don't even know how this all happened," I said rubbing a hand over my bald ass head, trying to alleviate the headache that was threatening to build.

"I have some insight into that," Yale said darkly from his seat. Aly was sitting next to him, her hand beneath the table and either gripping his thigh in a comforting massage or giving him a hand job. With them two, you never could tell, and I didn't wanna know. Yale, Driller, and Narcos were the real freaks in the sack around the table. Yale, for the most part, kept it on the down low but we all knew he wasn't quite right – controlling – but a real good dude and hyper-focused on consent and shit.

I don't know. It was way too complicated to me. I didn't need all the extra bells and whistles surrounding sex. I just needed Ellie and me and whatever the moment called for and I didn't share unlike Driller and Narcos. More power to those fuckers, anyhow. Everleigh was gorgeous.

"Well spill it, Yale. What 'cha waiting for? A Golden invitation?" Driller grinned from under a tangle of his brown hair and Yale scowled.

"Shit, we doing puns now?" Golden complained.

"Shut up!" the table chorused grinning and everyone fell out laughing.

"You son of a bitch." He wrinkled his nose at me from across the table and grinned and I held up my hands.

"That was all them! Mm-mm, you ain't pinnin' that one on me."

I turned and winked at Ellie who was genuinely smiling at the comradery around the table. The first genuine smile I think I'd seen her make all day and some of the apprehension binding my heart, making it hard to beat, loosened up for me.

Coco came back with our drinks as Yale started filling in the blanks.

"For some unknown reason," he said, and turned to Ellie, "and forgive me if any of this is difficult to hear. You tell me to stop and we'll table it for now."

Ellie nodded, paling a bit, and said, "Okay," softly.

Coco handed her the drink she ordered, and she took a healthy mouthful, wincing as it went down.

"For some unknown reason, the coroner originally assigned to the case wasn't exactly truthful in his findings. He put down that Elka's sister was indeed shot and that the bullet retrieved was consistent with the type of bullet fired from the initial aggressor's handgun but that is where the filing stopped. The ballistics report went conveniently missing."

"Wait," Youngblood held up a hand, "so was it the coroner trying to cover shit up or is this on forensics and the ballistic's panel?"

"We still aren't sure. All we know is that upon mandatory review, the review panel noticed the shoddy or outright missing work and ran it themselves and everything has now blown up into a departmental corruption scandal and it looks like one big intentional coverup."

"I had no idea," I said soberly, downing some of my Hennessy.

"There was no way for you to know. It was out of your hands," Yale said.

"How the fuck you keep this shit from rolling downhill?" Narcos demanded.

"That was more than a bit of pure dumb luck," Yale said. "As most of you know, Oz knows everybody, but Internal Affairs Bureau, despite looking and looking *hard* might I add, couldn't find a single connection between Oz personally and any of the people involved in trying to cover this up. Hence, why Oz is off the proverbial hook."

Ellie sagged in her seat and all eyes directed toward her.

"Then why would they try to hide this?" she asked.

"The ICPD has been taking a beating in the media over race relations lately," Golden said with a sigh. "Maybe the thought of a black cop shooting an innocent white girl curled the toes of some top brass somewhere enough to make it want to go away."

"That's precisely it," Yale said. "The review team was going to let it slide but for a whistle-blower in their midst who went to IAB."

"Oh, what the fuck?" Driller scowled. Everyone turned some surprised expressions his way. "Not that I am on board with any fuckin' coverups going down, don't get me wrong," he said holding up a hand. "Just if they'd just been straight to begin with this wouldn't be going down and if they'd just fucking let it lie, there would be a lot less pain and anguish going around right now."

Yale nodded. "I agree, which is, of course, why I did some quiet digging on my own when it came to said whistle-blower."

"Aw, shit, here it comes," Golden said.

"He's got some white nationalist undertones to several of his social media posts and some attachment to our old pals the Blue Templars."

"Oh, snap!" Backdraft said.

"Okay, alright, alright, settle down!" Skids declared waving us down as fury blazed up in several of the cops' eyes around the table.

"We're gettin' way too far into club business and into what is far from polite conversation to be having in front of the ladies. Let's go on and change the subject some. Now the damage has already been done, what we need to do now is focus on the fallout and how to handle things from here on out until the dogs that are the media lets go of this particular bone."

"We both got the rest of this week off through the weekend," I said, the wheels and gears turning in my head.

"Well, that's something – even under the shitty fuckin' circumstances," Golden declared.

"Our phones keep blowing the fuck up so bad we're gonna have to change our numbers," I said and there was some cringing, and some scrunched up faces around the table.

"Baby, what do you want?" Narcos asked, eyes leveled on Ellie who was sort of collapsed in on herself in her seat, her fingers threaded through mine beneath the table, gripping my hand in a death grip.

"Honestly, I wish I had the money to just go somewhere until Sunday. Somewhere where I can sit and paint and breathe and deal with what's going on with me for a few days. I just want to leave the rabble behind."

"I have an idea." The feminine voice was an unfamiliar one. Sweet, clear, and almost too soft to hear even in the silence that followed Ellie's wish.

I looked up and down the table and with a bit of a startle, fixed eyes onto Everleigh and blurted, "Was that you?"

She blushed and tucked herself between Narcos and Driller and nodded.

"I'm picking up just what you're puttin' down baby. You're cool, I'll take it from here if you want," Narcos declared. Everleigh nodded a bit too rapidly and we all let it go. It was enough that she'd been comfortable enough to put it out there like she did. Outgoing she was not when it came to other people, especially new people and for good reason.

"We got a summer cabin out in one of the West Virginia hollers, out on the river. Sound like just the place?" Narcos asked. I felt Ellie perk up just a bit beside me.

"Yeah," I agreed.

"It's a hell of a long ride," Driller said.

"That's okay if it gets us away from here for a minute."

"Could leave tomorrow morning," Narcos declared.

"Shit, yeah, brother." It was sounding better and better the more I thought about it.

"Well alright then," Skids declared. "It sounds like that's all settled."

I eyed Narcos, Everleigh, and Driller who were exchanging happy looks and thought this shit was gonna be interesting for sure.

"I'll have to go pack some things," Ellie murmured.

"Yeah," I agreed, nodding.

"Which means I'll have to go home."

Shit, I knew she was thinking about the reporter that morning and whether there would be more waiting to ambush her or not.

"Yeah," I agreed.

"Why don't you guys get something to eat here, get your shit, and come stay at our place tonight," Golden said. "I'll call up Lys and give her and *Hombrecito* the heads up, so they know you're comin'."

I nodded. "Much appreciated, man."

"Anytime, my brother."

I checked with Ellie who looked thoughtful and finally nodded her assent.

"It'll be all good, baby. I promise," I murmured against her temple and kissed her there. Her eyes slipped shut and she took a fortifying breath.

"Promise?" she asked and I smiled.

"Promise."

28

———

*E*lka...

We three went to my place first. Golden accompanying us in case there was an ambush, he could call it in and have them potentially criminally trespassed if the law would allow for it. Meanwhile, Oz was there to help me get things together for our trip. He was dubious about my plan to take paints and an easel, but I had that all covered and in a fairly compact fashion. All carriable on my back.

We lucked out. There wasn't anyone waiting, but then again, by the time we had left the *10-13*, as Oz and the rest liked to call it, it was fairly late in the evening.

Oz watched me as I packed light, a bag of clothes to wear that could go in his saddlebags on his bike, and my art kit. He raised an eyebrow at the paints I selected out of my big industrial tool box on wheels in my little art studio.

"That's it?" he asked.

"What? Yeah. I mean, I don't really need that many pigments. I can honestly mix whatever colors I need with a few basics."

I pointed at my smaller French easel in the back of the closet and said, "Can you grab that one for me? I think it might be better for a trip like this."

"Yeah sure, what's it do?"

"It's a French easel and allows me to carry the canvas back even though it might still be wet – which if I use oils, it will be. It takes forever for oils to dry."

"Yeah? About how long?" he asked.

"Okay, I'm sort of misspeaking in layman's terms a little bit, oils technically never dry, it's the solvents in them that make the paint pliable that dries and it can take anywhere from twenty-four hours on up to twelve days depending on conditions."

"No shit?"

"No, shit," I said and slid my smaller pallet, my roll of brushes and paint knives, and my wooden box of pigments into my artist's satchel.

"I'm gonna look forward to watching you paint," he said and I laughed.

"It's seriously about as boring as watching paint dry – which I guess comes with the territory, to be honest."

He cast his gaze to the painting of Mia and his expression softened.

"Would it be selfish as fuck of me to ask you to keep this one?" he asked softly.

I cocked my head slightly and went to him, wrapping both my arms around his one that held my French easel by the leather top loop to carry it by. I shook my head.

"No," I said gently.

"I feel so fuckin' guilty," he said, tearing up and I teared up with him.

"It was an accident," I said and hugged his arm tight. "You were trying your absolute best to stop those men. It was just a stupid accident."

He nodded silently and said, "They weren't even men," he told me. "They were just boys."

The crushing weight of what he was dealing with hit me like a freight train in that moment. Soul crushing guilt about how I had been leaning on him so heavily followed.

"God, Oz… I'm so sorry. Here you've been silently suffering all of this time and I've just been leaning on you like I've been the only one hurting all this time."

"Hey, no. You lost your sister –"

He sighed out harshly as I began to cry. Setting down my easel, his own eyes rimmed with red despite shedding no tears of his own, he pulled me against his chest and held me tight. Once again, Oz was the stronger of us both while I dissolved into tears and a fresh batch of useless emotional goo over our mingling and mutual pains.

"Everything alright?" Golden asked from the door a moment later as I was slowly pulling myself back together.

"Yeah, man, yeah. Just a couple minutes more. It comes in waves, dude."

"Yeah, I get it," Golden said and disappeared from the studio doorway as silently as he'd appeared. "Take your time," he called back down the hallway.

I blew out a shaky breath and detached myself from Oz.

"God, I am getting so sick of crying," I said, voice still unsteady.

"You and me both, babe," he said with a nod. "It definitely ain't my usual thing."

"Think we will ever get to a point that we won't feel so crappy?" I asked, smoothing the wetness off my cheeks with my middle fingers.

"Someday," he said with a crooked grin. "Not today, and probably not tomorrow, but someday soon, yeah."

A silence fell between us, but it was one of comfort, one of healing, as the truth of his words sank in.

I loaded a fresh canvas of an appropriate size into my French easel for transport and hooked the leather backpack-like straps to it for ease of carry.

"Let me just change into something a little more appropriate for the road and we should be good to go," I said standing.

"Sounds good, I'll be right out front with Golden packing this shit on the bike."

"Leave the easel and the satchel out, I can carry those. The only thing that needs to go into a side case is this." I tossed him my small cylindrical duffel of clothing for the next almost-week and he caught it.

"Look at you go, we'll make you a bad biker bitch yet."

I laughed. "And just when I was getting to be fine just being me."

"Who says the real you ain't bad?" he asked.

"I'm an art restorationist and nerd, ain't nothing bad about that," I declared.

"You work on five-hundred-year-old shit without batting an eye. You got nerves of steel and ain't nothing more badass than that."

He had me there.

"I'm going to go get changed," I said deflecting.

"You do that," he said hefting my bag and heading down the hallway. It never seemed to get old watching that crest on his back, those silver rays of justice shining behind that dark indigo chess piece.

I sighed silently and slipped across the hall to my bedroom. Sometimes, there just wasn't any justice surrounding a given situation. Sometimes it was just one big raw deal for everyone involved… like the situation at hand. My family, Oz, the families of the gang members shooting it out in the middle of the street in the first place… we were all hurting. All of us except for the men who had started it all. They didn't have to hurt anymore, unless Hell was real, and they were burning in it.

I dressed swiftly to ride, in better and proper protective gear. My sister's boots, my poured-on jeans, a light tee, and my sister's jacket. I pulled my hair into a ponytail and put everything I had been wearing in their proper place, shoes in a rack in the closet, belt on a hanger, the rest in the laundry hamper – washing in one side, dry cleaning in the other.

My little apartment was as neat as ever and I felt a little sad, like I was being driven from it, but my heart thirsted to get away, to just get out of the city for a little while.

I stepped back across to the studio, picking up my satchel and slinging it across my chest. I slipped first one arm through one strap, and the other arm through the other and secured the leather and canvas straps by pulling them tight, hitching the wooden framework into a more comfortable position on my back.

"You ready?" Oz asked from the mouth of the hall.

"As I'll ever be," I murmured, staring for a fraction of a moment at the painting of my sister. *God, I miss you, Mia… but I think I am going to be okay,* I said silently, before snapping out the light.

Oz gave me a quick kiss in the hall and with a brave smile, took my hand and led me out to the living room. Golden stood from where he had his butt leaned on the back of my couch and looked up from his phone.

"What the hell is that thing?" he asked, waving in my general direction.

"Art supplies," I said.

He raised his eyebrows and said, "Okay, better hang on. Looks like that thing'll drag you right off the back once you catch some air."

I frowned. "He serious?" I asked Oz.

"Naw, he's just a dick," he said and Golden barked a laugh.

I shook my head and took up my purse, awkwardly slinging it across my body over everything else, the strap riding awkwardly above and against the framework of the easel but not too badly to make me want to fix it. I mean, it was as secure as anything else.

I locked up with a heavy heart and we left the front stoop, returning to the bikes parked under what seemed the lone working streetlight on the block.

"You're gonna come back feeling as good as new," Golden said, sitting astride his bike and pulling on a pair of gloves.

"I don't know about all that," I said dubiously. "The break will be nice, though."

"You'll see," he said with a wink and I put on the helmet Oz handed me.

"Right now, I just want to get some sleep," I said.

"Me too," Oz echoed. I think we were both mentally and emotionally drained from the day.

We rode to a nicer part of the city. A part that ten or even twenty years back hadn't been so good at all. Now? Now it was flipping *beautiful*, the street idyllic, lined with old-fashioned streetlights – or at least replicas, in front of huge beautiful old brownstones on both sides of the street.

"Come on down into the garage!" Golden called and we waited, turning down a steep drive into a lower-level garage, just big enough for Golden to pull a tight turn to face out. There was no way for Oz to do the same, so he just pulled down into it nose-in and parked beside Golden.

"I'll let you out in the morning," Golden declared, hitting the button on the nearby support post for the garage door to come down.

The door to the inside of the garage opened, a woman with dark brown hair and brown eyes like mine smiled from it and said, "Hi, I'm Lys."

"Hi, I'm Elka," I said getting off the bike.

"*Hombrecito* asleep?" Golden asked.

"Yes," Lys rolled her eyes. "Almost couldn't get him to go to bed once he found out his Uncle Oz was coming over to spend the night."

"Is he here then?" a young man's voice asked from behind Lys.

"Yeah, I'm here, but you're supposed to be in bed!" Oz called.

"Uncle Oz!"

A boy no more than nine or ten flew past Lys and into the garage in his pajamas, holding out his fist in 'rock' fashion. He and Oz did some kind of elaborate hand shake that made me rear back some.

"Wait, do that again, I couldn't catch how you did it," I said. The boy smiled and turned to me eager.

"Wow, you picked a pretty girlfriend, Oz," he said and I laughed a little, blushing. "Okay, hold out your fist."

The boy eagerly walked me through it twice, but it was still almost too much.

"*Hombrecito*, it's a school night," Golden reminded the boy. "C'mere and give your *Tio Rodrigo* a hug goodnight and get on up to bed."

"Awww, but they just got here!" the boy whined.

"*Hombrecito!*" Golden's tone turned admonishing.

"Okay." The boy gave an exasperated moan.

"We'll see you in the morning before school," Oz promised him, giving him a hug.

The boy nodded at me politely and hugged Lys on his way by. She hugged him back and kissed the top of his head. "Get some good sleep, Manolo."

"Night, love you," he said.

"Love you, too, buddy!" Oz called after him.

"Sorry about that," Lys said with a chuckle once he was out of earshot.

"Takes after his uncle," Oz said side-eyeing Golden with a sly grin.

"Isn't that the truth?" Lys rolled her eyes and stood aside, holding the door open for us.

We filed past as soon as Oz grabbed my bag for me.

"We'll have to stop at my place tomorrow on the way out of town," he said.

I simply nodded.

"As I was saying," Lys said when it was my turn to pass her, "my name is Lys. Welcome in."

"Thanks," I said with a smile. "I really appreciate it."

"It's no worries." She smiled brightly. "Oz can lead the way."

Golden nearly attacked her, smothering her in kisses and causing her to shriek, laughing as she fended him off with lighthearted slaps against his leather.

"Missed you, baby," he murmured and she smiled against his mouth, kissing him.

"Missed you, too."

The scene warmed my heart.

"You guys have a good night, now," Golden called after us and I looked back and said, "Thank you." Having to keep myself sideways almost as it was to keep from scraping a wall with my easel.

The hallways widened up more upstairs, which I was grateful for, and I loved, loved, loved, their brownstone. It was beautiful inside and I had visions of regency era ladies descending the staircase all a flutter at the latest gossip, which I know was funny… regency era was likely long before this place was built. If I had to say, I would place it around the turn of the twentieth century, maybe a little earlier. I would get a better sense during the day.

We climbed the stairs to the first floor, then went up the big, impressive staircase to the second floor and crept down the hall.

"Goodnight, Oz!" Manolo called from his open bedroom doorway as Oz paused outside what I presumed to be the guest room's door.

"Night, buddy, now go to sleep before your uncle finds out you're still up messin' around."

Manolo laughed and Oz sighed and shook his head letting us into the room and closed the door behind us. "Swear to God he's just like his uncle Golden. My momma would have whooped my ass by now – or had my pops do it. Mm-mm, that woulda been worse."

I smiled and said, "Once or twice Mia and I would collect a wooden spoon across the ass. Depending on how far we pushed it."

"We had to pick our own switch off the damn tree in true southern momma style," he said and I giggled, tangling myself up when I tried to remove the easel before my purse.

He laughed and said, "Hold still; let me grab the light."

The overhead light was harsh after the near perfect dark, but he got me untangled and unburdened, which felt wonderful.

We were too tired for any sexual shenanigans. Simply opting to strip each other down to basic underwear and crawl into bed. Oz snapped out the light and got in beside me, pulling me into his chest and I laid myself across him, cuddling up to his side, my leg over his, my head on his chest.

I was usually the one that took a thousand position changes and a sacrifice to the gods to fall asleep, but not tonight. Tonight, I think I was asleep faster than he was, even after the benefit of a nap in the middle of the day.

29

———

*O*z...

"Oz! Oz! Come on, wake up! You said you'd see me before I went to school!"

"Manolo!"

I was already up, pulling open the door for the kid as Ellie put a pillow over her head and groaned.

"Whoa! Hey, little man!" I caught him before he could charge into the room and disturb Ellie any more than he already had. That, or see something he shouldn't. "Take it easy, and let's take it out into the hallway now," I said steering him in the other direction, shutting the door behind me.

Golden was just finishing up climbing the stairs and lit off in his nephew's ass in a string of Spanish. I smiled and rattled off at him right back, *"Come on now, he's just being a kid."*

"Yeah, he's just being a kid *who won't listen.* Now get your little butt back down those stairs, pronto."

214

"Awwww, *Tio Rodrigo!*"

"*Now, Hombrecito!*"

"Fine, sorry, Oz."

"We're cool, buddy. Just listen to your uncle sometime, huh?"

"Okay," he said sullenly and went back down stairs.

"Sorry about that, brother."

I waved G. off and said, "Nah, it's fine."

"She still sleepin'?" he asked.

"No, but she wants to be!" Elka called out from behind the closed door with an exasperated groan.

G. and I both chuckled and he said, "Come on down when you want breakfast."

"Thanks man, we'll be down in a little bit."

I went in to see to my lady. She took her head out from under the pillow when I entered the room and sighed, hugging it to her chest and propping her head on it as she lay on her stomach.

"Mornin' sunshine."

"Mm, morning," she said and she looked exhausted.

"You sleep at all last night?" I asked, sitting down on the edge of the bed, laying my hand on the smooth skin of her back.

"I did," she said, "but I sure don't feel like it."

"You need some coffee," I said with a smile.

She nodded. "Yeah. Yeah, I do."

"Wait here, I'll go get you some."

I pulled on a pair of pants for both Golden and Lys' benefit and padded downstairs in my bare feet. I found them both in the kitchen, Manolo still putting up an argument.

"Didn't I just talk to you about listening to your uncle not five minutes ago upstairs?" I asked. "Gol-lee, kid! My momma woulda slapped the holy hell shit outta me if I still sassed her after a talk like that."

Manolo's mouth dropped open. "Nuh-uh!"

"Yeah-huh!" I turned to Lys and gave a wink asking, "I get a cup of that coffee for my lady?"

"Yeah, yeah! Absolutely. Rough morning already?" she asked with a smile.

"Just a rough wake-up call," I said fixing Manolo with a look. He had the grace to look embarrassed.

"Car, *now*," Golden ordered. "I'll run him to school. Be right back," he said and went around to kiss Lys goodbye.

"Good deal, see you when you get back," I said.

"Yeah, man."

"Will I see you?" Manolo asked.

"Next week, at the Cuban block party – for sure."

"Aw, man!" he gave an exasperated kid's melodramatic sigh and grabbed his backpack off the counter.

Golden made a rage face, crossed his eyes, and mimed wanting to strangle the kid and I laughed silently.

"Man, you are killin' me!" G. said putting a hand on his nephew's shoulder, catching up to him.

"Can we take the bike to school?" his nephew asked.

"Sure as shit ain't dropping you off in the patrol car," he said.

"Well you could have taken Lys's car." You could *hear* the eye roll in the kid's voice from all the way down the hall.

Lys and I stifled our laughter.

"He is just like G."

"Tell me about it," she said grinning.

Her face lost its easy smile as she handed over two mugs of coffee and she asked, "How is she doing?"

"Eh, I think we'll both do a lot better once we're on the road. I think we both need some serious distance from this shit."

"I can't agree more," Lys said with a sigh. "I may not have been around for it, but I've heard enough first-hand accounts from Lil and from Chrissy to say I hope I *never* get my fifteen minutes of fame. Especially for something so tragic."

"You ain't lyin'," I said as I finished doctoring the coffee up. "This is some bullshit."

"Take your time, I'm working from home on the books today. I'll fix you something to eat whenever you come down."

"You ain't have to do that," I said.

"You're right, I don't, but you're family and I like to feed my family – okay?"

I smiled at her and shook my head at her. "You and G. are a perfect match."

"Why thank you," she said.

I went back upstairs to find Ellie up and mostly dressed; she dropped heavily onto the end of the bed and stared at the coffee cups in my hands with longing. I held hers out to her and she took it from me with both hands. God, she did everything, even the smallest movements, with elegance and grace.

Even now, sleep tousled, exhausted, and crabby, she was beautiful to me. The type of beautiful that made my heart feel funny in my chest. Like it was simultaneously heavier than lead and lighter than air at the same time.

There were times I looked at her like this and I got choked up. Choked up for no reason at all other than it hurt to look at her because she was just so damn pretty.

"What?" she asked staring at me over the rim of her coffee cup as she took a slow drink.

"Nothin'," I lied, unable to put it into words for her anyway. I mean, I could think it, but saying it out loud was a whole different thing. One I just didn't think I could do.

She arched one brow like she didn't believe me and I smiled, chuckling lightly and said, "Just shut up and drink your coffee."

"I didn't say anything!" she cried.

"Yeah, but you were thinking it."

She rolled her eyes and shook her head.

"Whatever."

"Yeah, don't you 'whatever' me."

She scoffed and I laughed.

"In other news," she said. "When are the others supposed to get here?"

"Who, Narcos, Driller, and Everleigh?" I asked.

"Thanks for that. I have a hard time with all the weird names sometimes."

"Road names, not weird names, and they'll be here when they get here," I said shrugging. "Them three run on their own time."

"Mm, how long is the ride?"

"*Long*. Longer than any ride you've taken with me, so far. Something like four and a half to five hours. You're gonna be saddle sore after this one."

"Fantastic," she said with a sigh.

"Antsy?" I asked.

"Yeah, I'm beyond ready to go."

"Well, let me call and see where they're at." I picked up my phone from the nightstand and switched it on.

"Oh, no, don't do that," she said.

"It's cool," I said, ignoring her and phoned up Narcos. It rang and rang and went to voicemail which meant one thing – well, maybe two.

"Either they're on their way or they're fuckin'," I said.

Elka nearly spat coffee through her nose.

"Wow, and you're up on their sexual proclivities how?"

"They ain't exactly shy about it," I told her. "Those three are freaks."

"Good to know," she said laughing.

The three in question showed up not long later. We had breakfast, thanks to Lys and Golden and we packed up my bike down in the garage. Ellie, suited up as best she could, and ready to go, was chomping at the bit to get the fuck up outta Indigo City and I couldn't say as I blamed her. I was right there with her.

The ride was just what I needed and by the time we pulled up in front of what was supposed to pass for a cabin, I felt much more like my old self. I eyed the ramshackle hut on its stilts and cut the engine to my bike.

"What kind of white-bred, dueling banjo, *Deliverance* kind of shit did you two fuckers just get me into?" I demanded as soon as the last bike engine had cut.

The guys and Everleigh laughed it up, but Ellie smacked me on the shoulder and cried, "Oz!"

"What?" I demanded.

"That's so – so –"

"What?"

"Racist!" she sputtered.

"Mm-n-mm," I said patterning the sound after 'I don't know.' "Kinda hard for me to be racist," I sniffed and she climbed off the bike.

"Oh, and how is that?" she asked pointedly.

"I got a color T.V. at home same as you."

Her mouth dropped open and the guys fell out laughing all over again.

Everleigh whispered in Narcos' ear and he looked at the two of us, me and Ellie, thoughtfully for a minute saying, "We could do that."

"Do what now?" I asked, standing up and stretching.

"Nothin'," he said with a reckless grin. "You two can head on down and around back that way," he said pointing out a dirt track. Twin ruts had been worn into it over the years, the center humped and grassy. "River is down there. We're going to head on in and open things up, air it out and the like."

"Copy that. Fancy a walk?" I asked Ellie. She had shrugged out of her easel and was pressing her hands to the backs of her hips, arching in a luxurious stretch that made me think of a cat.

"I would love to stretch my legs," she said and took up her satchel, looping her arm through, and dropping the strap over her head. Her easel she hefted by the loop at the top. "Lead the way," she said.

We took the track, walking slow, bandanas down around our necks, pulled down from our faces. We'd left our helmets back at the bike, and I had my sunglasses on, while Ellie had perched her safety glasses on the top of her head.

"How you feelin'?" I asked when we got about halfway down the track cut into the hillside.

"Better," she said. "Like a thousand-pound boulder's been lifted off my chest."

"Yeah? That's a good way of putting it," I nodded sagely.

"Is that how you feel?" she asked.

"Yeah, actually. It was a good idea to get away from the bullshit, even if it is only a short reprieve."

She sighed heavily as we came around the bottom of the cabin and I hated that I reminded her that we would be back in it come Monday morning.

"Oh, wow! They weren't kidding. They're right on the river," she said, and I was grateful for the swift distraction.

"Guess now we know why it's on stilts, still don't make no damn sense why the garage is down here, though."

She laughed. "No, it doesn't but it is beautiful."

"Now *that*, I'll give you."

"Reminds me of *Midsummer Eve* by Edward Robert Hughes," she said.

"I have no clue who that is." I shook my head.

"You do, I *promise*. If you saw it, you would know it."

"I'll have to take your word for it." I smiled and she set her easel down, leaning it against a stump that was a little ways back from the riverbank.

"This should do," she said and lifted her satchel off over her head.

"Looks like it'll work for a seat," I agreed.

"I am so going to dip my feet and cool off."

"Alright, now. Now you're talkin'."

We each took a seat on the broad, low stump to take our boots and socks off and to roll up our jeans as far as they would go. It may have looked like something straight outta *Deliverance* up in here, but I had to give it to the guys, it was peaceful.

The sound of running water loosened things up in my shoulders and neck from the ride, the tension draining outta me as I waited for Ellie to stand back up. I took off my jacket and cut, slipped my cut off from around my jacket and donned it again.

"Oh, good idea." She slid out of her sister's jacket and laid it over the top of mine next to her satchel.

She looked good in her light pink tee, jeans rolled up to just below her knees. She took my offered hand and we walked through the low brown grass, spotted with green here and there, to the water's edge.

"Hey! Don't go out too far! The current can be a bitch!" Driller called from up on the back, screened-in wrap-around porch.

I put a hand up and waved that I'd heard him, and Ellie and I got our feet wet, just past our ankles.

The cold water was a shock, but it felt damn good.

She was quiet and reserved as she scanned the tree line across the shallows, the sound of river water babbling over rounded river rocks the only thing to fill the silence.

"What you thinking about?" I asked finally.

"I don't know," she murmured. "Nothing, I guess. It's kind of nice, actually. The quiet."

"Yeah, I'm not used to it. Been a city boy all my life. It's like I need the noise and the hustle."

"I can understand that," she said with a sigh.

"C'mere," I murmured and she fitted herself against my front, laying her head on my shoulder. I held her close, the water running past our feet and we just absorbed the peace and quiet, the comfort in each other's arms.

"I love you," she whispered.

"I love you, too, babe."

"We're going to get through this, right?"

"Damn straight," I told her. "It's you and me against the world, baby."

She sighed and cuddled a little closer. We stood like that for I don't know how long, the river moving lazily around our ankles, carrying a lot of the tension and the bad shit downstream – at least for now.

I didn't know what I did to deserve having this woman in my arms, loving me, after what I'd done – unintentionally or not – but I would take it. I would stand here, in the here and now, and breathe the clean green smelling air and her fresh vanilla scent and I would let it all go for just a minute. I would lay the burden down and let myself rest, and I hoped I could get her to do the same.

"I wish this feeling could last forever," she said after a moment and I smoothed a hand up and down her back.

"Me, too."

"Son of a bitch!" Driller swore from back up on the porch and Ellie and I sputtered, laughing.

"Way to ruin the moment," she said with a rueful grin.

I sighed, "Ahhh, boy," and shook my head.

"What are they even doing?" she asked curiously.

"Who knows, when it comes to them two; I learned a long time ago – don't ask questions."

"Oh, come on, they can't be *that* bad," she said.

"Bad? Naw. Different?" I gave a slow nod. "Definitely different."

"How so?" she asked curiously.

I chuckled lightly. "Stayin' around 'em a whole weekend I'm sure you'll see. Those two have no inhibitions and that shit's only gotten worse since Narcos hooked up with Everleigh last year."

"Aww, they seem really sweet on her."

"They are, but I just don't get that dynamic."

"What? Poly?"

"If that's what you call them sharing her."

Ellie shrugged.

"Doesn't bother you?" I asked.

"It's not for *me*," she said. "But who am I to judge anybody else's decisions about their life? If they're not hurting anyone and it's not toxic, I don't see anything wrong with it."

I smiled and said, "Me either. It's just not how a brother from my hood was raised, you know what I mean?"

She smiled faintly. "I understand, but that's more your hang up than theirs, yeah?"

I thought about it and turned down the edges of my mouth impressed.

"No, you know what? You're absolutely right."

"Live and let live," she murmured.

I nodded and kissed her forehead.

"Sounds good."

30

*E*lka…

We relaxed by the river. At one point, Everleigh carefully picked her way across the stones and disappeared into the woods while Narcos and Driller appeared with fly-fishing rods. Oz professed his rustiness at fly-fishing but like a good sport, joined the guys in trying his hand at it while I set up my easel and got out my drawing pencil.

I sighed and stared sightlessly across the river and contemplated what I wanted to paint. I mean, I couldn't get the image of *Midsummer Eve* by Edward Robert Hughes out of my mind. The enchanted young girl in the woods, leaning forward with her hands on her knees, the fairies dancing at her feet, a crown of flowers in her red hair.

The scene before me had the same vibe but there was just… something missing.

Then the magic happened.

Everleigh, in her long, flowy hippy skirt and peasant blouse stepped out from between the trees to the river's edge. She held something in

225

her hands – what, I wasn't quite sure until she held it up to the light, a jar filled with amber-gold liquid. She peered up at it, hair long and flowing wild behind her, a soft smile on her lips and I sucked in a sharp breath.

It was perfect. One of those singular moments in time, only a fraction of a second but burned into my memory and I swiftly began to sketch before I lost it.

I didn't have the ability to make this painting as photo-realistic as I had the painting of Mia back in my studio, but I would do my best to get it as close as mere memory would allow with just a few tweaks here and there.

I worked for hours, roughing out the image with pencil on the canvas, the basic shapes, before I set to work mixing pigments on my palette.

I worked until the light failed and I found myself squinting at the canvas. I looked up at the clear sky and sighed, wishing I had an hour or two more but having to give it up, for now. Oz came up behind me, ice rattling against the sides of a mason jar and I turned smiling appreciatively, accepting the iced tea he offered and sipping at the sweet brew.

"Thanks," I murmured. "Where did you get the ice?"

"We been here a minute, baby. Everleigh got ice going in the freezer just as soon as they turned the power on in the cabin. Plenty of time for the trays to freeze over."

"Oh, wow, I guess I didn't realize we'd been here that long."

He looked over my shoulder and nodded slowly. "Nice," he declared and I smiled.

"Call me inspired, it's beautiful out here."

"Yeah, it's not half bad," he agreed and I laughed.

"You're a city boy through and through, aren't you?"

"Guilty as charged," he said with a reckless grin.

"You catch us some dinner?" I asked.

"Me? Not so much, but I had some fun trying. Driller and Narcos caught a few, though, so we won't be going hungry tonight." He winked at me and I looked back over my shoulder. The rest of our little party sat around an outdoor firepit style cowboy grill, the fish wrapped in foil on the coals, beers in hand. Everleigh was smiling in our direction but they were far enough away I couldn't make out what Driller was saying as he stirred the coals with a poker.

Whatever it was, Narcos grinned and Everleigh brightened considerably.

"Bugs are gonna be coming out soon," Oz said. "We got some citronella candles going. Why don't you come on now and pack it in?"

"Okay," I said softly.

I packed it in, intent on coming back out to paint some more the next day, weather permitting. When I joined everyone by the fire, it was to soft greetings and an almost intimate kinship. It reminded me of family camping trips when Mia and I were kids. Of long car trips and making s'mores. It evoked good memories long forgotten and I was grateful for that. To remember something good amid all of the bad come my family's way.

Dinner was lovely, the star-shot sky even more so, and all too soon I found the day's events, hell, *all of the things*, catching up to me. The alcohol from the beers with dinner definitely didn't help things. So, with a full belly and sagging eyelids, I begged off in favor of an early night.

"You know what? That sounds like a plan. I think all of us are a little beat," Driller said kindly.

Everleigh leapt to her feet excitedly and held out her hand to me, waving me on excitedly. I laughed a bit at her sudden enthusiasm and looked to Oz.

"Well, go on!" he said. "Don't keep the lady waiting."

I took her hand and let her drag me along to the stairs leading up to the corner of the wrap-around, screened-in porch. We went up the two flights of switchback stairs and she pushed open the screen door on the landing.

"Oh!" I declared, when she swept her arm out from her body in a grand revealing gesture and I *was* duly impressed.

A day bed had been brought out onto the porch, old apple crates set on end to serve as end tables. Citronella candles winked in every available rustic container from old tin cans, to jelly jars, and even crafted from an old chipped earthenware bowl or two.

I went to the bed and sank down onto its edge and asked, "This is for us?"

Everleigh nodded excitedly, and with her auburn red hair and the excitement in her eyes it reminded me of a certain little mermaid. I smiled and asked, "Can I hug you?"

She laughed and came over and hugged me tight, Narcos, who was leaning a shoulder against one of the porch roof's supports said, "It's cooler out here. Thought you could use it. I know city boy down there can't live without his air conditioning."

He rolled his eyes but the joke was on him. Oz was on the stairs and called up, "I heard that!"

"Don't believe I was trying to hide it," Narcos said coolly.

"Yeah, fuck you."

"Didn't think you swung that way, brother."

"Nuh-uh, I ain't into all that gay shit you and Driller get up to," he said and Narcos looked over his shoulder at Oz, flashing a grin.

"Oh, stahhhhhp," he gave an effeminate wave and Oz laughed.

"You fucker."

"Can't shame a guy that ain't got none," Driller called out. "Now you wanna make a hole?"

"Why, you wanna fuck it?" Oz asked and Everleigh and I exchanged a roll of eyes at the guy's ceaseless banter.

"You know me," Driller said edging past Oz in the doorway, "I'll fuck anything."

"Now I *know* that's right," Oz declared.

A low sweeping chuckle went through the lot of us and Narcos stepped past where I sat and put an arm around Everleigh's waist.

"We'll let you two get comfortable and settle in."

"Thank you," I said softly.

"Bathroom's inside, only door in the place besides the front door," Driller said on his way past.

"Thanks." I smiled up at him.

"You stay put, baby. I'll go get our bags." Oz bent down and kissed me on his way by and I drew in a slow steady breath full of beeswax and citronella and smiled, looking out over the backyard, the stars in the sky, the flicker of the fire down below, the faint shimmer of the water moving slowly by beyond it all but before the deep black of the wood.

God, I needed this... I thought to myself and was overwhelmed with gratitude.

Oz returned and handed me my bag and motioned around the corner from the windows. I smiled and bit my bottom lip. I hadn't considered changing *out* here, but it was vaguely naughty, and I liked the idea.

I went around the corner and stripped down, sliding my sleep shorts up my legs and pulling the ribbed cotton tank over my head.

I stepped back around to Oz already stripped to his boxers and tucked beneath the light quilt on the bed. His arms open, he threw back the blankets to let me into the bed and I joined him.

We settled in the circle of each other's arms and lay quietly, listening to the insect song and the three of them get ready for bed. The playful slap of a hand against flesh, the light yip and feminine laughter that followed made Oz and I both chuckle faintly. The good mood of our travel companions infectious to a degree.

We listened to the bed creak, the sounds of them settling, then *different* sounds began. A light, soft, feminine moan, the gentle wet sucking sound of an intense kiss, a masculine chuckle.

I held my breath and looked up at Oz who was staring at me fixedly, an amused smile on his lips.

"Are they?"

"I told you they were freaky."

"I heard that!" Narcos called through the open windows and screen door.

"Y'all are more than welcome to come in here and join us," Driller called, and the invitation was punctuated by Everleigh's high and lilting laugh.

"Mm-mm, I don't share," Oz declared.

"Fine, stay out there and fuck," Narcos called and you could hear the shit-eating grin in his voice.

Oz raised his eyebrows and said low enough for only me to hear, "Sounds like a plan to me."

I felt my mouth drop open in surprise, but it was quickly stifled by his mouth on mine, his hand sliding down my body, dipping below my waistband, fingertips teasing my clit and getting me all worked up.

I moaned into his mouth, my hips rising off the bed to meet his hand, my own hand delving below the waistband of his boxer briefs to wrap sure fingers around his velvety cock. I stroked him as he stroked me, putting a little twist in my wrist causing him to moan into my mouth.

I sucked on his tongue, rolled the sound in my mouth like candy – decadent like rich dark chocolate as we worked each other up.

My nipples tightened, pebbling beneath the thin cotton-blend tank I wore. He palmed one of my breasts over the material, pinching one swollen and sensitive peak between thumb and the side of his palm, rolling it between them, making me writhe just as the rhythmic creaking of the bed inside started up, Everleigh giving a throaty moan of pleasure.

Oh, my God… there was something about that sound. Something erotic that deepened the fire of my desire, sending it coursing out through my veins, flooding out from my middle. My pussy throbbed, contracted and pulsed with a deep and abiding need to be filled and there was only one man present I wanted to fill it.

"Oz, please," I whispered, nipping his earlobe even as his teeth scraped lightly, grazing my shoulder in a tender love bite.

"I got you, babe," he whispered against my skin, but he wouldn't be rushed.

He tortured me sweetly, even as the sounds of sex intensified within the cabin. I rolled and Oz let me, lying on his back as I slipped my sleep shorts and panties off, pushing his boxer-briefs down in front.

"Side pocket of my bag," he said from between clenched teeth and I leaned way over the side of the bed, dragging his bag across the area rug they'd lain on the porch beneath our bed.

It left my pussy exposed to him, my ass up, and Oz took advantage – massaging my most intimate parts, teasing my asshole with his thumb, delving his fingers through the slick wetness collecting at my pussy.

God, I was so wet. It took everything in me not to pause. Not to writhe against his hand, not to get him to finger fuck me for the immediate pleasure, to take the easy route to orgasm.

No, I wanted his dick. I wanted him to stretch me. I wanted him deep inside me as I rode him. I wanted to look down upon him, his hands on my tits as I teased my clit myself and came around him. I wanted to make myself come again and again until I was drunk on his love and the ecstasy and couldn't take anymore.

Until I floated on that river of pure warm bliss that was afterglow to the sounds of the real running water just yards away, lulled by the lullaby of insect song and Oz's panting breath.

Everleigh cried out from just inside the cabin and my pussy constricted around Oz's invading fingers. I echoed her cry with a sultry moan of my own and faltered in my purpose, pausing, letting him finger me, the condom gripped in my hand.

"You better get up here and get that on me," he said in his demanding way and I lived for it.

I crawled back up on the bed and straddled him, candlelight glowing against our skins as I tore the condom open with my teeth. I watched him, watching me, writhing, my hips rising and falling under his kneading hands as I was too worked up to hold still. I rolled the sticky condom with its spermicidal lubricant down his length, making eye contact the whole while.

"Ride me, baby," he ordered, and his voice was filled with the tight, barely controlled grit of a man who was on the edge.

I put him at my opening and worked him inside me slowly, watching his face as my hair fell around me. With the light summer breeze against my naked skin, the glow of the candlelight, the soft rhythmic panting and light feral moans emanating from Everleigh's throat as we both gave and took our pleasure. I felt freer than I ever had ever in my life before.

I felt like a goddess fallen to earth, like I should be the subject of some of those sensual and erotic old Roman paintings.

I felt beautiful and serene. I felt bold and beholden to no one and nothing but the wind against my skin and the firelight that kissed my skin and the man who panted and groaned beneath me as I fucked him. God, the way he looked up at me. The adoration in his eyes, the longing in his gaze, the reverence in his touch.

I both worshipped and felt worshipped. I both gave everything of myself and felt I was given everything this man had to give me in return. We were a perfect ebb and flow of erotic energy. A perfect circle, the cycle of life and death playing out between us over and over again with every rise and fall of my hips, with every stroke of his cock inside me.

His hands on my tits, gripping hard, I threw my head back and caught a glimpse of the threesome inside. Of Everleigh riding Narcos in a mirror of what Oz and I were doing. Of Driller positioning himself behind her, hiding her from view, licking his palm, stroking himself, lubing her ass from the tube in his opposite hand.

He fit himself inside her ass and she threw back her head and cried out. A wild sound pure and feral and free and accepting of their love.

God, the pure and beautiful sight of it alone made me tighten up around my man. Made him grunt, sent my hand drifting from his chest to where our bodies met.

I watched the threesome fucking just inside through the window, at the eroticism of it, the poetry in motion, the pure, fantastical, beautiful work of living art in front of me and I let it fuel my fire, stoke the blaze in my belly ever higher, the pleasure coiling, spiraling high and higher still.

I was a falcon in the wind, riding the thermal of sex and power, climbing higher and higher, wings outspread, inhibitions forgotten? Damn if I didn't fly too close to the sun.

Just like Icarus, the fire of that glowing unattainable ball of pleasure flared, the wax holding my wings together melted, and with the stars falling from the sky to flit at the edges of my vision I plunged. Falling, falling, falling from such unearthly heights, I convinced myself for a split second that falling was all there was and that falling was all there would ever be until with a mighty devastating crash, I hit the warm bathwater state of that unending river of afterglow and came back to my senses slowly.

What I came back to, was Oz's hands low on my hips, fingers wrapped around to my ass, his body still fitted inside mine despite the impossible angle I lay in, heels at my sides, head between his feet, the tops of my thighs slightly screaming and buzzing with the stretch.

I panted, muscles still spasmodic with little aftershocks as I panted, reaching blindly in front of me. Oz's hands left my hips, tangled with mine and we pulled me upright again, both of us breathless, both of us laughing as Everleigh let out a pleasure-filled wail of her own release and both Narcos and Driller cheered.

There was the clap of hands and Oz and I exchanged a look and burst out into a gale of laughter at the audacity of those two high-fiving each other over their girlfriend's orgasm.

To be fair, it was a well-earned celebration.

31

*O*z...

Fuck, the weekend was too short. All too soon it was Sunday fucking morning and we had to head back to the city. To the maze of rage and pain with its endless twists and curves that even Ellie with all her book smarts couldn't predict and me with all my street smarts, I just couldn't seem to navigate.

It was an oil slicked street fresh after a rain, or worse – a street full of grass clippings. Dangerous as fuck to ride and unpredictable the outcome, and I fuckin' hated that I couldn't hedge my bets. The only thing I could do was stick to the rule of the street and be and act impervious to all the bullshit.

I felt like I could do that now. I felt like I had to. One of us had to be the rock and my Ellie had already taken more than the brunt of it, more than her fair share.

"You alright?" she asked, eyeing me, as she shrugged into the straps to hold her easel with its still, slightly slick in places canvas to her back.

She wasn't done with the painting, but she was close, and it was straight fire. Something that looked like it needed to hang on a gallery wall somewhere.

"I'm good, babe. How about you?"

"Could use about a week more of this, but I'm alright. Better, now." She took one more wistful look at the cabin where Driller locked up behind us and I smiled.

"You're welcome to come back anytime," Narcos called from where he sat astride his bike, Everleigh climbing on the back behind him.

"We're all good," Driller called, trotting up to us. Ellie got on behind me and settled on.

Driller flung a leg over his ride and Ellie called out, "Thank you, you guys. Really, I mean it. This weekend has meant the world to me. I'll be forever grateful."

"Think nothing of it," Narcos said and started his bike. We all started up and just before letting out his clutch and rolling out he yelled back over his shoulder, "Welcome to the family!"

Ellie covered her smile with the bandana I loaned her for the ride out here and back and eyes sparkling with joy behind the clear lenses of her safety glasses, we hit the road.

The ride back was an easy one and almost went by too fast. All too soon Driller, Narcos and Everleigh split off from our small pack with a wave, taking their exit for home and it was just me and Ellie, crossing the expanse of the Chesapeake Bay Bridge – Indigo City looming on the east shore of the bay, waiting for us to come home. With every quarter mile that passed beneath the bike's tires, the gravity of our situation and the shitshow we were riding back into weighed me down just that little bit more.

It was okay, though. I'd had my much-needed rest and I was ready to carry this burden to the finish line. Looking at Ellie's pensive and pinched look in my side-view mirror only deepened my resolve, carving it into the bedrock of my being.

We pulled up to the curb two doors down from her place where there was parking and I shut off the bike. She immediately climbed off with a loud groan and I was with her on that one. It was a long hard ride, even if it was a good one with fair skies.

She took off her helmet and up ended it while I pulled down my bandana. Her safety glasses went into the bowl of her overturned lid while I got up, joints creaking a little more than they used to, so I could get her bag for her.

She gave a heavy sigh, and pulled the cover from off her nose and mouth and I could see it already, all over her beautiful face, the lines of worry, the stress; it was already settling in. Whether she wore it with grace or not, it still sent a pang through my chest at the sight of it.

"Stay with me," she said abruptly. "I don't want you to go."

I sighed and did the hardest thing I'd ever had to do and said, "I ain't got no clean uniforms for work or nothin'. I gotta go home."

She looked dejected but nodded her understanding.

I sighed and pulled her close, kneading the back of her neck with my fingertips as I pressed lips to her forehead.

"Then ride safe and text me as soon as you get there," she said. "I'll turn my phone on."

I felt my shoulders drop and said, "You know what? Fuck it. I ain't gotta be in until late. I'll go home, do some laundry and be back in a couple of hours. You good with that?"

She looked up at me and the light in her eyes told me all I needed to know. Yeah, she was more than good with that.

"Okay," she said, and sounded much stronger.

"Let's get you inside and off the street," I murmured and I walked her to her door. She dug out her keys from her jacket pocket and let herself in.

"Don't open it for no one but me, mmkay?"

"Okay."

I leaned down and kissed her soundly and with a whole lotta reluctance, let her go inside, handing off her bag once she crossed the threshold.

"See you soon," she said and I nodded.

"Real soon," I promised.

I went home, texted her as soon as I got in, and got my laundry going. I shot a text to Driller and Narcos and let 'em know the eagle had landed and Ellie was safe and sound at home. A few cursory texts back and forth giving each other a ration of shit and I sighed, hauling my ass into a hot shower to shave the mountain man Steve look off my head and face so I could feel somewhat human again.

My phone rang mid-way through shaving my head and it was Youngblood's ringtone. I answered, putting it on speaker and said, "Yeah, yo, what's up my man?"

"Are you in the bathroom?" he demanded.

"Yeah, yeah, just shaving my head, not taking a shit or nothing. We may be close but we're not *that* close."

"Fuck no we're not, you save that shit for your butt buddy, Golden."

"Ha, ha – fuck you, dude. So, what's up?"

"This Little Havana thing this coming weekend, you good to handle it or you want to pass the baton?"

"Shit," I sighed. "Ah, boy – with everything going on it skated clean outta my mind, but I got it my man."

"You sure?"

"Yeah. It's my thing, I'll follow through."

"You sure you're good, because –"

"Yes!" I insisted. "I'm good, I'll make some calls before I head back over to Ellie's."

"Oh, it's like that now, is it?" he asked, and I could hear the devilish grin over the line.

"Ain't nowhere near whipped as you, brother."

"Ha, yeah right – welcome to the club, my brother."

"Man, I already been in the club."

"Not this one. So, what's it like to be *in loooove?*"

"Man, don't ever say it like that again, why don't you go fuck your woman if you need a reminder?"

He laughed outright and I shook my head at my reflection. "A'ight, I'ma hang up now, I got shit to do."

I tapped the icon to end the call to him still laughing. It was fair enough, after all the shit I been giving the lot of 'em gettin' themselves ball and chained.

Ellie was different. So very different from any other woman I'd been with before. I sighed and rinsed my razor in the sink and took a good look at myself in the mirror. She softened all my hard edges. Okay, well, not *all of them*, but a good majority of 'em and once upon a time I thought that made a dude weak.

I'd been wrong, though. Before this whole thing, before Ellie – I was only living half a life. Together we were strong as fuck, and I intended we should stay that way.

I played a couple rounds of a shoot 'em up on my console while my clothes finished drying so the load I had in the wash could go in and the time just fucking dragged mercilessly. I shot a few text messages back and forth to my girl, keeping her updated and she did likewise.

I did laundry, she got her painting out of one easel and onto her main one at home. I showered, she showered. I played a stupid video game, she made some of her fancy tea. I couldn't wait to see her, she couldn't wait either and was on the couch with a book, just waiting on me.

That felt good. Incredibly good, actually, and I looked around this shithole apartment, this half-lived existence and wanted more. A lot more.

I packed up as much of my shit as I could carry in one load and headed back over. When she answered the door, her eyes widened in surprise.

"Are you moving in?" she asked.

"Yeah. You got a problem with that?" She blinked and looked pensive for a moment and opened the door wide enough for me to pass through with my big duffel bag and extra gym bag.

"Nope."

"Good," I said and stepped inside.

She shut the door behind me and said, "Don't you have a lease?"

I shook my head. "Month to month."

"What about your furniture and stuff?" she asked.

"Don't give a shit."

"Oh, damn." She looked a little disappointed and I laughed.

"Why?"

"I like your bed better."

I grinned. "That we can keep, then."

"Okay, good. Let's put your stuff away."

And that was that. Just like that. It was the easiest transition I think I'd ever made in my life and she genuinely seemed one hundred percent committed and cool with it as she knelt on her bedroom floor and shifted things around in her dresser to make room for my socks and underwear.

"You're kind of amazing, you know that?" I asked, sticking a hanger in the top of one of my tee shirts.

"And you're kind of a clothes horse," she said dryly.

I laughed. "Oh, she's got jokes!"

She smiled faintly and murmured, "She's got jokes."

"You know that Little Havana block party is this weekend," I said.

"That's right," she said chewing her bottom lip as she put a bunch of my undershirts in a drawer. "You still want to go to that with me? I mean, have me there?"

"Yup. I mean, I been thinking about it."

"Yeah?"

"We ain't got shit to be ashamed about, right?"

She looked a touch startled and shook her head. "No! I mean, you don't feel like I am, do you?"

"Nope. Not at all. I'm just sayin' that what we do or don't do ain't none of these motherfuckers' business, but at the same time, we ain't gotta be runnin' scared neither. Who gives a shit what people think? Mmkay? We know the truth. The people closest to us know the truth, and that's all that matters. Am I right?"

She thought about it, the wheels turning for an exceptionally long amount of time and as much as I loved her for thinking everything through, the wait liked to drive me nuts. Finally, she reached the same conclusion I had by nodding slowly at first before picking up speed, the motion becoming resolute.

"You're right," she said. "You're absolutely right."

"Fuck them motherfuckers," I said, and she smiled and nodded.

"Fuck those motherfuckers," she agreed and it was adorable coming from her.

"You hungry?" she asked.

"You cookin'?" I asked.

"Actually, I was thinking about ordering Thai from that place I took you to. You're still dressed, will you pick it up if I do?"

"Absolutely."

Life was gonna get good if we had more nights like this and not less, and I was determined to make that happen.

32

*E*lka...

The week went by in a blur, and I admit to some difficulty with our somewhat mismatching schedules. I would get up in the morning and Oz would insist on getting up with me and would take me to work. He didn't like the idea of me taking public transit anymore. Once he would drop me off, he would either return to our apartment and would sleep a little more, or he would go off to the gym to get a workout in.

At two he would text me every day that he got to work safe and he would see me at home.

I would work, and depending on if I could or not, would catch a ride home with one of my coworkers headed that way. On the one occasion I couldn't get a ride, and I'd told Oz? I'd stepped out to a patrol car waiting for me and a couple of officers on their meal break ready to take me home.

I have no idea how Oz arranged that, and I honestly didn't want to know. I was deathly afraid it would get him into some kind of trouble, and I didn't want that for him at all. If anything, I wanted to be the least troublesome thing in his life, right now. I already felt like I caused him so much grief.

When he would come home late at night, he would usually find me painting or on the couch, curled up with a book. At least once, maybe twice, he found me fast asleep with the book that was supposed to be in my lap on the floor.

Once, I woke up to him carrying me to bed. Once, I woke up the next morning to my alarm, cuddled up against his nice warm body and I couldn't tell you how I got there.

Today was the big day of the Cuban block party thing he was volunteering for and with a change of clothes in a small gym bag, he'd left early.

He had told me to open the door for Everleigh and the girls and that Yale would give me a ride later but wouldn't tell me why the girls were coming. Just that he figured we could all get ready together here.

In my tiny shoe closet of an apartment? Wasn't there anyplace better?

I was going through my closet trying to decide on just what to wear when the knock fell at my door. I looked through what my sister and I had always called the spy-dee hole and caught the crown of all of that gorgeously dyed auburn hair that was a familiar trait of Everleigh's.

I opened the door and she squealed happily, for all that she had never really spoken in my presence and threw her arms around my neck in a joyous hug like she hadn't seen me in absolutely forever. Never mind that we'd only seen each other just last week.

"Hi!" a bubbly little blonde cried from just behind her, another redhead next to her wearing hippy glasses clutching a white cane for the blind.

"Hi," the redhead called, without seeing me, just turning her head in a vague notion of where I might be.

"Hi," I exclaimed half-dubiously.

"I'm Aly, this is my best friend Dawnie, we're here to help you get ready."

"Did Oz just seriously send…" I faltered and Dawnie grinned.

"A blind chick as your fashion consultant?" she asked. "Yes, yes he did. Guess that doesn't account much for your style, does it?"

I was taken aback at her abrasiveness, and then she grinned wider and I realized that she and Oz shared the same dry, sarcastic brand of humor. I laughed and Aly rolled her eyes.

"No, that's all me," Aly declared. "Lead the way into your bedroom, lady. Let's get you all dolled up!"

Everleigh nodded happily and looped her arm through mine and practically dragged me into my own apartment, a woman on a mission.

That's when I spotted him bringing up the rear – the city prosecutor who always seemed somehow bigger when his picture was in the newspaper. He raised his eyebrows and smiled and said, "I'm Yale, I'll be your chauffer this afternoon."

"Hi, Yale, I'm sorry," I said and he laughed and shook his head.

"Absolutely think nothing of it." His dark eyes sparkled with good humor and I smiled back.

"Help yourself to the couch – um, sorry I don't have T.V.," I called as the girls herded me up the hallway and back into my room. Everleigh sat me on the edge of my bed and Aly immediately went to my closet whisking things along the rod. Dawnie tapped and swung her cane getting the lay of the land and dropped down next to me on the bed.

She leaned over into me and said, "Not to sound all rapey, but with these two? It's better if you just sit back and let it happen."

"That sounds exceedingly rapey when you put it that way," I said.

She shrugged and said, "I gotta work on my delivery, I know this about myself."

I laughed and watched as Everleigh and Aly went through my closet wrinkling their noses at this or that and contemplating the other. Finally, they reached the far back, the dregs of my dresses that weren't really things that I could or would wear on the regular and Aly lit up, mouth dropping open and pulled whatever it was out so Everleigh could see it.

The quiet woman gave an excited peal of laughter and they both turned with the bright turquoise retro 40s dress in their hands. A consignment shop find that I wore for a June Cleaver Halloween costume a couple of years ago. The dress had fit like a dream! Hugging my upper body, the skirt flaring at the hips with the help of a light petticoat, and I had hated to part with it, but at the same time, I had never had occasion to wear it again. At least, apparently, until now.

"I think this, with some victory rolls and nix the apron because wrong era," she tossed the frilly white 1950s apron into the bottom of my closet, " and finish the look off with a bold red lip and Oz'll be tripping over his own tongue," Aly declared. Everleigh nodded happily and enthusiastically beside her, looking at me with a sparkle of excitement in her green eyes.

"Should I be intimidated?" I asked, leaning slightly into Dawnie perched beside me.

"Are they looking at you like you're a snack?"

"Little bit," I confessed.

"Run."

"Dawnie!" Aly cried.

"Don't you Dawnie me! I wasn't born blind, bitch. I remember that look."

I smiled and chuckled as Everleigh came over to me with the dress holding it out to me. I took it and asked, "You want me to dig out the stockings that go with this? I think I have them in a drawer here somewhere."

"They got the line in the back?" Aly asked.

"Yeah, I think so, if I remember right."

"Ooo, yaaaas."

Everleigh and Aly set to work on me. I dressed in the pinup style dress and smoothed the skirt, slipping my feet into the sling backed peep-toe pumps that my sister and I had found with the dress.

Everleigh brought a chair in from the dining room and she and Aly set to work on my hair and makeup in a flurry of activity that left me blushing, unused to being taken care of like that.

I felt like my hair had been bobby pinned to within an inch of its life, but there was no denying, I looked really damn good when I looked in my bedroom mirror.

"Oh, my God, you guys, I think I'm gonna cry," I said.

"Don't you dare!" Dawnie cried. "They just did your makeup."

"Right?" Aly asked, wrinkling her nose, but she looked well-pleased.

Everleigh raised her eyebrows, looking amused and took up her macramé shoulder bag straight out of the nineteen-seventies and tugged on the shoulder of Aly's shirt.

"Right, our turn. Bathroom?"

"Across the hall," I said turning this way and that in front of my mirrored, sliding closet doors. "Mind the paintings!" I warned.

Aly and Everleigh trouped across the hall and a minute later Aly called, "Um, Elka?"

My heart sank, worried what I was about to walk into, a knocked over canvas, a solvent spill? What I hadn't expected was to walk in and see

Everleigh standing in front of the painting I had finished up over the week from the cabin trip, her hands over her mouth and her eyes glistening.

She turned to me, eyes wide and brought her trembling hands from her mouth and pointed at me and then pointed to the painting. I was surprised when she asked me, "Is this how you see me?" I couldn't recall her ever having spoken to me before.

"Well, um, yeah. I mean, that's what I saw, how I saw it in the moment… I maybe took a few creative liberties."

"Can I have it?" she asked.

"Sure," I said with a faint smile. "I didn't exactly have any other plans for it. Consider it a thank you for getting me out of the city when I needed it most."

She rushed me and wrapped me up in a great big hug and I laughed and hugged her back.

"It should be dry, let me check it while you all do your thing and let me get back across the hall. I don't want to leave Dawnie alone.

"Dawnie is just fine!" she called from my bedroom and I smiled.

Everleigh joined Aly in the bathroom where Aly had already plugged in her wand and was starting in on her hair.

Thirty minutes later, they were ready, and I had my French easel loaded with a new canvas, a satchel with some drawing pencils, pigments, and the out-of-era apron shoved in the top to protect my dress.

Yale had made himself at home on my couch and stood, turning, a smile lighting up his eyes when he looked at Aly who looked beautiful in her sunflower spangled sundress. Dawnie looked like a hippy chick in her light and airy patchwork skirt and airy evergreen silk peasant blouse. And then there was Everleigh in her strappy leather sandals and white, ankle length country-perfect sundress.

We were each uniquely different but no less beautiful in our own styles, even if mine felt borrowed.

"Wow, you ladies look incredible. Shall we?" Yale held out his arm for Aly who took it.

"Yes, we shall," she said with an impish smile.

The love that radiated from them both was enough to warm the coldest of hearts and I think, even the blind woman knew. Could hear it in their voices, feel it like warmth from a hearth. I brought up the rear, Everleigh clutching the sides of her painting, holding it out from herself carefully as if it was still wet, which a few places weren't *quite* set, but the paint layer was definitely stable nonetheless.

Yale led us to a big black Escalade parked down the row and chirped the locks. They disengaged with a slight thump, and he opened up the rear cargo area for me which was pristine and empty.

I stowed my gear inside and he hit a button on his remote, the tailgate smoothly coming down and closing.

"Thanks," I murmured.

"You're welcome."

The ride to Little Havana was full of chatter between Aly, Dawnie, and Yale. The latter trading good-natured barbs back and forth that had me and Everleigh howling in delighted laughter. Both were master social chess players, equally quick-witted and equally hilarious.

He parked as close as he could get to the closed-off street, which was still several blocks away. When we got out of the Escalade, he looked down at my heels and frowned. I smiled as I retrieved my satchel and easel with its freshly mounted canvas. A larger one than I had dared take to the cabin on the back of a motorcycle.

"It's a bit of a walk," he said. "You sure you're going to be okay in those?"

"What?" I looked down at my shoes. "Oh, yeah. I think Mia and I inherited the same genes when it comes to heels, they've never bothered either of us much. Stilettos or sneakers, it's all the same to us… or was for her."

He raised his eyebrows and shut the back hatch, eyes still fixed on my pumps.

"I'll take your word for it," he said and Dawnie smirked from the curb, her hand in the crook of Aly's elbow.

"Adding a shoe fetish to your repertoire, prosecutor?" she asked, amused.

"Hey, you watch yourself," he said sharply and though he smiled his eyes held worry.

"Duh, blind chick, and sorry about that," she said.

"It's fine."

I went over by Aly and Everleigh and made a face like 'eek' and Aly smiled, mouthing 'later' at me.

"Nothing needs to be said later," Yale declared behind me. "I just very much so like to keep my private life private and you all know that. You never know who might be listening out here."

I thought it a little paranoid, but then again, I would absolutely die of embarrassment if any of my colleagues discovered what I'd gotten up to at the cabin. We all had our kinks, I guess, and they really were nobody's business but our own.

I dismissed it out of hand as we traversed one block then the next. Music and delicious smells swept along by the summer breeze enveloped us the nearer we drew to the celebration. There were those police saw horse looking barricades up across the road at the next block, freshly painted a navy blue with reflective tape on the legs and to either side of 'Indigo City PD' that was stenciled across the crossbar in silver.

An opening had been left between the stations and an Indigo Knight stood next to it with an off-duty, but still in uniform, Indigo City police volunteer. As we got closer, we recognized the Knight as Backdraft.

"Hey, Backdraft!" Aly called for Dawnie's benefit. Dawnie's chin rose slightly and a faint smile graced her lips.

"Batting for the other team today, huh?" she asked him and the cop beside him snorted.

"Hey, I liked playing 'cops and robbers' when I was a kid, it's nice to revisit every once in a while." He stepped aside so we could pass, and we slipped beyond the barriers.

"Have fun," he said to me with a wink, eying my easel and satchel.

"Thanks, I will. Have you seen Oz?" I asked.

"His shift just ended, I think he went to go change to actually join the party."

"Privileges of putting the security for this shindig together, huh?" Yale asked, grinning.

"Yeah, he took first shift, but can't say I blame him. This is his jam, after all."

"He's actually taking two," I said, feeling the need to defend him. "He doesn't get to drink – he's closing things down at the end, too."

"My bad," Backdraft said, holding up his hands in gentle surrender. "Didn't mean anything by it."

I nodded and looked down the block. The street was lined to either side with classic cars, their rich paint jobs sparkling in the sun. Each one from the nineteen-fifties, beautifully restored in fabulous colors. People wandered up and down the aisle between them that must have spanned an entire block of the three-block length of Ninth Avenue they had closed down. At the far end was the stage, a live band playing

Salsa music, a dance floor in front of it with figures on it, barely discernable through the thick crowd on the street.

Past the line of classic cars, they had the next side street blocked off in either direction with rows of portable bathrooms. Portable round sinks connected to garden hoses were perched in front of the restrooms, step on a lever at ground level and the water would turn on. Big trash cans on wheels were filling quickly with the rough paper towels provided, and volunteers would regularly take the trash bin past the portable bathrooms down Oak Street to the waiting garbage truck to empty.

It was a clever system, and I smiled and nodded at one of the teens wearing a juvenile detention center work vest who was refilling the paper towels. He smiled back and gave me a nod and seemed somehow grateful for the small recognition. It was a good way to work off some of his community service hours and no doubt, it was Oz's doing that the teens were here with trash bags in hand and those grabber stick things, intermittently picking up litter.

Non-food vendors were next, a whole block of them, selling all kinds of wares. Dolls and baskets, hand-painted hand-fans, traditional clothing, jewelry, baskets, paintings, photography, you name it, it was there. I paused at the booth with the paintings and prints and the gentleman who was running it came over my way.

"Ahhhh, a fellow artist, I see!" he smiled and I smiled back shyly, biting my bottom lip.

"I dabble," I confessed, and Everleigh stepped in front of me holding out her painting. She looked back at me over her shoulder and rolled her eyes dramatically. I laughed.

"You did this?" the booth owner asked, eyebrows going up in surprise.

"Um, yeah, I have a degree in fine arts. Work at the museum up town doing restoration work."

"Noooo waayyy, really?"

"Yeah," I grinned, and he looked over the painting with a practiced eye. He handed it back to Everleigh who beamed at me.

"Hey, Ev! There's Narcos," Aly called.

Yale asked me, "You good?"

"Yeah! I'll catch up."

They wandered on without me and the vendor introduced himself, "I'm Silverio Pérez." He held out his hand.

I took it and said, "Elka Köhler, it's nice to meet you, Silverio."

"Likewise, likewise! Always nice to meet a fellow aficionado of the brush."

"These are really beautiful," I said looking over the paintings he had on display. "When were you last in Cuba?"

He smiled faintly and said, "My parents put me on a raft when I was two. I'm a first-generation refugee."

"Oh, I'm so sorry, I thought…"

"Nah, my paintings are mostly from photos and imagination."

"Well, I would have never guessed," I told him honestly.

"That does my heart good to hear you say it," he said tipping his straw panama hat in my direction. He was handsome, in a distinguished sort of way, with silver just beginning to grace his temples, a little heavier in his goatee that offset his angular jawline.

He wore a Cuban style guayabera shirt in a light peach over khaki pants and a pair of loafers with no socks. In fact, that seemed to be the almost uniform dress code for the Cuban men wandering by over the age of thirty or so. It was an attractive look.

We chatted a bit more and with a polite farewell, I took myself deeper into the festival's fray, alone this time – though I didn't feel unsafe at all, not in the slightest. There was a good turnout of uniformed officers and Indigo Knights alike. I just couldn't seem to spot Oz among the crowd.

"Hey, Elka! Is that you!?"

I turned to the nearest food truck and grinned. "Enrique, hi!"

He had a brisk business going so he couldn't stop what he was doing, but he held out his hands almost beseeching and put them both over the center of his chest as though he'd been struck by Cupid's arrow.

"You look great!" he called out and I laughed.

"Why, thank you!"

"Come see me later!" he called.

"Better watch it, now!" Oz's familiar voice came from just over my left shoulder. I jumped as his hands settled on my hips and he called out to Enrique, "Might get the idea you be hittin' on my woman!"

"Oh, man! I been tryin' to! She's loyal though! You got a good one, there!"

Oz laughed and waved him off and Enrique got back to work.

"Wait, he has?" I asked, confused.

"Probably," Oz agreed.

"I had no idea," I said, mystified.

Oz laughed and turned me around in his grasp and looked me over giving a low appreciative whistle.

"I think you found yourself a signature style," he said. "You look damn good."

I blushed faintly and mumbled, "I wore it for Halloween a couple of years ago when I went as June Cleaver. It was Mia's idea. Aly found it in the back of my closet."

"Well Aly's on to something, you look beautiful, babe."

"Thank you." I took him in.

"You look amazing yourself."

He did, too. A navy-blue ribbed tank top with a short-sleeved white shirt with tiny navy-blue dots. He wore the short-sleeved shirt open over the tank which was neatly tucked in to a pair of matching navy chinos. The cuff of which had been rolled up slightly over grey suede loafers with no socks.

A white trilby with a navy band around it and gray accents in the weave of the cloth completed the look, and the overall effect curled my toes.

"I was about to go have a cigar with some of the boys from work," he said.

"Okay, lead the way."

He took my hand and we crossed the street to an area roped off in front of a narrow Spanish-colonial style apartment building. Oz took a seat midway up the steps of the front stoop and pulled a cigar tube from the front pocket of his shirt.

I pulled the easel off my back and set it up, right in front of him, struck with inspiration.

"Hold that thought!" I declared and he blinked.

"What?"

"I want to paint you, so don't do anything yet."

Conveniently, one of those green power boxes was located in the planter strip between the sidewalk and the curb, just off to one side a little further than I initially would have liked, but it could make for a unique composition.

I got set up, tied on my apron, poised my pencil over the canvas and said, "Okay, action!"

He shook his head smiling and pulled his cigar out, did whatever it was you did with cigars, pulled a lighter out of his pocket and putting the cylinder of tobacco to his lips, lit up.

It was perfect, I sketched furiously; roughing out the image I wanted to paint on the canvas before loading my pallet with paints.

"What have we got going on here?" Skids called, joining Oz on the stoop with a cigar of his own.

Coco stopped beside me, and I looked up and smiled. She raised her eyebrows and looked over what I had on the canvas with a nod. I went back to loading the canvas with paint, easing into my happy place, listening to the music playing from the stage, the light summer breeze rustling the leaves of the sycamore tree providing me shade from the punishing summer sun.

"Hey, babe, can I move yet?" Oz called after a while and I called back, "Yeah, go ahead!"

He got up and made to come over and I frowned at him. "It's not done yet! You can't come look."

"Sor-ry! I'm gonna head over to the food trucks and get us something to eat, you know what you want?" he asked.

"Surprise me," I answered distractedly, working on some edge of sky.

"Copy that," he said and wandered off.

He came back with an overloaded Cuban sandwich, which of course was to die for. I stopped long enough to eat, suddenly famished and asked, "What time is it, anyway?"

"Something like two o'clock," Oz declared.

"Oh, wow. No wonder I'm hungry."

"Yeah, but are you *happy*, though?"

"You know what?" I said. "I am. I really am."

He smiled down at me and leaned over, stealing a kiss. I giggled lightly and said, "No peeking, yet."

"Alright, alright. You better hurry up though. I want a dance with my woman before I have to go back on shift."

"I think that can be arranged," I murmured.

I finished eating and Skids and Coco swung back by. Coco tucked a flower behind my ear and offered to watch my stuff for me while Oz and I took a spin around the dance floor. I thanked her and for a while it was just Oz and me.

"You having a good day?" he asked.

"A very good day," I agreed. "Sorry if I'm so boring."

"Nah, you're never that. I'm glad you're having a good time."

"It's a beautiful culture and the vibes are really good, everyone is super proud of their heritage and so willing to share it with the rest of the community. It's a really beautiful thing that's going on here."

"The Cuban people are a passionate and resourceful people," he said.

"Absolutely, and it's really carried over and showcased here. I mean, one of the cars I passed earlier? I heard them talking about how it didn't have an engine when the guy bought the shell, and so he improvised and adapted a boat motor to power it when he couldn't find one."

"Ah, yeah, just like they do back home," Oz said.

"Are you originally from Cuba?" I asked. Realizing we had never talked much about his early childhood.

"Naw, I was born in Virginia. My mom, she was American. It was my pops who was from Cuba. His parents were smart and jumped ship with him before things got real fucked up. He and my mom were high school sweethearts."

"Were?"

"Yeah, he died when I was sixteen. Knifed on the way home from work over five dollars in his pocket."

"Oh, my God! I'm so sorry."

He made a dismissive face. "Don't be. Don't get me wrong, I loved my pops, but he was a flawed man. Drank too much and sometimes hit my mom. Ah, boy. She's an iron lady, my mom."

"Yeah?"

"A house with two teenage girls and a teenage son, husband murdered, cut down to only one income overnight? Yeah. She didn't take no back talk from none of us, I'll tell you what."

He chuckled.

"What?" I asked, a slow smile spreading my lips at his expression. He'd thought of something in particular, it was plain to see.

"Right, so my mom is short, only something like five foot three, right?"

"Uh huh."

"So this one time, when I was like seventeen, I was at the kitchen sink and I can't remember exactly what I said, but I was back talkin' her somethin' fierce. We were arguing about something dumb – I really can't remember, but she –" he started laughing and I smiled bigger, patiently waiting him out.

"She pulled the stepladder over and got up on it and man, that slap came down from outer space – *pow!* Right across my cheek, like hand-print raising up and everything. And she gets down off that stepladder and was like 'good, now go put some Vaseline on that and get your little ass out to that school bus on time boy, or I'm gonna make you walk.' She was *not* playin'."

"Oh, my God!" I choked on a laugh picturing the whole thing.

"Yeah, it's pretty funny now, wasn't so awesome back then. Man, *all* them kids made fun of me that mornin' and I gotta say, I deserved it."

"That's *crazy!*" I declared. "My mom would have never dreamed of doing something like that, although I'm pretty sure Mia and I more than earned something like that a few times."

"See," he spun me out and back in, "that's the difference from ol' white folks families and black folk. Black folk just don't care. You earn an ass whoopin' you gonna get your little ass whipped. Southern mommas like *my* momma, they just don't play."

"I'd imagine not," I said. "Especially becoming a single mother so suddenly like that."

"True. Right up 'til then, it'd always been my dad to hand out the punishments."

"Sounds like your mom was doing the best she could."

"Oh definitely, she was. Ain't nobody denyin' that. I got nothin' but mad love and respect for my mom. She's downright amazing."

"I can't wait to meet her someday," I said.

"My sisters drive me nuts, but there ain't no reason we can't ride down on some weekend soon."

"Weather is supposed to start turning, soon," I mentioned.

He gave a one-shouldered shrug. "So, we rent a car for the weekend. Ain't no big deal."

"I hadn't thought of that," I said. "That's not a bad idea."

The song ended and we broke apart to politely applaud. The next number was much faster, and I begged off.

"Sure, you want I can get you something to drink?"

"That would be amazing, see you back over by my painting?"

"Yeah, yeah, I'll be right over there."

"Okay, cool."

He gave me a quick kiss and I smiled, drifting through the crowd back the way we'd come. I was just nearing the electrical box when I heard my name, "Elka! Elka Köhler!"

I sighed in frustration and turned, scowling hard as Anthony Rivers, the blogger who had accosted me at work came trotting up.

"Looks like you went out of town last weekend," he said with an oily smile.

"In case you hadn't noticed it was in an attempt to avoid you," I said dully.

He smirked and I frowned harder.

"Can't run forever," he said.

"Don't have to talk to you, don't want to talk to you, how about you just leave me alone?" I demanded.

His grin turned nasty and I rolled my eyes. Hopefully Oz would get back to me sooner rather than later.

33

$\mathcal{O}$z...

I heard the slap as I was threading through the crowd, halfway back to Ellie. There was a universal *'Oooooh'* from the onlookers and so you *know* that had to hurt. I sighed and didn't even imagine it could have been her but then I heard her voice rising in anger.

"I've asked several times to be left alone by you and now I'm telling you! Leave. Me. Alone! I don't want to talk to you. I won't answer any of your rude, sexist, and inappropriate questions – take the hint and *fuck off!*"

A cheer went up as I pushed through the crowed and some dude was standing back from Ellie, a tape recorder in one hand and the other pressed to the side of his face. The crowd was cheering, and Skids was holding Ellie back, a couple of the uniformed officers on OT blocking the side streets were coming up in tow behind some kid someone had sent their way for backup.

Shit. One of 'em was Bartle, a Blue Templar and a real fuckin' asshole.

"What's going on here?" he demanded as the crowd parted, and he stepped up behind Ellie.

He took a look at dude as she turned to me. I passed my drinks off to some random chick who was a bystander and went to my girl. Ellie immediately huddled against me, miserable.

"Did she assault you?" Bartle asked the dude and the dude made a great show of wobbling his jaw back and forth and nodding miserably.

Bartle brought out the cuffs. "Whoa, hey now – that ain't really necessary is it?"

"No! You need to arrest that guy! He put his hands on her first!" a feisty little Cuban lady with a heavy New York accent barked. "She was just defending herself!"

Ellie held to me tighter as a real dustup ensued. A bunch of the bystanders all started talking at once as I put heads together with Skids and asked what the hell had happened. He said he didn't know, he was over by Ellie's paints, on his phone, when the shit went down. The feisty New York Cuban honey gave me the rundown, said dude had grabbed Ellie's wrist and shoved his recorder in her face, said a bunch of shit that would make her mamma blush and Ellie had been cringing back from him and finally lost it. She'd open-handed slapped the creep and the rest I already knew – sort of.

"He's the reporter that came to my office," she mumbled miserably, tears streaming down her face.

"Shit."

Yale was here, and he was arguing with Bartle who had his hands up.

"That's not my job," he said. "She hit him, that's assault, the rest is all up to you guys."

Yale had his hands on his hips, staring at the cracked asphalt, a scowl on his face as he thought furiously, but I could see the way this was about to go from a mile off. Bartle, the fucking prick.

"Coco, go find Chrissy," I ordered and Coco bobbed her head and trotted off without a second glance in search of the former defense attorney who, until she'd flipped sides, had been the best in the business. Skids was on the same page as me, nodding as he ran through the series of events over the phone.

"Baby, these here officers are gonna arrest you," I said calmly and Elka's eyes went wide as she stared up at me. "Don't you say anything to anyone about nothing, you hear me?"

She nodded her head a little too fast.

"I mean it. Nothing at all, to anyone. You wait for me or Chrissy. You understand me?"

"Yes," she said, her voice mournful as Bartle hooked her up. She jumped and winced as he slapped the cuffs on her and I scowled.

"Hey!" I barked. "Take it easy, man. Jesus."

"I don't tell you what to do with perps once I hand 'em off at the jail, Jones. You don't tell me how to do my job out here," Bartle grated. He was spoilin' for a fight, but I wasn't about to give it to him.

Elka looked back over her shoulder looking lost as they led her up the street. I looked back at Yale who thrust his chin at me and said, "Go, I'll cover." I nodded and trotted up the street after my girl, Chrissy materializing out of the crowd blocking the path of the two dipshits that had her in custody.

One of the off-duty cops was getting a statement from the mother-fucker she'd clocked, Skids standing by and listening to everything.

"You'll get your chance at her in the courtroom prosecutor."

"You mean I'll get my chance at *you*, officer. I'm Ms. Köhler's defense attorney. Elka, as your attorney, I am advising you to speak with no one.

"Okay," Elka said, fresh tears leaking from her eyes. Backdraft and Lil appeared behind me, flanking me to either side.

"Come on," Lil said grabbing my elbow. "I'll get her bail."

"Thank you," I breathed. I didn't know how I was gonna swing that. "You'll get it all back, I promise."

"I don't have to worry about that, Oz. Let's just get her out before she has to go through too much of the process – I mean, I'm not sure how all that works."

How it worked, was for a simple assault like this, was she would get booked, wait around a while, and a judge would review and set a bond amount remotely. We paid and she got bonded out before she even had to hit the orange overalls.

Lil ordered up an Uber and we got to the jail pretty quick. Just as Bartle was pull in' out the garage, waving at me through the windshield as he turned to go back to his post. I was straight fuckin' steamed but couldn't do shit about it. It was up to the arresting officer's discretion after all, problem was, Bartle didn't fuckin' have none. I was looking forward to the day he passed through my jail under arrest for the dirty dealings I *know* he had a hand in. It was only a matter of time.

Let Karma sort that motherfucker out.

Lil and I trotted down into the garage and went into intake. Miller looked up from behind the counter and frowned.

"What're you doing here?" he demanded, and I felt my shoulders sag with relief.

"Could ask you the same thing."

"I got a kid in college, I'm pulling all the OT I can get."

"Wish I was here on a social call," I said thrusting a chin past him where Elka was being printed.

"Some dumbass reporter got all up in my girl's face, scared the shit out of her, she slapped the holy hell shit out of him and Bartle brought her in."

Miller hung his head, letting it bounce on his shoulders twice. He sighed.

"You know the grind," he said and I nodded.

"Lil and I are here to post bail as soon as you got a number," I said.

"I got you. Why don't you both have a seat over there, I'll see what I can do about expediting the process a little – for *real*," he added as a distracted afterthought.

"What did he mean by that?" Lil asked.

"Usually when we tell a person comin' in we're gonna expedite the process for 'em what we really do is drag our feet. Depends on how much of an asshole they're bein'."

"Charming," she said with a smile.

"A lot of these motherfuckers don't seem to get we ain't a concierge service. We protect and serve the people out there, you get in here it's not supposed to be a trip to club fed. Ain't no camp cupcake up in here. You pass through those doors in cuffs, it's game over. You runnin' with the big dogs, now."

Lil put a hand on my back and rubbed it back and forth comfortingly, giving me a side-hug squeeze.

"I know you're worried about her, but I'm sure everything is going to be fine. Just make sure to give her a lot of extra love when she gets out. Take her home, draw her a hot bath, and make her some tea or something."

"You're the boss," I told her, and she kind of was – at least when it came to the romantic shit. It's how she made her bread and butter, after all. Writin' all them damn books of hers, getting movies made out of them. It's why I didn't think twice or even sweat it when she offered up to pay Ellie's bond, whatever it was. Lillian Banks *made bank*. She had enough to spare and then some and probably wouldn't even miss it while it was gone.

We waited for two hours before Miller came to call us back and knowing how things worked, that was fast as hell. It still took too damn long for my tastes. Ellie sat in the DMV style rows of chairs, handcuffed to the metal frame work on one side as was protocol, twisting in her seat to follow me and Lil with her eyes, expression softly pleading.

I gave her a nod, promising with my gaze that I would be getting her out of here in no time.

Her bond was two-fifty. Not bad at all. Lil paid it with cash from her wallet and we were led back out to wait in the lobby. Around fifteen minutes later, Ellie was buzzed out the security door and she flew right into my arms.

"Not how I ever pictured seeing you at work," she mumbled against my chest and she shuddered in my arms.

"I know that's right," I said disgusted.

"I have my court date," she turned her head so she could look at Lil and said, "Thank you for bailing me out."

"No problem," Lil declared. "Just don't leave the state," she said with a wink.

Ellie sighed. "That's just what I *want* to do right now. I never should have lost my cool. I'm so embarrassed."

"Come on, let's get out of here," I said.

We went out and hoofed it up to street level. Once there, Lil ordered up another Uber to take us back to the festival where I could get my bike and Ellie could get her stuff. Skids said it was at the vendor booth with the guy selling paintings.

"Listen, you ain't got nothing to be embarrassed about," I told her when the car pulled up.

"Except that makeup," Lil chimed in. "Get in the car and we'll get you fixed up."

"Oh, God!" Ellie cried, sniffing and patting her cheeks. "I must look awful."

"A little bit," Lil agreed. "Nothing we can't fix, though."

Lil fussed over Ellie in the back of the Uber, cleaning up her face with makeup wipes from her purse and giving her some fresh powder, eyeliner, and mascara to even things out. By the time we pulled up to the festival, Ellie was mostly back together, and the sun was sinking below the horizon, casting long fingers of shadow as it dipped behind the buildings.

We got out at the main entrance, Yale and Youngblood at the barriers, welcoming us back with glad cries. The rest of the Knights were comin' up the way between the classic cars that were left. Owners still lingering and talking, some closing up their hoods and doors getting ready to take off.

"Thank you!" Lil called back to the driver as he waved us off.

Ellie tucked herself into my side and I put an arm around her shoulders, kissing the top of her hair which was coming undone without her bobby pins to hold it. They'd been taken at the jail. Protocol.

"How you doing?" Skids asked us.

"Embarrassed," Ellie muttered and wouldn't really look at him.

Skids sniffed. "No need to be, not after what he said to you. We got it all on video and his own recording is apt to dime him out."

"Really?"

"Yup. This is a slam dunk," Chrissy said, and she straight had her barracuda game face on. "You got a court date?" she asked.

"One of them." Ellie handed over her sheaf of discharge paperwork from the jail and Chrissy started to immediately devour them, her eyes rushing over the lines of text in a thorough read-through.

Yale sighed. "It's out of my hands on prosecution on this one. I have to recuse myself for obvious reasons – there was no guarantee it would have landed on my desk anyway."

"You're just a cog in the machine like any one of us, man. Don't sweat it," I told him.

"There's a very real possibility that whoever gets it, they'll decline to prosecute," Chrissy said. "If they do, I'll be taking them apart." She shrugged.

"Can you do that?" Ellie asked.

"Do what?" Chrissy asked.

"Work as a defense attorney while also being a prosecutor?" she asked. "Isn't that a conflict of interest or something?"

Chrissy gave her a charmed smile and said, "I can see where you're going with this, and no, I won't get into trouble if that's what you're worried about."

"Okay." Ellie nodded. "If you're sure."

"I'm sure. Thanks for worrying, though." Chrissy winked at her.

"So how about it?" Driller asked as Everleigh rested her head on Narcos' shoulder nearby. "You good to finish the party or are you all partied out?"

Ellie took a deep breath and let it out slow. "I could really use a drink, and something to eat," she said. "Lunch was a long time ago."

"Alright!"

"Yeah!"

The guys and girls of my club put up a rowdy cheer and I pulled my girl's temple against my lips.

"Thatta girl," I said grinning and she looked up at me with an impish smile that was still fragile around the edges and said, "Just feed me."

"You got it."

We had dinner, a few more dances, and wandered on over to the stall with paintings to pick up her stuff.

"Ah, there you are!" the artist guy called out when he spotted Ellie. "I can see where you got your inspiration this time." He produced her easel, all packed up, and her satchel of paints and shit from against one of the legs of his easy-up tent.

"Hey, what up, man. Good lookin' out," I greeted him with a firm handshake.

"Ah, you know; us artists have to stick together," he told me and passed my girl's gear off to me. I hefted both onto one shoulder.

"Silverio Pérez, meet Oz. Oz, this is Silverio," Elka introduced us.

"Nice to meet you, Silverio. Thanks again for hanging onto my girl's stuff."

"Absolutely, anytime. You've got quite a talent, Elka."

Ellie blushed, "Thank you."

"Here, let me give you my card. I'd like to stay in touch. There aren't a lot of other artists that I know. I could always use another person to talk color theory and you said you were a preservationist?"

"I am," she said with a nod.

"I may need help cleaning a painting I have at home. It was supposedly painted by my grandfather and was one of the things my mother brought with us. It meant a great deal to her, but I am afraid time has not been kind to it."

"Absolutely, I'd be willing to take a look." Elka beamed at him. "It's the least I could do."

"Ah, God bless you," he said and wrote his number on the back of one of his business cards, handing it over to her. She slipped it into a pocket of her satchel hanging from my shoulder.

"Thank you. I'll be in touch."

"Are you leaving?" he asked.

"Yeah, man. We gotta get home."

"Well, it was good talking to you. Safe travels."

"Alright, thanks man, we'll see you around."

"I look forward to it," he said with a smile and I took my lady's hand and steered us in the direction of my bike.

"I think you made a new friend," I said with a smile.

"You know," she said, "I think I did, too."

"Not a bad day over all," I said and she made a face like she'd just sucked on a lemon.

"I don't know about all *that*. You didn't get arrested and go to jail," she said.

I nodded and was about to say some smart-ass sarcastic remark but the look on her face stopped me.

"What? What is it?" I asked.

She came to a stop, dragging on my hand a little and I watched them, our hands interlinked, swinging between us, the distance between her body and mine only about a foot and a half but for all intents and purposes, it felt like an entire gulf had just opened up between us and I wanted to bridge that gap real quick.

"It's not going to look badly on you, my getting arrested, is it?" she asked and shifted uncomfortably.

I gave her a half-assed grin. "No, and even if someone wanted to come at me like that, fuck 'em. You were justified in slapping the shit outta that asshole. I just wish you'd thought to kick him in the nuts."

She stifled a laugh behind her hand and tried to school her expression immediately into something more appropriate – whatever that honestly meant.

I closed some of the distance between us and touched the side of her face. She looked at me and I couldn't keep the charmed half-smile off of my face if I wanted to.

"I love you," I said. "And what you did today isn't going to cause me any problems with the department. Even if it did, I'd find something else to do if they wanted to play it that way. You're everything to me. You have to know that."

She stared at me, searching my face, eyes wide and uncertain, looking for any hint of deception, a lie in my voice, a look, I don't know what. I just held still and let the truth radiate from me, let her pick it up with that sense we all had but rarely used.

"You really mean that, don't you?" she asked after a little bit of silence.

"I really mean it," I told her. The dead certainty in my voice clear as day.

I leaned forward and put my lips against hers, kissing her gently. She kissed me back, arms creeping around my neck as the street lights flickered on overhead.

"Let's go home," I murmured and she nodded slowly, gently.

"Let's go home," she agreed.

She tucked herself into the side of me that wasn't laden with her art gear and I put a protective arm around her as we strolled the rest of the way up the side street to my bike on the next block.

I got out my jacket and cut, secured in my locking hard case and peeled my cut off my jacket. I handed her my coat, putting it around her shoulders while my cut was trapped between my knees.

As soon as I had her squared away with my coat and her art stuff, I swung into my cut for the ride. She got on behind me as soon as I pulled around into the street and held on tight for the ride home which was a bit of a brisk one with the cooling temperatures brought on by night and a stiff breeze coming in off the water.

Ellie shivered when she got off the bike and hugged herself.

"First order of business, a nice hot shower."

"I know that's right," I said and took her art gear off of her. "Let me carry that."

I handed her my keys and we paused under the next street lamp so she could find the key to her door on the ring. She took my hand when she found it, her fingers frigid, and we double-timed it the less than half a block to the apartment's door.

She keyed us in the lock, stepping aside so I could get in after her. I shut the door and said, "Go on and handle your art stuff, baby, I'll put some water on for that tea you like and meet you in the shower."

"Okay," she readily agreed.

I went in the kitchen and filled her electric kettle from the tap while I listened to her unbuckle this and unstrap that. She made an impatient noise and an 'ah' of success and I smiled to myself.

"You alright in there?" I called.

"Yeah, just fingers are a bit stiff and he had this knob turned really tight. Everything looks good, though. Minimal shift in the paint layer, and the marks in the corners are easily brushed out."

"Good deal." I set the kettle on its base but didn't switch it on yet.

She made small talk, asking me, "You really liked me in this style of dress?"

"Yeah, I mean it. I think you got a signature look there. It really suits you, you know?"

She was quiet for a moment and finally called back, "I really like it, too. Makes me feel pretty and sassy."

I chuckled.

"I think that sass may be me rubbing off on you some."

"Ha! As far as I'm concerned, it needed to happen. It felt good to stand up to that asshole." She stepped around the corner of the kitchen and leaned a shoulder against the archway, crossing her arms over her stomach.

"Go get in the shower, babe. Go get warm."

"Towels are out, just waiting on you, Princess."

"Oh, you're funny!"

I grabbed a hold of her and she shrieked, laughing, and it was the best sound I'd heard all day. I kissed her soundly as she giggled against my mouth, her fingers still cold, touching the sides of my face as we swayed from our mock little struggle.

"How do you feel about maybe someday becoming Mrs. Jones?" I asked suddenly.

"Are you asking me to marry you?" she asked, face coated in a thick layer of surprise.

"Not yet," I said. "But maybe someday."

"Oh, the thought had crossed your mind?" she asked with a devilish grin.

I gave her one right back. "Just now, yeah."

She laughed.

"Elka Jones doesn't sound half bad. It's got kind of a nice ring to it," she said.

"Damn right it does," I said and pulled her tight against me. I kissed her more soundly, slipping my tongue past her lips. She kissed me back deeply, her hands at the back of my head, holding my face to hers.

I pulled back and said, "No matter what happens, we got this. It's you and me against the world, babe. Don't you ever forget that, mmkay?"

"Okay," she whispered and her smile was everything.

I led her into the bathroom, started the shower, and unwrapped her body from its pretty pastel blue-green dress like it was a present. She gave as good as she got, kissing me, nimble fingers working my belt, pushing my over shirt back off my shoulders.

"Mm, I should start the water," she said against my mouth and I nodded awkwardly, refusing to take my lips off hers.

"Mm-hm."

She laughed and pulled back, turning around and leaning into the shower to start the water giving me the absolute best view of her perfect ass.

"Mm, boy," I moaned admiringly and slapped her on one ass cheek. She yipped and stood up straight, looking at me affronted over her shoulder.

"Hey, you put it out there," I reminded her.

She smiled and shook her head, sticking her hand under the shower spray to test the temperature.

I swiftly finished stripping down and Ellie did likewise. "Ladies first," I murmured over the babble of falling water and she stepped in under the showerhead, stepping back to give me room.

I joined her, shutting the shower door and put my hands on her hips as she tilted her head back and wet her hair with a groan of pleasure.

"God, I don't know how you do it every day," she said. "That place left me feeling like I was just coated in a thick layer of depression."

I gave a bit of a bitter laugh and said, "It's easy for me. I get to go home at the end of the day. Makes all the difference."

"Mm, sorry, honey. I don't think I'll be visiting you at work again anytime soon."

I chuckled and leaned in, kissing her in the center of her chest over her heart. I straightened up and said, "I'm cool with that. You don't belong anywhere near a place like that, anyhow."

She smiled and it held an edge of sadness when she said, "You don't either."

"I signed up for it," I said with a shrug. "I'm all about keeping people safe, baby. Keeping the animals in line and helping those guys that wanna change – and I'm tellin' you, there are a lot more of them than you'd think. Problem is, the street is geared toward keepin' men down, keepin' 'em in their place. Breaking that cycle is hard as hell and the ones willing to do it? The ones willing to put in the work? Somebody's gotta be there to give 'em a hand."

"And that somebody is you."

There was no accusation in her tone. Just pride. Pride and a statement of fact.

"That somebody is me. Some of the other guys and gals that work the jail, too. Ain't all of us like the Bartle's of the world."

She made a face and I chuckled.

"That guy was an *asshole*. For no reason, no less."

I put some of her shampoo in my hand and massaged it into her hair. She groaned in pleasure and turned around, tipping her head back so I could reach better.

"He say anything to you on the ride over to the jail?" I asked.

"No, mostly just had this sickening satisfied and smug look on his face. Like he was sticking it to you."

"Ha! I wouldn't give that prick the satisfaction," I said.

"I wouldn't either," she said. "Let Karma sort his miserable ass out."

"K, rinse, and I agree. It'll come one day and when it does, I'ma park my ass in intake with a bag of fucking popcorn."

"You better call me when that happens, I love popcorn and you better share."

I laughed and pulled her close, kissing her soundly.

"I love you," I said and she smiled up at me.

"I love you, too."

I nodded and thought to myself again, that our love was forged under blue fire, hot to the touch and stronger than any steel. We'd been through it, and anything else that tried to come at us from here on out? We'd just be tempered and made stronger for it. As I washed my woman's troubles down the drain, I smiled knowing that I'd found a forever partner, a worthy partner in crime. A love that could withstand anything.

EPILOGUE

$\mathcal{E}$lka…

The judge looked over the papers in front of him and stared disapprovingly down through his bifocals. He took off his glasses and pinched the bridge of his nose and sighed out.

"While I am loath to advocate violence as a solution to *any* matter, I cannot in good conscience say," he paused and looked at me, "that Ms. Köhler was out of line. There she was, on a crowded street of onlookers, a man thrusting a recorder in her face demanding answers to questions he asked despite repeated pleas from Ms. Köhler for him to stop and leave her alone. His physical actions were overbearing at the least and clearly left Ms. Köhler feeling threatened. Therefore, I am dismissing this case with prejudice."

He stacked the sheaf of papers on his bench and looked over the courtroom.

"Quite frankly, I am disgusted this even got this far. This is a waste of the court's time. I would hope the prosecutor's office would use more discretion in the cases they brought before the court in the future.

"""

Again, case dismissed with prejudice, this court is adjourned." He banged his gavel on the bench and I turned to Chrissy a bit stunned.

"That's it?" I asked.

"What do you mean, 'that's it?'" Chrissy asked, rolling her eyes. "You *won!*"

"Yeah, but what does *with prejudice* exactly mean? Does that mean if they want to, they can re-try me?"

"No, silly. It means the exact opposite of that. That's it, you're done, you're free to go. No record, no more court dates, you're just done. Another one in the books for Chrissy Franco, Attorney at Law." She raised her hands in victory and did a little booty shake and Oz cracked up in the gallery behind me.

"You stupid!" he declared and I blinked.

"You mean, all of that – for nothing?" I asked.

"Yup, and now Yale gets to go ream someone's ass for dropping the prosecutor's office conviction rate."

"Wow." I sagged with relief. "Thank you. I don't know what I would have done without you." My hands were shaking, and Chrissy smiled.

"I have no problem defending people who are genuinely good people getting railroaded for no good reason other than to satisfy some imaginary vendetta." She rolled her eyes as she shuffled file folders into her briefcase.

"Man, those assholes really need to get over themselves," Oz declared, holding open my coat for me to shrug into.

I pulled the lapels closed and remarked, "It's sad really, you're all supposed to be playing for the same team."

"Right?" Chrissy sighed and shook her head.

"They just don't like it that we don't play dirty like them. In fact, ain't a one of us that would think twice or even hesitate to dime their asses out," Oz declared. "They're so dirty it could fuck up the whole damn department."

"Problem is proving it," Chrissy said flatly.

"All these motherfuckers tryin' to ice skate uphill. Eventually they'll figure out they ain't going nowhere. Hopefully by the time they do that? The rest of the system'll be all caught up to 'em."

"I will drink to that," Chrissy declared. "You buying?" she asked.

"Hell yeah, I'm buying."

"The *10-13* it is," she said with a smile, hefting her briefcase.

"Here, let me have that." Oz carried it for her.

"How'd you guys get here?" Chrissy asked.

"We took a car," I answered.

"Good, we can share one over to the *10-13*, then."

"Sounds good," I said smiling.

When we arrived at the *10-13*, we dashed from the car and through the biting rain to the front door. It was still technically fall but right on the cusp of winter and this damn charge had been dogging my every step since the Little Havana Block Party weekend. We stepped through the door, shaking off the rain and everyone just stopped and stared in our direction.

"Well?" Yale demanded.

"Case dismissed!" Chrissy crowed and a cheer went up. "*With* prejudice, might I add." She blew on her nails and polished them against her trench coat, and we all jumped when a champagne cork popped behind the bar.

"What?" Skids demanded. "This calls for celebration!" He poured along a line of flutes and said, "Everybody come grab one! You think this is some high-class joint that's gonna serve you?"

Laughter swept through the club and glasses were passed out among the men and ol' ladies.

"A toast!" Reflash declared, holding up a glass and tossing his kitchen towel over his shoulder and everyone settled down.

"To Elka, for putting up with our crazy and Oz for bringing us the best damn addition to family this club could ever hope to get. We don't know how you do it, honey – but more power to you!"

Oz laughed and flipped Reflash off and I snorted.

"Here! Here!"

Glasses clinked and we all sipped, and I went to the bar and asked Skids, "Can I have the thing?"

"You sure can." He pulled out the wide, flat, colorfully wrapped parcel and handed it over. I took it over to Oz.

"This is for you."

"For me? What for?" he asked.

"Because I love you, you dorkasaurus rex!" I rolled my eyes.

He tore the paper down the middle and took a double take.

"Are you fuckin' serious?" he demanded and pulled the rest of the paper off the painting.

"Uh huh."

"This is the most badass thing I've ever been given."

A chorus of 'aaaawwwws' went around the room as he covered his mouth and his eyes got misty. It was the painting of him, alone on the stoop, lighting his cigar. I'd painstakingly finished it in secret, swapping between it and another painting after guiltily lying and saying I hadn't liked how the painting of him was turning out and had said I had painted over it.

"This is," he choked up. "This is really something."

I smiled softly, touched that he was so touched. "I'm glad you like it," I said gently.

"I don't like it, I love it," he declared.

"How about you let the rest of us see it?" Golden called out.

"You shut up! I'm having a moment here," Oz declared and we all laughed. I leaned in and kissed him soundly, smiling, happy, relieved that he liked it.

"Just don't let his ass become your favorite subject," someone said and we laughed.

"He'll always be my favorite subject," I said, and he kissed me again to another chorus of cheers.

THE END

ALSO BY A.J. DOWNEY

The Sacred Hearts MC

1. Shattered & Scarred

2. Broken & Burned

3. Cracked & Crushed

3.5 Masked & Miserable (a novella)

4. Tattered & Torn

5. Fractured & Formidable

6. Damaged & Dangerous

The Virtues

1. Cutter's Hope

2. Marlin's Faith

3. Charity for Nothing

4. Stoker's Serenity

The Sacred Brotherhood

1. Brother to Brother

2. Her Brother's Keeper

3. Brother In Arms

4. Between Brothers

5. A Brother's Secret

6. A Brother At My Back

7. A Brother's Salvation

ABOUT THE AUTHOR

A.J. Downey specializes in writing real and relatable contemporary romance stories. She's from Seattle, WA and loves the Pacific Northwest. She finds inspiration from her surroundings, through the people she meets, and likely as a byproduct of way too much caffeine. An avid reader all of her life, it's now her turn to try and give back a little, entertaining as she has been entertained.

Stalker Information:

Website
www.ajdowney.com

Sign up for her newsletter at
http://eepurl.com/dkQiIH

Facebook Group - AJ's Sacred Circle
https://www.facebook.com/groups/authorajdowney/

facebook.com/authorajdowney

twitter.com/authorajdowney

instagram.com/ajdowney

bookbub.com/authors/a-j-downey